who killed OSHO?

ABHAY VAIDYA

Om Books International

First published in 2017 by

Om Books International

Corporate & Editorial Office
A-12, Sector 64, Noida 201 301
Uttar Pradesh, India
Phone: +91 120 477 4100
Email: editorial@ombooks.com
Website: www.ombooksinternational.com

Sales Office
107, Ansari Road, Darya Ganj,
New Delhi 110 002, India
Phone: +91 11 4000 9000
Fax: +91 11 2327 8091
Email: sales@ombooks.com
Website: www.ombooks.com

This book is a journalistic endeavour and the result of nearly three decades of reportage on the Rajneesh Movement. It is based on extensive audio and video interviews with Osho's closest followers and a mass of official documents, testimonies and press reports.

ISBN: 978-93-86410-02-3

Printed in India

10 9 8 7 6 5 4 3 2 1

Photo courtesy: Vilas Avachat

Abhay Vaidya is an independent journalist based in Pune. He has worked previously as *The Times of India's* Washington Correspondent, the newspaper's Assistant Resident Editor and as *DNA*'s Resident Editor.

A gold medalist in journalism from the University of Pune, he graduated with a Master's in Political Science from Indiana University of Pennsylvania under a Rotary Foundation Scholarship. He is a fellow of Lead India.

Abhay has reported extensively on the Rajneesh Movement in his career of nearly three decades. Other noteworthy news stories include the genesis of the multi-billion dollar Lavasa Lake City project and issues of political patronage and environmental concerns around it; IIM CAT paper leak in 2003, banker-borrower nexus and fraud at a nationalised bank and the seemingly unchecked proliferation of fake currency in the country. He writes commentary on social and political issues and media ethics on a regular basis.

Passionate about journalism and the role of a free press in the rocky odyssey of Indian democracy and secularism, Abhay is a visiting faculty at most leading journalism institutes in India.

सत्यमेव जयते

Truth Alone Triumphs

For

Prof. Kiran Thakur

who taught me

the fundamentals of good journalism

Contents

Among the Believers

Mentioned below are some of Osho's closest followers who were witness to dramatic developments inside Osho Commune International, Pune, on the day he died—January 19, 1990. In a few cases their sannyas (initiation) names and legal names underwent multiple changes.

Nirvano: Ma Prem Nirvano, Osho's girlfriend and caretaker for many years. British citizen who gave her name as Christena Woolf Smith, also written as Christine Woolf Smith. Her first sannyas name Ma Prem Vivek was changed to Ma Prem Nirvano. Died in suspicious circumstances at age 40 on December 9, 1989, barely 41 days before Osho's death. Was in a romantic relationship with Jayesh at the time of her death.

Jayesh: Swami Anand Jayesh. Age: 69. His legal name was Michael O'Byrne which changed to Michael Byrne. The all-powerful, Canadian-born Chairman, Osho International Foundation (OIF), Zürich is one of the two persons present when Osho died. The man who controls the Osho empire. Elusive and secretive.

Amrito: Swami Prem Amrito. British doctor, in his early 70s. Was Osho's personal physician and by his side when he died, but did not sign his Death Certificate. Previous sannyas name: Swami Devaraj. Current legal name: Dr. John Andrews. Previous legal name: Dr. George Meredith. Was victim of a murder attempt in Oregon by a rival faction led by Osho's disgraced secretary Ma Anand Sheela. Was accused by other sannyasins of misusing his medical knowledge.

Anando: Ma Deva Anando. Susan Heffley, formerly Sue Appleton. Age: 70. Osho's legal secretary and his caretaker at the time of his death. Was present in Lao Tzu House when Osho died but was not called to see him even though Osho named her as his 'medium'. Left the Commune in 1999–2000 and was no longer associated with any trust or foundation of Osho. Now settled in Italy.

Dr. Gokul Gokani: Swami Anand Krishna. Age: 81. Indian ENT surgeon who had never treated Osho but was urgently summoned and asked to issue Osho's Death Certificate. Said in an affidavit that he did not know the real cause of Osho's death. Emigrated to the U.S. eight years after Osho's death.

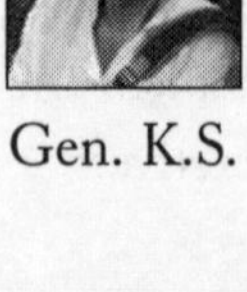

Chitten: German sannyasin, now known by his new identity, Santosh Thomas Hoehne. Around 65 years. Played a vital role on the day Osho died. Married to Ma Prem Amrita, granddaughter of Gen. K.S. Thimayya. Left the Pune Commune abruptly and re-settled in Almora, Uttarakhand, where he runs an organic foods and cosmetics manufacturing company.

Tathagat: Swami Anand Tathagat; legal name Ashok Kumar. Age: 68. Was Commune in-charge during Poona-II and member of the Inner Circle. Was asked to hurriedly make preparations for Osho's cremation. Witnessed Nirvano's condition at the N.M. Wadia Hospital where she died. Now based at Osho Nisarga Centre, Dharamsala.

Prem Anadi: Kishor Raval. Age: 55. Accompanied Osho sannyasins Dhyanesh, Dr. Gokani and Dr. Narayan Kshirsagar to get Osho's Cremation Pass from Pune Municipal Corporation office at Sassoon Hospital. Conducts music programmes and sings during Osho satsangs on special occasions. Is fighting several cases against Osho International Foundation (OIF) in the Maharashtra Charity Commissionerate and the courts.

Neelam: Ma Yoga Neelam; Neelam Dhall. Age: 68. Osho's India secretary from 1986 onwards. Was asked to inform Osho's mother, Mataji, about his death. Was denied entry into the Osho Commune on June 20, 2000 and told to keep away. Established Osho Nisarga Centre, Dharamsala after leaving the Commune.

Mataji: Saraswati Devi. Osho's mother. Took sannyas as Ma Amrit Saraswati. Wanted to meet Osho a few days before his death but was refused permission by Anando. Died on May 17, 1995 at age 81.

Klaus Steeg: Swami Pramod. In his late 50s. Director and member of the Board of OIF-Zürich. Head of Osho International Corporation, OIF's publishing headquarters in New York. President of American Multimedia Corporation, responsible for developing international publishing programmes for OIF.

D'Arcy O'Byrne: Swami Anand Yogendra. Michael Byrne's (Jayesh) younger brother, now in his mid-60s. Was inducted into the Inner Circle and was later member-Trustee, OIF-Zürich, OIF-India and Neo Sannyas Foundation. Director, Osho Foundation America Inc., Osho Media International Ltd., Master Zone Ltd.

Mukesh Kantilal Sarda: Swami Mukesh Bharti. About 62 years old. A key associate of Jayesh. Formerly trustee, OIF-Zürich. Trustee, OIF-India, Trustee, Neo Sannyas Foundation; Director, Zen Properties Pvt. Ltd.; Director, Osho Multimedia & Resorts Pvt. Ltd. and other companies. Sannyasins remember his early days as an LIC agent in Bombay and as a struggling Bombay-Poona courier boy for the Commune.

Amrit Sadhana: Amrit Belapurkar. Trustee, OIF-India. About 65 years. Spokesperson, OIF, Member of the Management Team, Osho International Meditation Resort, Pune. Said OIF made a mistake by creating Osho's Samadhi.

Satya Vedant: Swami Satya Vedant; legal name, Vasant Joshi. Age: 77. Indian-American scholar. Member, Inner Circle; Chancellor, Osho Multiversity. Left the Commune in 2002.

Laxmi: Ma Yoga Laxmi. Also known as Laxmi Thakarsi Kuruwa. Belonged to a wealthy Gujarati family in Bombay and became Osho's first sannyasin in the 1970s. Started the tradition of wearing orange robes and the *mala* (necklace) with a locket carrying Osho's picture. Was Osho's first caretaker in Bombay and his first secretary. Died of cancer in January, 1995, a month before her 62nd birthday.

Sheela: Ma Anand Sheela. Sheela Ambalal Patel, 67 years old. Was assistant to Laxmi and replaced her as Osho's Secretary in 1981. Played a key role in Osho's departure to the U.S. in 1981 and the establishment of Rancho Rajneesh / Rajneeshpuram at Oregon. Abandoned the Commune abruptly in September, 1985 and left for Germany. Was arrested and deported to the U.S. where she was convicted of various crimes, including attempt to murder Amrito.

Hasya: Wealthy Hollywood producer Françoise Ruddy, wife of Albert S. Ruddy, producer of *The Godfather*, took sannyas as Ma Prem Hasya. Was the most prominent celebrity of the 'Hollywood group' at the Commune which included some of her wealthy friends from California. Took sannyas in 1977 and brought glitter and glamour to the Commune. Became Osho's

International Secretary after Ma Anand Sheela left in 1985. Left the Pune Commune abruptly within a year of Osho's death. Died in her mid-70s on August 19, 2014.

Niren: Swami Prem Niren; legal name: Philip Toelkes, 71. Osho's personal attorney from 1982 to 1990. Presented a copy of Osho's Will dated 15th October, 1989 as an exhibit in a European Court while defending OIF's claim to OSHO trademark. The Will was produced for the first time, 23 years after Osho's death.

Premgeet: Yogesh Thakkar. Age: 56. Front Gate Guard Coordinator during Poona-II. Was among the few persons to attend Nirvano's cremation. Is in the forefront of fighting several legal battles against the OIF.

Shunyo: Ma Prem Shunyo. Age: 71. British national, Sandy Pengelly who met Osho in 1976. Accepted sannyas with the name Ma Dharma Chetana. Was later known as Ma Prem Shunyo. Handled Osho's laundry for 15 years as a part of his personal staff.

Chaitanya Keerti: Narain Das, 67, who took sannyas as Swami Chaitanya Keerti. Was Osho Commune's spokesperson during Poona-II. Left the Commune in 2000 after protesting over the creation of a publishing headquarters in New York and other issues.

1

Osho's Death: A Fairy Tale Account?

Osho's ardent followers the world over were shaken out of their complacency in June 2013, when a copy of Osho's Will was produced in a European Court as part of the evidence to lay claims and ownership to Osho's legacy. This was a good 23 years after his death on January 19, 1990. On that day and in the 23 intervening years since, the parent trust, Osho International Foundation (OIF) held that the Master did not leave behind a Will. Where then and how did this document surface from? Why was its existence never revealed all these years?

The Will had surfaced amidst a raging legal battle in the European Union for the right to trademark 'OSHO'. After it was presented, some of Osho's concerned disciples subjected it to forensic examination by three independent sets of experts in Italy, New Delhi and Aurangabad. All three concluded that Osho's signature on the Will was forged. Rather than counter and challenge this assertion, the OIF withdrew this document from the court proceedings. Chapter 15 in this book takes a more detailed look at the Will controversy which, since 2013, became a fresh talking point for Osho's followers and the media. For the author, however, this was yet another twist, yet another dot waiting to be connected among the many disturbing dots on Osho's death.

The fact is that the official account of the circumstances in which the controversial mystic, Osho, died reads more like a heart-warming, myth-inspiring fairy tale to those who are not aware of what really happened on January 19, 1990.

Osho was 58 at the time of his death.

Who Killed Osho? reveals for the first time the fast-moving developments that occurred inside the Osho Commune International, Pune, throughout the day on January 19, 1990. For the first time, many of Osho's senior-most sannyasins who were present inside the Commune on the day he died have revealed what exactly happened that day. Their testimonies—through interviews conducted in different parts of the country—raise numerous questions about the truth behind Osho's death. The author covered Osho's death as a reporter for the national media and has reported on every twist and turn in the affairs of the Commune since then. As such, this book is the result of extensive reportage on the Osho Commune since the late 1980s and investigation into his death.

Among his six brothers in a family of 11 siblings, only three of Osho's brothers now survive—Niklank and Amit in Pune and Shailendra, Osho's second youngest brother, who is based at his ashram, Oshodhara Nanak Dham at Murthal, Sonepat in Haryana, about two hours' drive from Delhi on the Grand Trunk Road. The 61-year-old who lives with his wife 'Osho Priya' is now a guru in his own right, and is known by his sannyas name Swami Shailendra Saraswati, and also as 'Osho Shailendra'—one of the three masters at Oshodhara.

During an interview at his Murthal ashram on July 28, 2016, Swami Shailendra appealed to the author fervently not to focus on the controversy of Osho's death. "You journalists have your point of view, but what constructive purpose will it serve even if you are able to establish that there was something odd or unusual or controversial about Osho's death? What has happened cannot be undone. We all have to die sooner or later. You are only presenting different versions; you cannot prove anything decisively. You will only succeed in creating doubts and confusion. Instead of that, why don't you focus and write on what is positive about Osho?"

If one were to accept this suggestion, what then happens to the search for the truth behind Osho's death?

Who Killed Osho? seeks to unravel a deeper angle to Osho's death, which relates to the ownership of the valuable assets that were created by him and accumulated in his name. The series of events inside the Commune in 1989—the last year of his life—merit closer scrutiny.

Although Osho did almost all his creative work in India, the ownership of the intellectual properties that he created, rests completely with entities outside India: while the parent trust, Osho International Foundation (OIF) is headquartered in Zürich, Switzerland, the publications headquarters, Osho International, is based in New York. The OIF has fought fierce legal battles in the United States and Europe to claim and exercise control over the 'OSHO' and related domain names on the Internet, and trademark in Europe. The name 'OSHO', his meditation techniques and therapies stand protected by trademark in Europe. Facebook and YouTube have been known to summarily delete accounts and archives of Osho Centres and remove pictures of Osho from individual accounts on receiving complaints of copyright infringement from the OIF.

A quarter century after Osho's death is a good time-frame to take stock of the Rajneesh Movement which took birth almost half-a-century ago in the mid-1960s.

Why did people by the thousands, many of them highly accomplished professionals from within and outside India, feel compelled to change the course of their lives and leave everything aside—family, job, education and careers—to be by Osho's side? What was it in Osho that acted like a magnetic force on thousands of people the world over? Osho was barely in his mid-30s when, in the 1960s, he began travelling across India, giving lectures on social issues, religion and spiritualism. His earliest followers were essentially Hindus from the towns and cities of Gujarat and North India, and later Bombay, where he was hosted by his Gujarati followers. Then known as Acharya Rajneesh, Osho was handsome, with jet black hair and a beard, piercing eyes and a wistful, captivating smile. Dressed in a white *lungi* (sarong-like ankle length garment) wrapped around his waist and a white *chaddar* (shawl) around his shoulders, he lived a Spartan life. During his lecture tours across India, his meagre belongings included a suitcase with two pillows, one bedsheet and one blanket. His listeners were primarily from Northern and Western India because Osho's earliest discourses were in Hindi. These were passionately delivered, mesmerising talks on Hindu scriptures and philosophy, human thought, state of the society, religion and culture. His lectures were provocative and questioned conventional wisdom. He offered deep and original insights into and interpretations of the scriptures and co-related ancient wisdom to modern life. He spoke with considerable depth and conviction and was far removed from the *pooja-paath* (religious rituals) associated with various religions. In fact, he rejected rituals and urged people to think and reflect for themselves. This appealed to the modern mind, especially to people who were well-educated, financially independent and in search of meaning and purpose to their lives.

Osho spoke brilliantly and beautifully in Hindi and his powerful oratory transfixed his listeners. It touched the innermost chord in them, stirring them from within, making them think and question their fundamental beliefs. He brought intellectual freedom to his followers and taught them to be courageous. He offered them a new vision and freedom from the tyranny of religion and tradition and urged them not to worry about the future but to celebrate life and live in the present, with awareness at all times.

Many young, Indian women from traditional families were attracted to Osho. They felt comfortable in his presence and were encouraged by their families to accept him as their guru. Osho did not shun women like most sadhus and babas but enjoyed their company. His secretaries were always women—Laxmi in Bombay and his first seven years in the Pune Commune (1974–1981) known as the Poona-I days; Sheela at Rancho Rajneesh, Oregon; Hasya in the U.S. and during Poona-II (1987–1990) and Neelam who was his India Secretary till his death.

Osho's talks would begin not with any familiar intonations but in his characteristic style, with the words, "*Mere priya atman*" (My dear souls). His forceful criticism of religious orders for attempting to suppress man's natural instinct in the form of sexual energy, was a part of this bold assault on religions and tradition. Interestingly, he did this while quoting extensively from ancient Indian scriptures, from the school of

Tantra, and therefore, his suggestion that sexual energy needed to be understood, accepted and used as a path to attain spiritual growth convinced his followers.

Alongside, Osho extolled the powers of the mind and meditation, held meditation camps, and went on to develop many distinctive meditation techniques and therapies for the modern man. That he was handsome and full of confidence and self-assurance, a forceful orator and a charismatic personality with powerful, expressive eyes, added to his charm.

The eminent writer Khushwant Singh who met Osho in Bombay in the early 1970s, described him as "perhaps the first of the great teachers who had carefully examined the tenets of other faiths." Himself an internationally-acknowledged authority on Sikhism, Singh said he could "personally vouch for the profundity" of many of Osho's discourses on ancient religious texts of different religions. He wrote about how stunned he was to hear Osho's interpretations of Guru Nanak's morning prayer, *Japji.* "I thought I knew everything worth knowing about this morning prayer till I heard Rajneesh's voice on tape propound esoteric meanings behind every line, quoting the Upanishads and writings of Bhakta saints. I had not heard anything as profound from scholars of Sikhism."[1]

It is precisely this kind of scholarship and oratory that attracted Indians by the droves to Osho. The disparaging 'Sex Guru' sobriquet which has defined Osho in the media, and consequently, in popular perception, hardly did justice to the man.

Why did Westerners flock to Osho by the droves?

The 1960s and '70s was a period of considerable social turmoil and upheaval in the West, with young people being caught in the midst of the Hippie Movement, sexual liberation of the '60s and the '70s, the Feminist Movement, and the lure of the spiritual East. Many were disillusioned with the Cold War brinkmanship between the U.S. and the Soviet Union and were distrustful of their politicians and community leaders. They found no answers to their questions in their religions and religious upbringing. The West was itself experimenting with a wave of human potential[2], counterculture movements with the promise of a superior, alternative way of living. Experiencing an 'inner emptiness,' they went in search of answers to life's many questions, either as part of the Hippie Movement, the Hare Krishna Movement which had become popular in the West or as youth icons who sought out masters like Maharishi Mahesh Yogi (made popular by the Beatles) and J. Krishnamurti. Osho, then known as Acharya and Bhagwan Rajneesh, was one among them and yet unique, because he spoke a new language of freedom from religious and social conditioning; offered solutions to relationship problems like an effective psychiatrist, and spoke boldly of the divinity of sex as a path to enlightenment. Added to this was the experience of new kinds of meditations which was exhilarating and the promise of a fresh new beginning with a new sannyas identity. Highly recommended by their friends back home, many Westerners came on holidays to India to see Osho for themselves and felt like returning again and again. They found a sense of fulfillment and inner peace in Osho's presence, and a guilt-free, sexually liberated environment wrapped in Eastern mysticism. It was all quite heady and yet inexpensive to visit and stay in India. The only nuisance they had to cope with was the tropical weather, the poor infrastructure, and dismal health, hygiene and sanitation standards in India.

Eva Cockova, a young Czech woman who was training to do therapy groups under the Human Potential Movement in England, found that Osho had far greater depth and understanding than Western psychologists on the subject of mind and meditation. "No one in the West had the understanding that Osho had and psychologists were running to him like bees are drawn to honey," said Cockova who took sannyas as Ma Deva Garimo in 1974.[3]

In fact, Osho represented the East-West synthesis rather uniquely. His ideas of Neo Sannyas[4], that man can pursue the goals of spiritual enlightenment without renouncing the pursuits of a worldly life, and his experimentation with meditation accompanied with specially composed music, had a strong resonance with the ideas of the early 20th-century Russian mystic, George Gurdjieff[5] whom he quoted frequently. The Gurdjieff influence was unmistakable on Osho although he went far beyond to experiment extensively with meditation and Tantra.

Osho had many British followers, one of whom was Sandy Pengelly who, in the mid-1970s had chanced upon his book, *The Silent Explosion*. She soon decided to experience Dynamic Meditation at a Rajneesh Meditation Centre in London. "Doing Dynamic Meditation changed my life. Everybody did the meditation naked and I soon realised that there was nothing sexual in this," Pengelly wrote later of this experience.[6] Like many others, she found her way to India, met Osho in 1976, and accepted sannyas with the name Ma Dharma Chetana. She later changed her sannyas name to Ma Prem Shunyo and was with Osho for 15 years, as a part of his personal staff, taking care of his laundry.

Osho was born in a Jaina family on December 11, 1931 to Saraswati Devi and Babu Lal at the residence of his maternal grandparents in village Kuchwada, about 120 km from Bhopal, in district Raisen, Madhya Pradesh. The child was named Chandra Mohan Jain. He was called 'Raja' at home and 'Rajneesh' was the nickname by which he came to be known in later years. His father Babu Lal was a cloth merchant at village Gadarwara, about 150 km from Jabalpur.

Osho displayed many traits as a child and as a teenager that distinguished him in later years. His love for nature, his powerful oratory, his fiercely independent and rebellious streak and an attraction for things spiritual and esoteric could be seen through his early years.

Till the age of 7, Osho lived at Kuchwada with his grandparents who doted on him and fulfilled his every wish. He was their prince, 'Raja.'[7]

His grandfather was a landlord and had the only brick house in the village. Osho had fond memories of his village life which he described in his autobiography, *Glimpses of a Golden Childhood*: "My birthplace, Kuchwada, was a village with no railway line and no post office. It had small hills, hillocks rather, but a beautiful lake, and a few huts, just straw huts. The only brick house was the one I was born in, and that was not much of a brick house. It was just a little house."

His grandmother Rani Ma, whom he called 'Nani' had a strong influence on him and he was more attached to her than to his own mother whom he called 'Bhabhi' as she was called by others in the extended family.

Rajneesh displayed a fascination for nature and as a child, gazed at the moon and the stars for hours together, "sometimes with a beautiful smile on his face." He loved pet animals such as deer and rabbits and one day released all the birds in the cage at home. Swimming was a passion with him and whether it was the Sakkar River near his village or the mighty Narmada which was not too far away, he spent many hours around the river, either performing acts of daredevilry while swimming in strong currents, exploring nature around the river or meditating on the banks, "in the stillness of early mornings before sunset and late at night."

The eldest of 11 children, which included five girls and six boys, Osho did not start his formal education till the age of nine. After schooling, he went to Jabalpur for college and university studies. He won numerous prizes in elocution, debate and storytelling competitions and from 6th grade itself, took to giving speeches and participating in debates. He loved to argue and was not intimidated by people much older than him. To the extent, his father recalled, he was disliked in the village "because he was always arguing with everybody" and even making fun of the village authorities. Osho spoke of this while recalling his childhood memories: "As far back as I can remember, I loved only one game, to argue—to argue about everything. So very few grown-up people could even stand me—understanding was out of the question."[8]

About his public speaking skills, he wrote: "I started speaking so early, yet it was not in any way what you call a speaker in the Western world. Not a speaker who says, 'Ladies and Gentlemen,' and all that nonsense—all borrowed and nothing experienced. I was not a speaker in that sense, but I spoke with my whole heart aflame, afire. I spoke not as an art but as my very life. And from my early schooldays, it was recognised, not by one but by many, that my speaking seemed to be coming from my heart, that I was not trying parrot-like to repeat something I had prepared. Something spontaneous was being born, then and there."[9]

A strong recollection from his childhood was his fascination with death. His grandfather's death when he was seven had affected him deeply and so had the death of his first love, a girl called Shashi who died of typhoid at age 14. In his own case, the family astrologer had said that he would draw Osho's birth chart only after he crossed the age of seven. He had predicted that Osho would not live beyond the age of seven. Eventually, Osho developed such a strong interest in death that whenever someone died at the village, he would follow the funeral procession and intently observe the rituals. On one occasion, Osho laughed uncontrollably at the residence of a saintly person who had died, angering his father who was deeply embarrassed. Osho said he could not help laughing because the man had died in a happy state of mind.

Osho believed in reincarnation and co-related the first three days of his birth to his previous life which he said occurred 700 years ago. As he told an interviewer: "Seven hundred years ago, in my previous life, there was a spiritual practice of 21 days, to be done before death. I was to give up my body after a total fast of 21 days. There were reasons for this, but I could not complete those 21 days. Three days remained. Those three days, I had to complete in this life."[10] Osho's mother told an interviewer that for the first three days of his birth, he did not suckle at her breast and this unusual behaviour in a new-born child confounded everyone.[11]

An incident from his teenage years highlighting his rebellious nature is of the time when his father, in a fit of anger, cut his long hair with a pair of scissors from his shop.

Without saying a word, Osho went to the village barber and got his entire head shaved off, shocking not just his family, but many villagers who thought that his father had died, and came to offer condolences. Among Hindus, the scalp is completely shaved only after an elder's death in the family as a sign of humility, and this rebellious act by Osho shocked one and all. After this incident, his father did not challenge him again.[12]

Osho's argumentative nature led to trouble at the Hitkarini College, Jabalpur, where he had enrolled for higher education. His persistent questioning during the classes in Philosophy and Logic led to a clash with the professor who insisted that the student be expelled from the college. The professor's demand was unreasonable; however, the college could not afford to lose him and Osho agreed to leave the college provided the college principal helped him secure admission in another educational institution. His college principal felt relieved when he managed to get him admitted to another college, the D.N. Jain College, on condition that he would not harass his teachers there with his incessant questions.

During this time, Osho suffered a series of headaches, inexplicable psychological trauma and a deep feeling of emptiness, none of which made any sense to him or his family. Visits to doctors proved futile till a *Vaidya* (practitioner of Ayurveda) said ecstatically that there was nothing wrong with Osho, but something was very divine about his experiences. Throughout this period, Osho continued with his meditations and he spoke of one particularly intense experience while visiting Sagar University for three days to participate in a debating competition. He would sit on a tree and meditate all night. During one of these intense meditation sessions, he fell off the tree and described that episode as an "out of body" experience.[13]

During a conversation with his cousin sister Kranti in November 1972, Osho claimed that he attained enlightenment on March 21, 1953 at the age of 21 when, after a week full of restlessness and inner turmoil, he had stepped out of their house at Jabalpur at around midnight, and gone to the Bhanvartal Garden. He once again underwent a deep psychological experience and felt pulled towards a maulshree tree and sat under it for about three hours after which the inner turmoil subsided and he felt overcome by a wave of serenity and peace. Osho wrote that those three hours which felt like "the whole eternity, endless eternity," was his state of enlightenment.[14]

Osho continued with his education and in 1955 completed his B.A. in Philosophy, followed by an M.A. in the same subject from Sagar University in 1957, where he was awarded a gold medal. In another of his rebellious acts, he took that medal and threw it in the university well in front of an astonished crowd after giving a short speech justifying his action. Throughout this period, two activities mattered most to Osho: reading voraciously and walking about in solitude at any time of the night or day in the hills of Sagar.

Throughout these years, Osho subjected himself to various experiments of the mind to understand and observe the experience. He spoke of how he decided to witness and experience a state of *tamas* or inactivity as discussed in Hindu philosophy. "I made it my first principle to refrain from doing anything. For the two years that I was in the university hostel, I never cleaned or swept my room," he mentions in *Glimpses of a Golden Childhood*, adding that he positioned his cot at the entrance of his room "so that from the door I could jump straight into my cot and from the cot I could jump straight out of the room."

After graduating from Sagar University, he secured a teaching position at the Sanskrit Mahavidyalaya, Raipur (Raipur Sanskrit College) in 1957 and later, became an assistant professor of Philosophy at the University of Jabalpur. He took to travelling and lecturing from 1960 onwards and held his first 10-day meditation camp at Mulcha Mahavir in Rajasthan where he taught meditation techniques that could be done early morning, and at night before sleeping. Osho described meditation as a "a state of no-mind." As he explained: "Meditation is the awareness that I am not the mind." As this awareness goes deeper within, a few moments of silence, of pure space, of transparency begin to appear "when nothing stirs in you and everything is still." It is in those moments of stillness that the mystery of existence reveals itself.[15]

Osho had been wanting to give up on his University job and focus entirely on travelling and delivering talks. In August 1966, he finally resigned from his post as Assistant Professor at the University, the provocation being the principal's objection to his attire of a *lungi* and a *chaddar*. His wealthy followers in Bombay had urged him to settle down in their city and had organised an apartment for him at the CCI Chambers, Marine Drive and later at Woodland Apartments on Pedder Road. Throughout this period, he provoked considerable controversy by speaking freely and boldly on a variety of topics ranging from the stupidity of religious orthodoxy, the true meaning of education, and socialism. He did not hesitate to criticise Mahatma Gandhi, who he said, was unscientific, regressive and knew nothing about meditation.

At the same time, Osho delivered immensely popular and deeply moving discourses on the most popular Hindu religious text, the *Bhagavad Gita*; religious icons such as Krishna and

Mahavir, and the Upanishads. The venues in Bombay were as varied as the open grounds of Cross Maidan, the sands at Chowpatty Beach, Podar College, Shanmukhananda and Patkar Halls. These were extremely popular, drawing crowds in the thousands; of more than 50,000 in open air venues such as Cross Maidan. However, none of the discourses were as controversial as the '*Sambhog se Samadhi ki Aur*" (From Sex Towards Super-consciousness) series of three lectures, the first of which was delivered at the Bharatiya Vidya Bhavan on August 28, 1968. The series had to be discontinued due to public outrage over the mixing of sex and spiritualism. Fearless as he was, Osho resumed the series on the request of his ardent followers and delivered the remaining two lectures on September 28 at Gowalia Tank Maidan. These lectures and his criticism of religious traditions and orthodoxy, not only provoked public outrage but turned many of his supporters into critics.

There was yet another reason the 'Sex Guru' tag got affixed to Osho. It was during one of his meditation camps at Mount Abu that a fierce controversy erupted when some women took off their clothes during a Dynamic Meditation session. Tathagat, who was then a young corporate executive,recalled reading about it in the newspapers. Tathagat, who later became the ashram in-charge during Poona-II explained what had happened: "Osho had been conducting Dynamic Meditation and after 45 minutes, during catharsis, the third stage of the meditation, was instructing, 'Throw everything out; lighten your mind, bring it out, faster, with greater effort; if your clothes are heavy on you, throw them; bring it out; throw it out…' It was at this stage, during the frenzy of this charged environment that some women actually removed their clothes.

This caused a sensation in the media and the headlines from Rajasthan were flashed across the country. It even caused an uproar in the Rajasthan State Assembly," Tathagat recalled.

Among those who met Osho in the late 1960s during his years of travel and lecturing was Neelam Dhall, who, after marriage, took sannyas and was Osho's India Secretary at the time of his death. Tall and attractive, Neelam was a newly-married 20-year-old Punjabi with a B.A. in Literature and Music. She first heard of Osho, then known as Acharya Rajneesh, in Ludhiana in 1969. Not in the least interested in religion, spiritualism or meditation, it was her businessman husband, and father-in-law who had attended a public lecture by Osho in Ludhiana. Both were thoroughly impressed. "When my husband came home, he was so happy and filled with joy that he insisted on taking me along the next day," Neelam recounted in an interview to the author at Dharamsala. Osho had been invited for a talk by the Ludhiana Police Commissioner and there was a crowd of about 8,000 people. Expecting to see a typical baba with his hangers-on in a noisy, mela-like setting with gossiping women, trash strewn about and children running around the venue, Neelam was taken aback at what she saw instead. Everything was well-organised, neat and clean and the crystal-clear voice of Osho could be heard over the loudspeakers. Since she was at the far end of the gathering, she could not see the Acharya clearly but found his voice magnetic, his Hindi poetic and his words insightful. Osho's words from that talk were etched in her mind and she recited a few lines while recalling that day. "Osho was speaking on the wasted life of the Indian youth," she said, recalling that she was "drawn to him like a magnet."

The next day, Neelam went well before the scheduled time with her entire family, including her mother-in-law, brother-in-law and others and took the front seats. She now got to see Osho closely. The gracefulness with which he walked and greeted the crowds with a *namaste* (respectful Indian way of greeting with folded hands) and his characteristic, opening line: '*Mere priya atman*', was unusual. "I had never seen a man so handsome, so good looking; so soft and fragile and yet so strong and fiery in what he was saying," Neelam recalled.

Such was the impact of Osho's talk on Neelam that by the time he ended, she had tears of joy streaking her face. "I was transported to a different world. I felt as though I had known him and had been with him before. There was overwhelming joy in me that I had found him again."

She attended many more talks by Osho whenever he visited Ludhiana; met him, participated in a guided meditation conducted by him, and also attended his talks in neighbouring towns and cities, and at Amritsar and Jalandhar. It was in October, 1972 that she took sannyas during a 10-day-meditation camp at Mount Abu. Her husband and father-in-law had also become Osho's disciples and Osho took a personal interest in Neelam, asking her to visit the newly-established Pune Commune twice a year during her daughter Priya's school holidays. Eventually, Priya too took sannyas with the name Ma Deva Priya and, on many occasions, was showered with expensive gifts and affection by Osho.

In those early days, the effect of Osho's words on many of his listeners was truly life-altering. Now close to 80, Swarnalata Batra, known by her nickname 'Soni' was among Osho's close followers in Bombay in the late 1960s. While managing her house and bringing up her children, she would often visit temples and gurudwaras in quest of inner peace. She felt that something was missing from her life and this made her restless. "I was in search of something within," she said of this period. Finally, there was a sense of enormous relief when she connected spiritually with Osho after she heard him at some public lectures in Bombay. As a four-year-old, she had heard a couplet sung melodiously by a Muslim fakir on the streets of Lahore:

Allah nu yaad karo baba
Jo dum gujare, so wah! wah!

(Remember the Almighty.
Celebrate every moment.)

She didn't grasp the full import of those words then, but they remained etched in her mind. Later, she heard them resonate in the words of Osho and felt electrified. There was no turning back now. She vividly recalled that day when Osho initiated his first batch of followers to their spiritual journey with him and introduced the concept of Neo Sannyas. She accepted her new name Ma Prem Sarita. "He said, 'This is *nav sannyas* (new form of sannyas), not *bhagoda* (cowardly) *sannyas*. Do whatever you are doing (to earn a living) and move towards enlightenment.' He said, 'Live in the present. Whatever is happening is for the good. Welcome it,'" Ma Prem Sarita recalled.

She remembered those early days when she and Ma Dharm Jyoti (Puspha Panjabi), 74, would wait at Dadar Station to receive Osho during his visits to Bombay. "He had tremendous grace. When he descended from the pedestrian bridge at Dadar Station, we would think a *farishta* (God's messenger) is coming down," Ma Prem Sarita said with considerable enthusiasm in her voice.

Swami Vitthal Bharti (Vitthal I. Thakkar), also a key disciple from those early years in Bombay, spoke of how difficult it was in the 1960s and '70s "to collect money for Osho's first class railway ticket to bring him to Bombay for lectures."

Ma Dharm Jyoti belonged to the very first group of Osho's followers who took sannyas during a meditation camp in Manali on September 26, 1970. She had been with Osho since 1968, while working as an accountant with BEST (Bombay Electric Supply and Transport Company). Born in Karachi in a Sindhi family which moved to Bombay after Partition, she had decided to live on her own and become financially independent. Like her friend Sarita, she too was in search of answers to life's mysteries. "I would think about life and death, read books, go to discourses, but none could touch my heart." Things changed dramatically after she heard Osho speak at Shanmukhananda Hall. It was a deeply spiritual experience. "I closed my eyes. My mind was washed away. There was complete silence within. I told myself, he is speaking from experience." She felt that she had found the guru she was looking for.

It was at the September 1970 meditation camp in Manali that Osho gave sannyas to his followers for the first time. Everything was somewhat fluid and unplanned. Before coming to Manali, Osho's secretary, Laxmi had decided to wear an orange *lungi* and *kurta* (loose, long collar-less shirt worn by men and women in South Asia) of her own accord because she felt blessed by her association with Osho. Osho liked that attire on her and asked his disciples to follow Laxmi's example. He organised a bundle of orange cloth in his room at the CCI Chambers, and asked his disciples to get *lungi*s and *kurta*s stitched for themselves and bring them to the meditation camp in Manali.

"At Manali, there were six to eight people wearing orange and I was one of them. Osho explained that he was launching a 'Nav Sannyas' (Neo Sannyas) Movement and thought of the sannyas name 'Dharm Jyoti' for me, on the spur of the moment. Another participant at the camp had suggested 'Jyoti' as my new name, to which Osho had said, "Jyoti" is incomplete, let me add "Dharm" to it—she will spread my message of *dharma*.""

Osho inspired her and convinced her not to worry about public ridicule and wear her orange dress to the BEST office where she worked. "If they laugh at you, you laugh along with them," he advised. When Jyoti Ma protested saying, "They will think I am mad," Osho laughed and said, "What's wrong with that? You are mad anyway." Laughing at those memories, Jyoti Ma said, "We were literally counting as our numbers grew... We would tell each other, today two wickets have fallen...We are now 30...We are now 35...We are now 50..."

It was during these years that a young woman from a wealthy Gujarati family in Bombay met Osho and went on to become his first sannyasin and secretary and was also instrumental in establishing the Pune Commune. Small and diminutive in stature but full of energy and enthusiasm, Laxmi Thakarsi Kuruwa lived in a large joint family which was devoted to Gandhian ideals. She spun khadi and wore khadi. Having decided not to pursue higher education, she spent her time in household work and social work. A bout of small pox in childhood had scarred her face and had also led to severe loss of hair which had been distressing. Sustained treatment from a *vaidya* had helped her regain her health and overcome her inferiority complex in her early years.

Osho had had a mesmerising effect on Laxmi when she first heard him speak before the women's wing of the Congress Party in Bombay, with which she was associated.[16]

Two months later, her mother met "a Jain monk" at a family friend's residence. That monk happened to be Osho and she too, was as impressed by Osho as was Laxmi. Laxmi, who died of cancer in 1995, recalled in her autobiography that Osho had a "unique charm" and was "neat, clean, immaculate and able bodied."[17]

The Kuruwa family soon offered their holiday home at Matheran for Osho, and Osho would stay as a guest at their Bombay residence during his visits to the city. The family consulted him during a crisis when Laxmi's brother had decided to marry his Parsi girlfriend, disregarding the family's opposition to this inter-religious alliance. Osho prevailed upon them to give up their opposition and bless the couple.

Laxmi's interest in Osho deepened over time as she discussed issues with him and attended his discourses and meditation camps. One fine day, she decided to wear orange-coloured *lungi* and *kurta* on a regular basis, to signify her new identity as a seeker on the path of spiritualism. Once when she went in this attire to receive Osho at the railway station, he liked it and called her his first sannyasin. "This marks the beginning of the 'Neo Sannyas' and you are the first sannyasin. Now I will begin giving sannyas to people who wish to be initiated," he said. She was there when he initiated 12 sannyasins, including a Westerner and a Japanese woman at the September 26, 1970 camp in Manali.[18]

Efficient in managing her time and organising things, Laxmi saw that there was no one attending to Osho's comforts and small needs; and visitors disturbed him at all times, not respecting his need for rest. She took it upon herself to organise things for Osho. He had been staying at the CCI Chambers, and as his Indian and Western followers grew in numbers in the early 1970s, the need was felt for a bigger place. A three-bedroom flat was purchased on the first floor of the posh, 27-storeyed Woodland Apartments, Pedder Road. Laxmi would take position at the front desk from 8 a.m. itself, giving appointments to visitors and managing Osho's schedule. She would also keep the flat neat and clean, take care of Osho's food and attend to other needs.

Rather unusually, Laxmi always referred to herself in the third person in an effort to break her identity with her body. For example, instead of saying, "I was joyous the next morning," she would say, "Laxmi was joyous the next morning." People found this extremely odd initially but soon got used to it.

Just as the idea of wearing the orange attire (which later became a robe) came from Laxmi, it was she who expressed the desire to wear a beaded *mala* with a locket bearing Osho's picture. Osho agreed to this and it was introduced as a part of the sannyas process. The former British sannyasin Hugh Milne (Swami Shivamurti) who was among Osho's earliest Western disciples and fell out with the Movement later, has recorded that Laxmi got the idea of the *mala* from one of Osho's disciples 'Pratima' who herself had a small following and whose followers wore a *mala* with her picture in a plastic locket. The *mala* with 108 wooden beads with Osho's picture in a locket was meant to signify that Osho was always by the side of the seeker and close to their heart. The many beads conveyed the idea that there are many paths to spirituality, all leading to the absolute truth.

Twenty-year-old Panipat resident Narain Das embraced sannyas on September 4, 1971 with the name Swami Chaitanya Keerti. He had come to Bombay by train with five rupees in his pocket and after making inquiries, had reached Osho's residence at Woodland. Keerti had never met Osho but had read his books, and the impact of Osho's words was so deep that it had drawn him to Bombay. At Osho's residence, Keerti was initially prevented by Laxmi from meeting the guru. Not willing to give up, he sent a note inside and was soon called by Osho. Overwhelmed by the guru's presence, Keerti was speechless and was staring at the Master's feet. Without hesitation, he decided to take sannyas there and then. Osho's words, *"Madhu, mala lao,"* (Madhu, bring a *mala*) still ring in his ears.

After a few years in Bombay, the number of disciples kept growing and the unsuitability of Bombay's weather for an asthmatic Osho became apparent. It was now decided to establish an ashram, a Commune in a 100-km radius from Bombay and a search was undertaken for a suitable location. Laxmi was in the forefront of this search and had scouted hill stations like Lonavla, Khandala and Matheran which were ruled out because of the heavy rainfall there. Pune was identified as an ideal location and soon, a bungalow at 33 Koregaon Park, which belonged to the former Maharaja of Jamnagar was identified and purchased after negotiations. The bungalow was financed by Greek shipping heiress Catherine Venizelos (Ma Yoga Mukta). Osho moved base to Pune on March 21, 1974, which coincided with the 21st anniversary of his 'Day of Enlightenment,' and named his residence Lao Tzu House, after one of his favourite philosophers. The Bombay flat was sold and another property purchased in Pune which became the main administrative block—Krishna House.

The author's personal discovery of Osho happened quite accidentally during final year B.A. at St. Xavier's College, Bombay, in 1986 and while staying at the college hostel at Tardeo. Over breakfast and tea, a friendship developed with a young South American tourist who was staying at the hostel. He was headed to the Rajneesh Ashram at Koregaon Park and since the author was headed home to Pune over the weekend, he offered to take him right up to the gates of the Ashram which he had never visited before. Something unusual happened while waiting for about 35 minutes in the Visitor's Centre while the young tourist proceeded with his registration formalities. A video of one of Osho's discourses was playing on the television monitor which made ample sense and had an impact. The author distinctly remembers feeling at that moment that Osho was making a valid point and was not the devil as portrayed by the media.

Barring that fleeting introduction, the author did not encounter Osho till the time of acquiring a journalism degree and entering the profession as a cub reporter in 1987 with the now defunct *The Indian Post* in its Pune bureau. Osho grabbed the headlines every now and then and from that point on, the author's association with the Commune continued through the decades, getting an opportunity to witness one of Osho's evening discourses in the Buddha Hall and being escorted on a tour of Lao Tzu House by Amrito, which included a visit to Osho's library, bedroom, the dentist's chair and the Rolls Royce in which he would be brought to the Buddha Hall.

As *The Times of India*'s Washington Correspondent in 1993, the author had contemplated visiting the ruins of Rancho Rajneesh in Oregon, but that didn't materialise.

However, there was an invitation from Satya Vedant to participate in an after-office demonstration of one of Osho's meditation techniques at the World Bank. This was an hour long 'Osho meditation,' with four, 15-minute sets of movements from a vigorous shaking of the body to *shavasan* (corpse posture in yoga), which was refreshing and invigorating. In early 2000, the Commune's spokesperson Amrit Sadhana asked the author to don a maroon robe and participate in an orientation programme as a pre-condition to gain access to Osho's Samadhi for a story for *The Times of India*. This was agreed to for the sake of accurate reportage.

Osho was a complex character, depicted on the one hand by the media as an outlandish sex guru; more of a madman than a godman who had foolishly anointed himself as '*Bhagwan*' (God). On the other hand, here was this man who was irreligious, irreverent, fearless, deeply spiritual, philosophical, mystical and thought-provoking. There was undoubtedly something extraordinary about Osho, and thousands of his followers saw him as an "enlightened soul," forsaking everything to be in his presence. They were not sex-starved people. As the stories of how ordinary folks took to following him make it amply clear, these were people who had been honest with themselves and had truly found their guru.

Apart from several profound discourses on spirituality and mysticism, and a series of meditation techniques that are followed avidly in many parts of India and the world, Osho left behind a priceless legacy in the form of his intellectual properties, trusts and prime real estate. His followers—and through them, society at large—are the true inheritors of this legacy. The physical and intellectual wealth that was created by

Osho, and in his name, cannot be allowed to be usurped by an unscrupulous coterie, if that is indeed what has been happening over the years. Osho's Samadhi, located inside the Commune in Pune, needs to be made accessible to the public, especially his followers, many of whom have been banned from stepping inside the Commune.

There is a need to look closely into the questionable circumstances of Osho's death—even at this late stage—to set to rest the truth of what really happened on the day he died.

Many lengthy interviews with a range of Osho's sannyasins across hierarchies were conducted by the author for this book and a mass of official documents and press reports accessed. Requests for interviews with Jayesh and Amrito were turned down by Amrit Sadhana, who also chose not to respond to several uncomfortable questions put to the OIF.

It is nearly half-a-century since the Rajneesh Movement began in India in the late 1960s, and more than a quarter century since the death of its founder, Osho. Many of his earliest followers and those who were around him at critical moments in the history of the Movement have either passed on, or are in the evening of their lives today. Some of them are privy to untold stories, especially the circumstances of his death. There was every possibility that the facts presented in this book would never have come to light and would have been lost forever. *Who Killed Osho?* is an effort to capture some of those stories for posterity.

It is extremely important that the official version of Osho's death be re-opened and re-examined through judicial verification and police investigations because it could otherwise tantamount to perpetuating a lie. A lie cannot be allowed to be passed down as a fact of history.

This book could not have been written without the willingness of Osho's closest disciples to share with the author the stories of their life with the Master. I am deeply touched by their kindness and generosity.

RTI activist Vijay Kumbhar and friends such as Mahesh Vijapurkar, Ratnakar Detke, Sandip Dighe, C. Ravindranath and Jaya Nair provided valuable assistance and suggestions.

Dileep Padgaonkar was a mentor throughout my career. I will always feel his presence, warmth and generosity.

My mother, Pramila Vaidya, wife Geeta and daughter Anshita inspired me wih their enormous love to plod on and on.

I am also deeply indebted to my friend and investigative journalist Josy Joseph, literary agent Kanishka Gupta, publisher Ajay Mago and chief editor Dipa Chaudhuri who provided valuable guidance during the writing of this book.

2

Poona-I: A Commune is Established

When the Shree Rajneesh Ashram was established in Poona[1] in March, 1974, it was the only place in the world where a mystic who effortlessly integrated and experimented with Eastern mysticism, new forms of meditation and Western psycho-therapy of the Human Growth Potential Movement, boldly led a Commune based on his ideas and spoke with sincerity, authority and conviction. The ashram did not begin as a Commune but as a place where Osho could reside in spacious environs and deliver his discourses. Initially, there was no place to do group meditations at his residence and these were done in a public botanical garden. Those interested in his ideas were expected to come for short periods of stay and return home in India or abroad. Only his closest followers, who had dedicated their lives to him, lived with him. However, such was the surge of followers from within and outside India in the early 1970s, that neighbouring bungalows were purchased in Koregaon Park, the ashram expanded rapidly and soon became a Commune.

Osho was the focal point and the Commune quenched a thirst for the believers like no other place on earth. It presented the opportunity of a fresh beginning for all open-minded seekers. There was the promise of new relationships and freedom from the bondage of tradition and social expectations. There was adventure in the form of sexual experimentation through Tantra and Encounter Groups within the safe confines of a gated Commune. This was not possible earlier when Osho was living in an apartment in Bombay.

Forty-three years old in 1974, Osho, known as Bhagwan Shree Rajneesh over the past few years, was at his peak and gave the fullest expression to his ideas and creativity. By the mid-1970s, several Indians were already following him in large numbers. There were many who had left him by the wayside because they found his ideas on sex and spiritualism too strong and unpalatable. From vocal supporters of a guru who had spoken brilliantly on the *Bhagavad Gita*, they had now become his critics. Criticism had never intimidated Osho since his childhood and now, a flood of seekers from Europe and America, Australia and Japan was finding its way to the gates of the Commune. They brought valuable dollars with them, swore by his name and stayed for a few weeks or months as this was easily affordable. The Commune's popularity was spreading rapidly by word of mouth, especially among the Westerners. Foreigners would arrive in Bombay, brave the heat and dust, the inevitable dysentery, and the ramshackle infrastructure of the 1970s India and find their way to the Bhagwan. Poona became an important stopover for hippies and other tourists for whom Goa, Manali and Pushkar in Rajasthan were important destinations. Many tourists would make it a point to visit the Rajneesh Ashram out of curiosity before returning home.

The seven years—from March, 1974 to June, 1981—when Osho quietly left for the United States, is known as the

'Poona-I' phase of the Movement. This was the phase when the Commune added more rooms to existing properties, expanded by adding several residential properties and undertook fresh constructions such as therapy chambers in the basement, and the marble-floored Buddha Hall with a capacity to seat 6,000 people. Residential blocks such as Jesus House, Francis House (a part of which was reserved for Osho's parents and relatives), Eckhart House, the Bookshop, Osho's fully-equipped Dental Room with a specially imported dentist's chair from the U.K. were added during this phase. During Poona-I, Osho's girlfriend and caretaker Nirvano, then known as Ma Yoga Vivek, was described as "his constant companion." His personal secretary Laxmi was the only other person who had complete access to Osho.

Soon after settling in Poona, Osho gave a series of eight discourses on the *Bhagavad Gita* in Hindi in April 1974, and a series of English discourses, in May 1974. He had realised the value of humour and his discourses would be interspersed with Mulla Nusruddin jokes in Hindi and several jokes in English, many of them ribald, picked from *Playboy* and other magazines. Peals of laughter during his discourses were a common feature. Dynamic Meditation[2] would be held in the mornings at the Empress Botanical Gardens and Sufi meditation in the evenings. After Dynamic Meditation at 6 a.m., the sannyasins would gather at the Chuang Tzu auditorium in Lao Tzu House for Osho's morning discourse at 8 a.m. He would alternate between Hindi and English discourses every other month, and a number of his foreign disciples would even attend the Hindi discourse, without understanding a word of it, just to be in his presence.

It was during Poona-I that Osho's parents, his brothers, their wives and children left Gadarwara and began living in the ashram since 1978. Like his mother, Osho's father also became his disciple and took sannyas with the name Swami Devateerth Bharti.

In keeping with a variety of skills that professionals such as doctors, engineers, psychologists, academicians, artists, architects, writers, photographers, accountants and others brought with them, Osho's sannayasins were delegated to various departments inside the growing Commune and were engaged in a range of activities. In return for a free-food pass and accommodation, they worked with complete love and dedication for the upkeep and growth of the Commune. The Commune was buzzing with activity and the term "work meditation" entered the lexicon of the ashram. In the main administrative block at Krishna House, Laxmi was in complete charge and the British psychotherapist Paul Lowe (Swami Ananda Teertha) led the immensely popular therapy groups. Osho's personal needs were looked after by Nirvano who headed his team of caretakers and lived in a room next to his at Lao Tzu House. There was a team of seamstresses who stitched his robes which became flashy, resplendent and 'messiah-like' in the U.S. after the Hollywood group gave Osho his new look, with diamond-encrusted watches and Gucci shades. The tape department had sophisticated recording equipment and sound engineers to ensure that Osho's discourses and his interactions with sannyasins were recorded without a hitch. In his early years, Osho insisted on having his talks recorded with a tape recorder. He went to the extent of halting his discourse briefly to give enough time to change sides of the cassette or stopping entirely when the recording stopped due to a power breakdown. Eventually, alternate stand-by arrangements were made for recording at his discourse venues.[3] The meticulous recording of his discourses and their laborious transcription to enable the publication of various titles soon became a standard practice.

The Commune had a full-fledged photography department with the latest equipment and a darkroom, and a videography department which not only recorded all of Osho's discourses and interactions, but also captured his various moods and movements.

During the seven years of Poona-I, the discourses delivered by Osho were transcribed into as many as 240 books. Apart from Dynamic and Whirling meditations, many other innovative meditation techniques were introduced during this phase and included Nataraj, Nadabrahma, Gourishankar, Devavani and Vipassana meditation, which was also being promoted by S.N. Goenka Guruji's Vipassana Meditation Centre at Dhamma Giri, Igatpuri. Swami Chaitanya Keerti once told the author that the Commune did not hesitate to suggest that those wanting to go deeper into Vipassana could gain from attending the advanced meditation camps at the Igatpuri centre which was famous for this form of ancient Buddhist meditation.

The Press Office which brought out press notes, attended to visiting journalists and produced a monthly magazine, was among the busiest departments. So was the Publications Office which not only worked with outside publishers but also produced a range of slickly designed and professionally edited books which won annual design awards. Stationery used by the Commune was designed in-house. The Silkscreen Department printed titles on book jackets and brochures and there was a lathe shop, a jewellery department, a carpentry shop and a *mala*-making workshop. The sound studio managed by Swami

Chaitanya Hari composed highly distinctive and original music for meditations and groups.

The Rajneesh Theatre Group went on to stage Shakespeare's plays such as *A Midsummer Night's Dream* and *Twelfth Night* to critical acclaim in Bombay and Delhi. Exceptionally creative work was done at the ashram workshops and studios in pottery, ceramics and fine arts. The demands on the Kitchen Department kept increasing year after year, with an effort towards improving the quality of vegetarian food, European cuisine, breads and pastries available inside the Commune. In many respects, the Rajneesh Ashram resembled Auroville in Pondicherry, except that it didn't have the land and expanse of Auroville.

The Medical Department with a team of sannyasin-doctors, had to combat water and food-borne diseases, outbreak of Hepatitis and tropical ailments among the foreigners. Added to this were sexually transmitted diseases as there was a surfcit of sexual activity with multiple partners. The Commune encouraged sterilisations and abortions on a large scale as Osho was against children on the Commune because they were a distraction and "interfered with a person's spiritual growth." However, a playschool and a 'No School' had been introduced in the Commune for the children of sannyasins who were already parents.

Like many Western psychologists including Freud, Osho had been emphasising that sex was a part of human nature and therefore natural. Man had become dysfunctional because of the conditioning by society and religious orders and the repression of natural biological urges. Unlike Western scholars, Osho linked spiritualism to sex, and said that the state of thoughtlessness, timelessness and bliss that was experienced during orgasm was similar to the highest state of super-consciousness and the ultimate goal of meditation. Thus, sexual experimentation now had the stamp of spirituality to it and therefore experimentation through the Tantra and Encounter groups began on a big scale inside the Commune during Poona-I. These groups were led by Teertha and participation in these groups was not open to Indians. Osho explained this by saying that Indians needed "more quiet and passive meditations" like Vipassana and Zazen compared to people from the West who came "from a very oppressive world" and therefore needed active therapies.

Britisher Paul Lowe, who had taken sannyas as Swami Ananda Teertha led the therapy groups. A pioneer in the field of Encounter group therapies, he with his wife Patricia, had co-founded Quaesitor, a prominent humanistic growth centre in London after training at Esalen, one of the leading centres of the Human Growth Potential Movement in California. A man with a voracious sexual appetite, Teertha was described by Patricia as "a great sexual adventurer."[4] The Encounter group was so called because participants gave free expression to whatever feelings and emotions they felt were repressed, and this led to shouting, screaming, violence and group sex. Some participants suffered fractures which would be treated at a local hospital where a variety of reasons such as "fell from the bicycle" or "hurt during construction activity" were given by way of explanation. The staff soon got used to such explanations without knowing the truth but provided treatment nevertheless. The violence in the Encounter groups was eventually banned after some negative reports appeared in sections of the international press.

According to Satya Vedant, the Encounter and Primal Therapy groups began at the Commune in 1975 and Teertha was joined by a well-known Western psychologist Leonard Zunin (Swami Prem Siddha) who had embraced the Rajneesh Movement. Apart from these front-ranking programmes, the Commune offered a range of other therapies such as Reichian, Gesalt, Bioenergetics and Rolfing, all at Western prices. In March 1976, there were seven group therapies offered at the ashram which increased to 30 in a year and by 1979, the therapy groups at the Commune numbered more than 100 under the Rajneesh International Meditation University (RIMU) which had been envisioned. The proposed university, however, did not get government recognition.

One of the first group therapies that Amrito attended in 1978 was the 'Tantra group' where the men and women sat in a circle in a padded room. "Here was a group of fairly typical young Westerners who barely knew each other, except for one couple. And yet, with so little provocation, we could become raging animals within a minute," he wrote of this experience.[5]

Later, he said in his memoirs, "The sexual encounters that happened in the group were unremarkable; it was the aggression it released that was startling." At the end of this Encounter group he noticed that the flowers that were laid out beautifully at the start of the session lay crushed all over the room.[6] The Tantra group therapy lasted for three days.

During these years, several delegations from established therapy groups and human potential movements in Europe and America made it a point to visit the Poona Commune, adding to its reputation. Americans from the Arica School came in 1976 and Richard Price, co-founder of the Esalen Institute also visited the Commune during Poona-I. In fact, the Encounter groups in the Poona Commune were reputed as the best in the world and Poona was called 'Esalen of the East' by *Time* magazine. The ashram introduced its own Arica Programme in December, 1975.

The specialists who came to experiment with various therapies sought to go beyond the boundaries of sex, violence, anger and rage and along with the therapies, most meditations were cathartic, encouraging the release of "suppressed madness."

Attendance of Indian and foreign disciples swelled to nearly 10,000, especially around the special celebrations that took place at the Commune every year: Osho's birthday on December 11, his 'Day of Enlightenment' on March 21, and Guru Purnima Day (Hindu custom of expressing gratitude to spiritual and academic teachers), also celebrated as Full Moon Day in July. Two prominent deaths that were marked by 'death celebrations' during Poona-I were those of Osho's father, 'Daddaji' on September 8, 1979 and Swami Anand Vimalkirti (formerly, Prince Welf Ernst of Hanover) on January 9, 1981. The death of the blue-blooded prince brought in condolence messages from Buckingham Palace and from Prime Minister Indira Gandhi. After Daddaji's death, September 8 began to be celebrated as 'Mahaparinirvana Day' in the memory of all those sannyasins who had died in the Commune.

'Energy Darshans' were introduced in 1979. These would be held at night with all the Commune lights switched off briefly, creating complete darkness during the ceremony that included loud, pulsating music and flashing lights, inducing a trance-like environment at its peak. During this ceremony, Osho would have 12 female sannyasins designated as his 'mediums' dancing in a circle with the sannyasin wanting an

'Energy Darshan' sitting in front of him. At one point, Osho would touch the energy centre (third eye) in the middle of the forehead of a 'medium' with one hand and that of the person sitting in front of him, with the other hand. Almost everyone who went through an 'Energy Darshan' described it as a powerful experience. While Shunyo called it a "psychedelic experience," Dr. Gokani said, "I was in the air for three days."

By the middle of Poona-I, foreigners outnumbered the Indian disciples inside the Commune. During his morning darshan, Osho answered selected questions ranging from personal problems, emotional and relationship issues troubling the seekers to spiritual queries. In the evenings, he gave a discourse. Osho was intensely photographed and videographed on every occasion; the question-answer sessions were transcribed and edited into a series of volumes titled 'Darshan Diaries' while the discourses became books and audio tapes were available for sale and distribution. The landscaping and beautification of the Commune was an ongoing activity.

The British physician who is known as Amrito and who emerged as a central figure in Osho's life at the time of his death, and later, has written about his adventurous life before and after he became an Osho sannyasin in 1978. His testimony at the Wasco County Special Grand Jury hearings on October 15, 1985 in the aftermath of the Rancho Rajneesh fiasco also provides rich details of his background. His story is that of a typically disillusioned Westerner who came to India in search of Osho.

In his testimony, Amrito gave his legal name as George Alexander Stowell Wynne-Aubrey Meredith; in short, Dr. George Meredith, and his sannyas name as Swami Devaraj.

Amrito had "the usual Church of England upbringing," and his parents were divorced when he was about four years old. His first marriage was to a woman named Eileen and while in that marriage he had an affair with a writer called Cathy. He felt imprisoned and miserable by the sense of guilt resulting from this affair. Young George was disillusioned with the Cold War, attracted by Communist ideology, and his readings in radical psychiatry and the break-up of families all around were issues that made him think. Amidst all this, he wondered, "Where was music and dance, fun and laughter, art and literature, not to mention sex and the mysteries of love?"

In 1974, Amrito worked in Kuwait as the head of medicine at a hospital, and later visited Karachi and India on a holiday. Delhi, Rajasthan and the Aurobindo Ashram at Pondicherry were among the places he had visited. The erotic sculptures of Khajurao in a sexually-repressed country like India puzzled him then, and after his holidays, Amrito returned to England overland via Pakistan, Afghanistan, Iran and Turkey. He was now romantically involved with an old friend of his named Wendy, one of whose friends was an Osho follower, wearing orange clothes and the *mala*. This piqued his curiosity.

Bored with hospital life in England, he came on a holiday to Goa with Wendy, and this time visited the Rajneesh Ashram in Poona. He found the environment of people dressed in "beautiful robes of bright oranges, pinks and reds" very exhilarating, with much laughter, hugging and the holding of hands. "Something in me was screaming to simply jump in," he recalled.[7]

Although he did not understand a word of Osho's Hindi discourse in the evening, the Master, by his very presence, had touched a chord in him: "He looked beautiful; his movements were graceful, and he had a delicate elegance about him that almost didn't fit with his laughing, fun-sized eyes," Amrito wrote. When Osho spoke of God, Amrito found it far more refreshing than that "crusty Church of England stuff" he had heard in his childhood. After that discourse, Amrito found himself in a queue leading to Osho and when he was in front of Osho, he didn't think twice, "just bent down, kissed his foot, *namaste-d* and moved on."[8]

The British doctor took sannyas on April 24, 1978 and was given the name 'Swami Devaraj'. He found that Osho had a deep understanding of the human mind and his meditations, therapies and advice during the question-answer sessions helped many Westerners deal with their frustrations, relationship problems, search for meaning and an alternative to mainstream religions which they found shallow. By now, his wife Wendy had taken sannyas as Devena (with whom he broke up later) and his son was named Deveda. In later months, in the highly promiscuous free love environment of the Commune, Amrito fell in and out of love with Nirvano. He was impressed when she showed him around in Lao Tzu House where she lived in a room adjoining Osho's, and where they made love. Most people in the Poona Commune, he said, had regular girlfriends and boyfriends and some people stayed together for years. "Others had a series of love affairs; some people lived alone and had none." Men and women had no hesitation in showing interest in someone they liked. They took rejections sportingly.

In 1986, Osho's bodyguard Shivamurti wrote in his memoirs how Amrito had happily boasted of his freshly-done vasectomy and encouraged Shivamurti to undergo the minor surgery. He agreed to it only to regret later.[9]

Osho's transition from 'Acharya' to 'Bhagwan' had already happened a few years before he came to Poona. Neelam remembered this vividly: It was during a 10-day meditation camp in Manali in 1970 that he gave a discourse on Krishna—the man and his philosophy. There were around 250 participants and they were so deeply moved that they said, "The way he is explaining Krishna, it feels as if he is Krishna. If Krishna were alive, he would be just like the person in front of us." It was a full moon night and there were many Gujaratis in the gathering. They asked Osho to sit in the centre and did a *garba* dance around him (*Garba* is a circular dance performed in Gujarat traditionally during the Hindu festival *Navratri*). "It was all very enchanting and we felt, if he is not God, then who is God?" Soon, Osho's followers were discussing among themselves about a new title for their guru and they decided on calling him 'Bhagwan'. "We told him we want to call you Bhagwan. He kept quiet. We kept repeating and bringing this up again and again, that we don't want to call you 'Acharya Shree' but 'Bhagwan Shree'." After a month, when he went to Bombay, a note appeared in the Rajneesh Movement's magazine *Jyoti Shikhar* that Rajneesh had agreed to be called 'Bhagwan Shree.' This was around November, 1970, said Neelam.

When this news reached the public, it at once sparked a controversy, with considerable criticism and ridicule that here was a person mixing sex and spiritualism and calling himself 'Bhagwan'—God. Didn't this caustic public reaction bother Osho? Osho had become used to being controversial since his teenage years. Instead of being bothered by the sharp comments from the public, he seemed happy that he had ignited another controversy. As Neelam said, "It served his purpose."

Poona-I was the period when Indian-American scholar, Prof. Vasant Joshi took sannyas as Swami Satya Vedant in December 1975. He had not heard of Osho when he completed his PhD in English Literature from M.S. University, Baroda, and headed to the United States in 1966. This was the period when, attracted by the Hare Krishna Movement, Maharishi Mahesh Yogi and the Hippie Movement, several Westerners were flocking to India. Prof. Joshi was invited by the University of California at Berkeley to look at these social upheavals closely and conduct a course on the cultural and literary traditions of India. That was when he received some booklets on Osho's discourses in Hindi which he found very illuminating. The interest in Osho continued as he undertook his second PhD in Education at the University of Michigan at Ann Arbor in 1973. He was deeply touched by an audio recording of one of Osho's discourses on Mahavir, and two years later, took leave and came to visit Osho at the Poona Commune. He arrived on December 10, 1975 and the next day, "while I was sitting in front of Osho, I was initiated with the name Satya Vedant."

One person who had a devastating impact on the Rajneesh Movement was a young Gujarati woman who came to the United States as a teenager and had married her American boyfriend when she was just 18. Born at Baroda, Sheela Ambalal Patel had first met Osho in her childhood when he had visited their home at the invitation of her father. When she met Osho again in the early 1970s in Bombay, she felt deeply inspired by him and took sannyas as Ma Anand Sheela. During the Poona-I days, she served as an assistant to Laxmi and less than a decade later, replaced Laxmi as Osho's personal secretary during the 1980s, planning and executing the entire re-location to the U.S.

Sheela had courageously married her American boyfriend Marc Silverman even though he had been dissuading her from marrying him as he had been diagnosed with lymphatic cancer. Eventually, both decided to tie the knot and spend the time available with them joyously. Following in Sheela's footsteps, Marc too took sannyas and was renamed 'Swami Chinmaya'.

According to Sheela, one incident that endeared her to Laxmi was her idea of raising money for the ashram through borrowings from sannyasins, especially the Westerners. On one occasion, Laxmi was in need of money to purchase a neighbouring bungalow in Koregaon Park for the ashram's expansion. Sheela went out with a notepad and checked out with the sannyasins how much money they could loan to the Commune and by when they wanted their money back. "Before lunch, I had more money for Laxmi than she needed," said Sheela in her memoirs. According to her, the informal 'Ashram Bank' soon became a permanent institution and the average daily turnover was more than $1,00,000, with liquid cash of half-a-million dollars available at any time. As the Commune grew, so did this bank, requiring three full-time sannyasins for its management.[10]

Since Osho was allergic to perfumes and strong smells, some sannyasins were designated as "sniffers" who would sniff at people and prevent anyone with a strong smell of perfume, hair oil or shampoo from going anywhere close to Osho. The decision of the sniffers was final and absolutely no one was spared, no matter how important the person was or how high on the celebrity index. Once, Sheela had been refused entry to an evening darshan with Osho as Sheela smelled of shampoo. She had exploded at Maneesha who was on 'sniffer duty' at the Lao Tzu gate and was later asked by Osho to apologise to Maneesha in front of the gathering and touch her feet to seek forgiveness.

Although the foreigners contributed substantially to the local economy, bringing good business to vendors, merchants, autorickshaw drivers, flat owners and property agents in the Koregaon Park area, they also offended local sensibilities with their thin, loose flowing robes and absence of underwear, the holding of hands, frequent hugging and open display of affection—a sight that the citizens of a conservative Poona were not used to. Added to this, Osho was hated for his controversial views. While sannyasins would be attacked by petty criminals off and on, the most sensational attack on the Commune occurred in May, 1980 when a knife was thrown at Osho. The knife which fell limply on the floor, a few feet in front of Osho, was thrown by Vilas Tupe, a member of a radical Hindu organisation. The attack took place in the Buddha Hall on May 22, 1980, during Osho's morning discourse and was the result of the overall resentment in a section of society against the Commune.

Towards the end of the 1970s, the Commune was spread over 6 acres of land in the Koregaon Park area and the need was felt for more space and greater expansion. This was no longer possible in Pune where the expansion had been done in a piecemeal manner. What was needed was a large plot of land where the needs of the Commune over the coming years could be addressed in a better way. Two locations were being considered seriously—one at Saswad within Poona district where negotiations were in an advanced stage with the property owner Amarsinh Jadhavrao, and the other location being Kutch in Gujarat which was being explored by Laxmi.

An ambitious plan was drawn up for a new Commune with the name Rajneesh Neo Sannyas International Commune on a 400-acre plot at Jadhavwadi in Saswad, about 32 km from Pune. An inauguration ceremony was also held on December 11, 1979 to coincide with Osho's 48th birthday. However, that plan fell through just as the plan for a Commune at Kutch was also still-born.[11]

There were other irritants in the form of a major legal dispute with the Charity Commissionerate over the charitable status and exemption of taxes claimed by the Commune, and constant friction between Osho and Prime Minister Morarji Desai. According to senior sannyasins, it was Desai—frequently criticised by Osho—who had shot down the ashram's proposal for expansion at Kutch, and the application for starting a university.

Sheela, who had now gained greater access to Osho and had also won his confidence, was strongly in favour of moving to the U.S. Finally, it was decided that Osho would fly to the U.S., and among the 5,000 odd sannyasins, a small team of Osho's closest aides and Sheela's confidants was put together and told that a date was being set for Osho's departure to the U.S. One set of sannyasins left in advance to make preparations and receive Osho in the U.S.

Osho gave his last evening darshan on March 23, 1981 and his last morning discourse the next day, March 24, 1981. He then entered a period of silence which he had done previously. Osho secured a temporary visa to the U.S. on medical grounds for seeking treatment for severe backache. His last *satsang* (spiritual gathering) was on the morning of June 1, 1981, after which he left Pune in a convoy of five cars which included two Rolls Royces. At Bombay airport, Osho's Rolls was allowed to go right up to the nose of the 747 Jumbo jet and the entire first class with 40 seats on the upper deck had been reserved for Osho and his aides. The final phase of the plan to leave India for good had been set in motion.

3

The Lure of the United States

If Laxmi was rooted in India, the Indian way of life, and was instrumental in establishing the Poona Commune in 1974, her assistant, Sheela, also a Gujarati, was rooted in the United States, enamoured by Western life and culture, and instrumental in re-locating the Movement to Oregon. Sheela was appointed Osho's personal secretary in January, 1981, replacing Laxmi. She served in this capacity during the Oregon years till September 1985, when she abandoned the Commune and was replaced by the Hollywood celebrity producer Françoise Rudy, also known by her sannyas name Ma Prem Hasya.

The four-and-a-half years that Osho spent in the U.S., from June, 1981 to November, 1985 proved to be a complete misadventure and most disastrous for him and the Movement.

Sheela, who had emerged as a very bright and efficient assistant to Laxmi, and had gained considerable influence with Osho towards the end of Poona-I, disliked India as vehemently as she loved America. She boasted that all her personal supplies "from Heinz tomato ketchup to tampons" were sourced from the U.S. Sheela found everything slow, annoying and frustrating in India. Indeed, the infrastructure and public conveniences in the 1970s were abysmally poor, especially when compared to the West. She found India hot and dirty. When she moved to Poona in the mid-1970s, she brought everything she needed from the U.S. and wrote that she could have "opened a small supermarket" with the contents of her suitcase. In the evenings, Sheela would warmly share her nostalgic feelings for the U.S. with like-minded friends in the Poona Commune.

In India, there was animosity towards Osho from the government, bureaucracy and a large section of the people, and Sheela reasoned that he should move to the U.S. because of the superior quality of life and greater tolerance among the people there. The Poona Commune was trying to live up to Western standards of perfection and professionalism, and to achieve that, it imported all its requirements, including gadgets and equipment at 125% to 200% import duty. Since Western followers had begun to dominate the Rajneesh Movement during the Poona-1 days itself, the U.S. with all its advantages and attractions as a leading nation emerged as the ideal destination to operate from. It would be far easier for people from the West to come to the U.S. and the Commune would be financially worthwhile too.

Osho's severe backache during 1980–81 and the need for advanced medical treatment in the U.S. were stated as the official reasons for his departure to the U.S. in June, 1981 on a temporary tourist visa. However, three developments clearly indicate that a detailed plan had been worked out to establish an ambitious Commune and settle there permanently.

Two months before he left for the U.S., on April 1, 1981, an agreement was signed between the Chidvilas Rajneesh Meditation Center at Montclair, New Jersey, and Rajneesh

Foundation, Pune, transferring Osho's copyrights to the Chidvilas Center. This centre was established in 1973 by Sheela who later abandoned Rajneeshpuram, driving it into a ditch, and moved to Europe.

Jeevan Jagruti Kendra was the first trust established by Osho on June 11, 1969, around the time when he initiated his very first disciples in Bombay. The name of this trust was changed to Rajneesh Foundation on October 23, 1975. On July 28, 1978, Osho gave this trust the complete rights to his intellectual properties.

The April 1981 agreement was the point at which the copyrights to the intellectual properties created by Osho in the form of books, discourses and meditation techniques moved out of India to the U.S. Neelam and Premgeet, who is a lead petitioner and complainant in several cases against the Osho International Foundation, contend that this transfer of copyrights on April 1, 1981 was illegal as the assignment deed was signed by just one of the nine trustees of Rajneesh Foundation, namely Manikant Ratansi Khona alias Swami Manu. They contend that this transfer was illegal as it was not accompanied by any resolution passed by all the trustees of Rajneesh Foundation.

In subsequent years, the Chidvilas Rajneesh Meditation Center changed its name to Rajneesh Foundation International (America) which later became Rajneesh Friends International. On August 18, 1986, Rajneesh Friends International signed an agreement of assignment of copyrights to Rajneesh Foundation Europe, which changed its name to Neo Sannyas Foundation, which in turn, changed its name to Osho International Foundation, Zürich. All rights to Osho's works now rest with this trust in Europe which is being challenged by many of

Osho's sannyasins in India, with support from sannyasins in Europe who are fighting their own battles against the OIF.

According to the official version, Osho had left for New York for a spinal surgery as a disc "was protruding onto the nervous tissue of his spine." However, that surgery never happened as Osho recovered "miraculously." About four months after arriving in the U.S., Osho was fit enough to travel, and was flown by a private jet to the ranch in Oregon. In 1981 itself, Osho's American disciples purchased the 64,000 acre—125 square miles—The Big Muddy ranch in Oregon for $5.75 million and invited him on a visit. "He eventually agrees to stay in the U.S. and allows an application for permanent residence to be filed on his behalf."[1] It was Sheela who had previously visited and identified the over-grazed, desolate property known as The Big Muddy ranch located in Central Oregon. It was renamed Rancho Rajneesh and the nearby town of Antelope became the city of Rajneesh after Osho's followers won the local elections and installed their own mayor.

The calculations of Osho's top managers were not off the mark because Osho's sannyasins, through their hard work and enterprise, had created an oasis in the desert. An estimated 5,000 people made their way to Rancho Rajneesh and contributed generously with their life's savings, time and talent to the Movement in the hope of establishing a successful Commune according to Osho's vision of the 'New Man'. Special summer festivals were held which attracted thrice that number.

At its peak, the Movement had a hotel and an airlines of its own called Air Rajneesh; at least one Swiss Bank account with 'contingency funds' specially reserved for Osho's needs,[2] and a growing collection of 97 Rolls Royces which had grabbed headlines not just in America but all over the world. With their ingenuity and hard work, the sannyasins took to farming, construction and road-building. The trailer apartments for the arriving sannyasins had central air-conditioning, and a bus service called 'Rajneesh Buddhafield Transport' was created.

Although the Oregon Commune made a spectacular beginning with its eye-popping fleet of Rolls Royces and the promise of an extraordinary experiment in Commune life, the four-and-a-half years that Osho spent in the U.S.—from June, 1981 to November, 1985—turned out to be the worst years of his life and the worst phase for the Movement. There was constant friction with the local community which made the 'Rajneeshees' unpopular with locals in the towns and villages neighbouring the ranch, and there was intense factional fighting within the Commune.

At Rancho Rajneesh, three factions were engaged in a power struggle: Sheela, who was the most powerful and the most domineering had her faction of loyalists and felt insecure by the 'Lao Tzu people'—those like Amrito, Nirvano, Devageet and Shunyo who were closest to Osho. Sheela was not only jealous of their proximity to Osho but also felt insecure with the strong ties emerging between them and the Hollywood group. Eventually, the Oregon Commune imploded with the intense jealousies, power politics and murder attempts between these groups.

The Sheela faction's attempts to repeatedly poison Amrito (who was not only close to Osho but also married to Hasya while in the U.S.), and Nirvano, were a part of the power politics. Sheela was eventually convicted and imprisoned in the U.S. on the charge of attempting to poison Amrito. According to Sheela's faction, a secretly taped conversation between Osho and Amrito discussing euthanasia was the provocation for the murder attempt on Amrito by Sheela's aide Shanti

Bhadra (Catherine Jane Stork) who stuck a syringe filled with adrenaline into his buttocks during a crowded gathering. One person who testified to hearing this conversation was David Knapp, also known as Swami Krishna Deva and 'K.D.' Appointed Mayor of Rajneeshpuram, Knapp testified that he "listened to a copy of a tape from a bug in Bhagwan's room where he (Devaraj) and Bhagwan discussed him assisting Bhagwan in committing suicide."[3] Sheela also suspected that Osho was a victim of dangerous drug experimentation and overdose and that Amrito was a threat to his life. Shanti B. confessed to her crime later and faced a prison sentence.

One of the highlights of the Oregon years was the presence of the 'Hollywood group' led by the wealthy film producer, late Françoise Rudy. Wife of the famous Hollywood producer A.S. Ruddy of *The Godfather* fame, Hasya brought glamour and glitter to the Commune with her closest friends and Osho sannyasins with strong Hollywood connections. These were Ma Prem Kaveesha (Joyce Scholozman) who later headed The Mystery School during Poona-II, Swami Dhyan Yogi, also known as Dr. Yogi and by his legal name Dr. John S. Hollywood, Kaveesha's nephew David and the super-rich Ma Shantam Avirbhava (belonging to the Kresge family, founders of the American retail giant, Kmart) who had gifted the silver Rolls Royce that Osho used in Pune. The high profile of the 'Hollywood group' at Rajneeshpuram can be gauged from the depositions that sannyasins made before the Wasco County Grand Jury in 1985 and in statements to the FBI when full-fledged investigations were undertaken into allegations of wire-tapping, murder attempts, sham marriages (immigration fraud) and mass poisoning at Rajneeshpuram. The testimonies of the sannyasins against one another suggested that all these allegations were true.

Hasya in her deposition on October 15, 1985 before the Grand Jury said she became a sannyasin in 1977 when she met Osho for the first time in India. Later, she stayed at Rajneeshpuram for three months in 1982 and returned in October 1983 to stay there permanently. She continued with her movie production work for which she would fly in and out of Rajneeshpuram by chartering a small plane. On September 15, 1985, she became Osho's personal secretary and was later appointed President of Rajneesh Foundation International which changed its name to Rajneesh Friends International. Hasya said that after Sheela left in September, 1985, Sheela's second-in-command at Rajneeshpuram, Savita, mentioned to her the existence of a Swiss Bank account "set up for Bhagwan's needs" with an undisclosed amount and that she would turn over the account number to her, which didn't happen. (The Indian sannyasin Ma Dharm Jyoti who was very close to Osho and worked in the Accounts Department at Rajneeshpuram told the author in February, 2016 that the Commune was able to access this account during Poona-II.[4]) Hasya said Sheela showed considerable animosity towards her, especially after her marriage to Amrito with whom Sheela had a rivalry from before as he was Osho's personal physician.

Giving her account of the events that followed after the attempt to kill Amrito by members of Sheela's team, Hasya said her friends such as Kaveesha, and to some extent Dhyan John took turns to be by his side during his recuperation.

In his testimony before the Wasco County Grand Jury on October 25, 1985, the wealthy 43-year-old former emergency room physician, Swami Dhyan John (legal name: John Wally) said he hailed from Kansas City where he qualified as a doctor and practised medicine. In 1980, he connected with some of Osho's followers in Beverly Hills, California, one of whom was his friend Kaveesha, and eventually moved into a home owned by Hasya. He took sannyas in January 1982, and bought a house in Hollywood Hills where he, Hasya, Kaveesha, David and a few other sannyasins set up a Rajneesh Center. This mansion was later donated by John to Rajneesh Foundation International after he moved to Rajneeshpuram to stay with his friends. After a brief stay of three months, he returned to California and came back to Rajneeshpuram in 1983 with Hasya and others.

One event, covered extensively by the American media was the departure of a convoy of three Rolls Royces from Rajneeshpuram driven by John, then in his early 40s, and Hasya and Kaveesha in their late 40s, to Hollywood to bring new followers from among the rich and the famous.

John said in his testimony that he and his friends did not compromise on their lifestyle while on the ranch which was under construction and required a lot of hard work and physical labour from the sannyasins. He had decided to lead a retired life which was resented by Sheela who tried to "blend" him and others from the Hollywood group into the Commune life. At the same time, Sheela did not want to push him too much as he was wealthy and a source of donations.

Amrito substantiated this version in his own deposition before the Wasco County Grand Jury on 15 October, 1985 and said, "...The fact is that Hasya's friends have money, they are not dependent upon Sheela's largesse in any sense. If they want to leave, they order a plane and fly out; when they come back, they rent a plane and fly in. This somewhat offends Sheela's notion that it's the queen who comes and goes, and if other people are doing such things, it rather weakens her childish need to be the boss."

Knapp appeared at the Portland office of the FBI and was interviewed periodically between October 29, 1985 and November 7, 1985 during which he revealed that one of the reasons for tension between Sheela and the Hollywood group was Hasya's decision to purchase a luxury Calista watch for $2.5 to 3 million which Osho wanted. Sheela wanted Hasya to turn down that request from Osho which Hasya said she could not do.

In their depositions, Osho's followers said that Sheela felt threatened by the growing influence of this wealthy set with Osho on the one hand and by Hasya's marriage to Amrito on March 22, 1984 on the other hand, which further elevated Amrito's status.

Finally, in September 1985, the Commune was hit by its worst crisis after Sheela abandoned it and took flight to Germany amidst allegations of failed murder attempts, mass poisoning and extensive wire-tapping. It was Hasya who stepped in with her sannyasin friends from California to do the fire-fighting, interact with the press, advise and protect Osho from the fallout of the crisis, and communicate important decisions. She had been appointed as Osho's International Secretary, as a replacement to Sheela, and was assisted in her task by newfound friend, the Canadian real estate developer and businessman, Michael O'Byrne who had taken sannyas as Swami Anand Jayesh. It was during this trying and frustrating phase that the Hollywood group provided a protective cover to Osho. Although Jayesh did not belong to their group, he had become indispensable because of his financial management skills and his close relationship with Hasya.

Handsome, charming and ambitious as a businessman, Jayesh had arrived on the scene in Oregon in 1984, barely six years before Osho's death. Habituated to an upper-class lifestyle, Jayesh had already experimented with the Arica group—one of the counterculture 'Human Potential Movements' of the 1960s. It was his curiosity about Osho that had brought him to Oregon and it was here that he had befriended Hasya who had introduced him to Osho, facilitating his entry into the topmost circle of Osho's followers. Jayesh and Hasya were later involved in a romantic relationship.[5] *The Oregonian* described Jayesh as a 37-year-old Canadian with permanent residency status in the U.S., serving as a trustee of the Rajneesh Financial Services Trust.[6]

While Osho and Hasya faced the American press and TV cameras, Jayesh worked in the background. He, however, could not avoid coming under the glare of the U.S. media when on October 28, 1985, he along with Osho, Amrito and Nirvano were arrested by the U.S. authorities when their two planes, including Osho's chartered Lear Jet, landed at the Charlotte-Douglas International Airport at Charlotte, North Carolina. Moved from prison to prison for 12 days, Osho was granted bail in Portland after being held guilty of immigration fraud and arranging sham marriages. He was fined $400,000 and deported to India in November, 1985.

Jayesh, Nirvano and Amrito were charged with "harbouring a fugitive" and were released on bail at $25,000 each. The entire group was accused of trying to escape to Bermuda.

4

Poona-II: A Reluctant Retreat

After being deported from the U.S., Osho and his entourage comprising his cook Ma Amrit Mukti, Nirvano and a few other top sannyasins arrived in Delhi on November 17, 1985, and proceeded to Kulu Manali the next day as he wanted to settle in the lap of the Himalayas.

The group moved into the Span Executive Holiday Resort owned by the family of senior Congress minister Kamal Nath. The resort had about 10 stone cottages centred around a large stone building with two walls of window overlooking a river. Shunyo, the British sannyasin presented a vivid account of Osho's brief stay here.[1] Shunyo had met Osho for the first time in 1976, and for the most part of the 15 years on his personal staff, managed his laundry. As she wrote in her memoirs, plans were being made to purchase the resort and the properties around Span to create a beautiful Commune amidst the hills. However, a crisis struck in early December, 1985 when visa extensions were cancelled for Osho's foreign disciples staying with him or headed to him at Himachal Pradesh. On December 10, the police arrived at the resort, asked for all the foreigners and stamped in their passports, 'Ordered to leave India immediately.'

According to Shunyo, the orders were coming directly from the Minister for Internal Security Arun Nehru, who was refusing to meet Osho's top sannyasins who wanted to plead their case with him. She suggests that it was none other than Laxmi (bitterly opposed to the Westerners) who had influenced Nehru to act against the foreigners by saying that foreigners were not needed to look after Osho. Shunyo says that the denial of visa / visa extension for his foreign disciples was the main reason for leaving Kulu Manali—and not Osho's deteriorating health or concern over the lack of medical facilities for Osho in Kulu Manali—as stated in an officially-approved version of the events.[2]

Forced to leave Himachal Pradesh, Osho and his entourage then moved to Nepal in what was to be the start of a 'world tour' in which he hopped in his chartered plane from country to country over a period of seven months and stayed in hotels while trying to get a permit to settle down. He had to leave Nepal after staying there for two months on denial of permission from the king. The next five months were a hectic period of travel as Osho and his core team of followers went to Greece in a bid to relocate there (February-March, 1986). On being refused permission, they moved to Uruguay (March-June), Jamaica and Portugal (June-July). Based on leads from Hasya and Jayesh, Osho's jet would land at a destination and within a few days or weeks of stay, he would either be forced to leave the country, if not flee out of fear of being arrested and incarcerated once again.

Tired of this constant upheaval, Osho finally expressed his desire to return to India and arrived in Bombay on July 29, 1986. Osho no longer wanted a Commune "but just a house where people could come and listen to him."[3] It was Osho's

Indian sannyasins who now swung into action, but found it difficult to get a suitable bungalow for him in Bombay. This city, which had once lent a liberal ear to him, seemed to be rejecting him now.

Post-Oregon, things had changed drastically and no one was willing to give a house to Osho for fear of opposition from politicians, fanatics and angry neighbours. Most of Osho's wealthy sannyasins were hesitant and finally, it was the Punjabi businessman and ardent Osho devotee, Swami Suraj Prakash, also known as Suraj Prakash Manchanda "who said he didn't care and stepped forward to invite Osho to his bungalow," recalled Sarita Ma in an interview to the author.

Osho stayed in Bombay for five-and-half months at *Sumila*, the Juhu bungalow of Suraj Prakash who owned the Prakash Road Lines fleet of trucks for goods transportation. The family vacated the entire first floor for Osho and lived on the ground and third floors. Osho's bedroom was on the first floor and he would meet his disciples in the evenings in a spacious hall, a few steps from his bedroom.

Suraj Prakash's son Rajan Manchanda spoke of how he met Osho briefly "just twice" during his five-month stay at his home. "Osho remained inside his bedroom almost all the time and stepped out only in the evenings to give darshan to his followers." About 100 sannyasins would silently walk into the bungalow, up the stairs to the first floor, and Osho would be escorted by his secretary Neelam from his bedroom for his evening discourse. About 20 top sannyasins, including his caretakers and Neelam, would be in the bungalow at all times and the family organised a "running kitchen" for this group. Osho's followers from India and abroad began descending on Juhu and throughout the day, the ochre-robed sannyasins would wait outside the bungalow and on the lawns of the nearby Pushpa Park. Not all of Suraj Prakash's family members were devotees of Osho and the guru could not stay indefinitely as a guest at the Punjabi businessman's residence. The Juhu neighbourhood was also up in arms against Osho's presence in their locality and at one point, the actor Manoj Kumar had to address a community meeting to cool tempers.

Sarita Ma remembers: "We were trying to get an alternate bungalow for Osho. He was shown many places but did not like any. We showed him places in Mud Island and Versova, but he said, 'the smell of the sea is very strong and I won't be able to stay here.'"

Osho did not want to return to Pune and for almost 14 months after his deportation from the U.S. in November, 1985, he tried—unsuccessfully—to re-settle in various places within and outside India. Hasya and Jayesh were in the forefront of trying to locate a suitable country for Osho to settle in. He had been denied permission by 21 nations in all and, as ambitious as Jayesh was, the possibility of living on an ocean liner was also considered. To explore this, Hasya and Jayesh "travelled to England to check out the situation with buying redundant aircraft carriers." They then went to Hong Kong to look at a ship, but that didn't work out either. The Hollywood group's contacts brought in offers of an island in the Pacific owned by the superstar Marlon Brando. The possibility of moving to that island was dropped as it had been "flattened by a hurricane."[4]

Given his unceremonious exit from the U.S., the intensely negative media coverage and his blasphemous attacks on Christianity while in Oregon, Osho was seen as a troublemaker and was unwelcome in most countries. His followers blamed the U.S. government of pressurising foreign governments against granting him refuge. There was now no option but to return to the Pune ashram.

To trip police surveillance, Osho left *Sumila* for Pune in the middle of the night of January 4, 1987. Having suffered neglect during his years in the U.S., the Pune ashram had a skeletal staff. There were heavy tax arrears to be cleared. The payments were made and the ashram was quickly readied for his arrival. Osho's troubles were far from over and on the very morning that he arrived unexpectedly—having left Bombay in the middle of the night—a police officer walked right into his bedroom to serve him with an order not to enter the city. There was shouting and acrimony in the bedroom and Osho refused to comply. The charming and attractive Nirvano stepped forward to offer tea to the police team and eased the tension. The order was finally suspended by the police commissioner, and conditions were laid down for Osho's stay in Pune even as the matter was challenged in the Bombay High Court by senior advocate Ram Jethmalani and a court order secured in Osho's favour.

Throughout this period, Jayesh played a spectacular role in managing the finances. As Tathagat said to the author, "We all loved Jayesh." He was handling the ashram's funds well and therefore had the fullest support and trust of all the top sannyasins in the years before Osho died, and till about four years after Osho's death. After that, sharp differences between the Jayesh faction and several other sannyasins, including Osho's last secretary Neelam, were out in the open.

"When Sheela left, we trusted Jayesh as if he was the best person around, and he certainly was," recalled Tathagat. Many other senior sannyasins agreed with this view. Jayesh began emerging as a brilliant planner and strategist when Osho was deported from the U.S. and was forced to travel from country to country in search of a refuge where a new Commune could be set up. When Osho was travelling internationally, Tathagat said, there was a continuous flow of money for lavish expenses. "It was parked somewhere...The planes were being chartered, hotel bills were being paid. The money was coming from somewhere. After all, someone has to manage it. That management was in Jayesh's hand."

The period from January 4, 1987 to January 19, 1990 marks the last three years of Osho's life and constitutes the 'Poona-II' phase of the Commune, the period in which he returned to Pune from the U.S. and the World Tour after five-and-a-half years.

Jayesh was officially at the helm of affairs during Poona II as he had emerged as a brilliant money manager and had won the confidence of Osho and all the senior sannyasins. He enjoyed the complete trust of the entire Commune as did Amrito and Anando. The Commune was indeed like a close-knit family which had suffered the trauma of harassment by U.S. government authorities, and a hostile press and public in the two years since Osho had been hounded in the U.S. and deported to India. His acerbic criticism of Christianity and his sharp, vitriolic attacks on the Ronald Reagan administration had not helped in the least.

Having returned to the Pune Commune, Osho's sannyasins did their assigned tasks, went out of their way to re-establish the Commune and make life as comfortable as possible for Osho and for themselves.

It was in such a setting that Jayesh handled the Commune's finances, chalked out its strategies, took all the top decisions and shuttled between his suite at the five-star Oberoi Hotel in Bombay and the Commune in Pune. Amrito and Anando exercised control in the Pune Commune and the other senior sannyasins were busy in the roles assigned to them. All attention was focused on Osho and everyone was busy in the tasks cut out for them. As many sannyasins believed in free love and had rejected the institution of marriage in keeping with Osho's philosophy, they went about their affairs, changing partners as and when they felt that love had dried up in the relationship. This did break hearts and arouse jealousies but by and large, the sannyasins were discouraged from nosing into other's lives and affairs.

Like a wilted plant that had found water and regained its vitality, the Pune ashram sprung back to life with Osho's return. The centre of gravity of the Osho Movement once again shifted to the up-market Koregaon Park locality; his devotees started flocking back from all over the world and a strong revenue stream started flowing. Lane No. 1 became lively, as during Poona-I, and Osho's sannyasins in maroon robes became a conspicuous element of North Main Road's street life. As Osho and his core team settled down and Pune became the hub of their activities, the Commune witnessed an explosion of creativity which was not affected by Osho's deteriorating health from the middle of 1989.

Foreigners began flocking during the cooler months from September to March and stayed in rented apartments in the Koregaon Park area for three months—or even six months—if they got visa extension. Many of them made short trips of less than a week to Nepal to re-enter India on fresh visas. The German Bakery restaurant (where a terrorist had set off a bomb explosion on February 13, 2010, killing 17 persons), close to

Lane No.1, and Prem's Restaurant further down was buzzing with people, mostly Osho's disciples. On the pavements were hawkers selling maroon robes, *mala*s, trinkets, cigarettes, imitation jewellery, Buddhist artifacts, slippers, and other such stuff that Osho's sannyasins loved. Fruit-sellers, retailers of almost every hue and colour, property agents, eateries and autorickshaw drivers began doing brisk business once again.

A well-maintained tree-lined avenue, clean footpaths and a row of shrubs marked the approach road to the Commune as all visitors first headed to the marble gateway to the main complex at No. 17 Koregaon Park. Strains of fusion music greeted the ears along with the familiar sight of maroon-robed people hugging one another and walking hand-in-hand amidst small swarms of gawkers and oglers who would be shooed away from time to time by the security guards. The reception, visitor's centre, a medical centre for the mandatory HIV/AIDS test for all visitors, the bookshop and the Buddha Hall were all located in this complex. The Commune also organised a daily guided tour of the ashram for visitors, which was discontinued in subsequent years.

While Osho and some top sannyasins lived in Lao Tzu House, Jayesh and Neelam had their business-like offices in Krishna House which also featured the office of Osho Global Connections (which coordinated with Osho Centres around the world). Osho's mother, Mataji, lived in Francis House.

A stickler for punctuality since his pre-Commune days in Bombay, Osho would arrive in his Rolls Royce at 7 p.m. for his evening discourse and darshan during the White Robe Brotherhood which was attended by all sannyasins. Bang opposite the main entrance was Meera House on plots 4 & 5 and in Lane No. 2, the expansive Mirdad House on plots

50 and 51 where pyramid-shaped buildings were constructed during Poona-II for the Mystery School. The scope of the Commune's activities continued to expand during this period and the Commune, in a long lease tie-up with the Pune Municipal Corporation, developed a magnificent 12-acre garden named Osho Teerth Park (also called 'Nala Park') on what was an open, mosquito-infested, stinking sewage canal.

Much attention was paid to the upkeep of the Commune in a neat, clean and aesthetic manner which adhered to high Western standards with modern amenities. There was lush greenery and landscaping all around. Undoubtedly, the Commune enriched the multi-cultural character and ethos of East Pune. Osho loved the sound of running water and had fond childhood memories of the 'marble rocks' at Bhedaghat, Madhya Pradesh. His sannyasins lovingly constructed a small marble waterfall and a rock garden outside his bedroom. A Japanese bridge, a rose garden, swan ponds and bamboo trees were part of the beautiful landscape around the bungalow. Osho's followers also constructed an air-conditioned glass walkway from the bungalow into the garden to allow him to enjoy nature without stepping out.

"Osho would have his meals in the huge verandah of Nirvano's bedroom. When Osho would come for lunch, our guard position would change. We would be asked to leave the spot to give him privacy," recalled Premgeet who had performed guard duties in the Commune.

During the peak season in Poona-II, the number of Indian and foreign disciples swelled to nearly 10,000 especially around the special celebrations that took place at the Commune every year. Art exhibitions would be held during the day and cultural events in the evenings, with many eminent poets, musicians, classical vocalists and dancers performing at the Commune. Equipped with all the modern communication facilities, the International Press Office would always be busy attending to local and visiting journalists and releasing press notes week after week while the Publications Department was busy with translating Osho's discourses, publishing its own books and coordinating with outside publishers.

Six types of meditations were conducted daily in the ashram which included Dynamic Meditation at 6 a.m., Vipassana and Mystic Rose, and an evening meditation when sannyasins gathered for Osho's discourse during the White Robe Brotherhood at 7 p.m. The Osho Multiversity and the Mystery School offered a range of therapies, programmes and courses. Teachers of the Mystery School wore black robes with white sashes, and offered courses in Zen Archery, Osho Alchemical Hypnotherapy, Synchronicity with the Master (a transmission of energy from the beyond), Tibetan Pulsing Healing, Tantra Budo and The Art of Dying. The Multiversity headed by Satya Vedant as its Chancellor had 10 faculties including School for Centering and Zen Martial Arts, School of Mysticism, Club Meditation and Creative Leisure. The Basho Spa was introduced during Poona-II, with facilities for tennis, volleyball, swimming and Jacuzzi in the first signs of the Commune's transformation into a 'meditation resort'.

Osho's caretakers Nirvano, Anando and Shunyo, his personal physician Amrito, his India secretary Neelam, the British dentist Devageet (Dr. Charles Newman), Mukta, Yogi from the Hollywood group, and Maneesha were among those who had rooms in Lao Tzu House and were, in a sense, close to Osho. However, they could meet Osho only when he asked for them and a message would be communicated primarily by Amrito, Anando, or Nirvano when she was around. Inevitably, the sannyasins living in Lao Tzu House had an aura of a special status as they were living in Osho's residence.

A lot happened during Poona-II: In the wake of 'harassment' from immigration officials and denial of visas to his followers from abroad, Osho instructed them to stop wearing the orange robe and discontinue displaying the *mala*. At the start of Poona-II, Osho was no longer defiant. His followers were told that the *mala* could be worn under the clothing. He later introduced maroon robes for the day and white robes for the evening gathering, specifying that they had no religious significance. The robes were to be worn only inside the Commune premises. On January 7, 1989, he dropped the prefix 'Bhagwan' and reverted to the earlier Shree Rajneesh and nine months later, around October, 1989, dropped that also. While the Commune states that he agreed to a suggestion by his followers to be called 'Osho' (meaning Zen master), Christopher Calder, a follower-turned-critic of Osho has written in his essay, *The Enigmatic 'Bhagwan,' Osho Rajneesh*, that the suggestion for the name change to 'Osho' actually came from Anando.

Poona-II was the phase when Osho's discourses were transcribed into 48 books, and three new forms of meditations were introduced. This was the period when the Commune purchased several properties and expanded its area to a total of around 30 acres, which included the Nala Park of 12 acres. This was the phase when all buildings were painted black with dark blue windows, and black pyramid buildings were constructed on new properties.

5

The 1989 Coterie: Jayesh, Amrito & Anando

In effect, 1989 was the last year of Osho's life and the firm foundations of a Commune without Osho were laid systematically that year. At the helm of affairs was a small coterie of his senior-most followers led by the highly secretive, 41-year-old Canadian sannyasin, Jayesh. Two years had passed since Osho's return to Pune in January, 1987. 1989 was a year of many behind-the-curtain developments before his death in suspicious circumstances, on January 19, 1990.

The suave and handsome British doctor Amrito, was a key member of this coterie. A former boyfriend of Anando and Nirvano, Amrito, was married to Hasya while at Rancho Rajneesh at Oregon. Since Osho and his followers did not believe in the institution of marriage, this marriage on March 22, 1984 was largely viewed as a bit of paperwork to get permanent residence status in the United States. Even *The Oregonian* made a similar observation on December 30, 1985, stating that Amrito's marriage to Hasya provided him "with a wife who was a U.S. citizen, seeming to assure his continued presence in the United States."

Over the years, Amrito had acquired a seriously dubious reputation of indulging in questionable medical practices. It was not just the guru's disgraced secretary Sheela who had accused him in Oregon of assisting Osho and Nirvano in drug abuse[1]; there were others who suspected that Amrito abused his medical knowledge. *A Year in Lao Tzu-1989*, the blog by Australian sannyasin Antar Navjot who worked in the library in Osho's residence, carries a detailed post under the heading "Usage of drugs in the Commune—questionable practices." Relating an anecdote, Navjot accused Amrito of prescribing "an almost lethal dose" of a drug to the senior sannyasin Ma Prem Maneesha (also known as Maneesha James) to control her severe migraines.[2] On the very day that Osho died, Mataji had lamented loudly that Osho had been put on "heavy medication" in the last days of his life, suggesting that was the cause of his death.

Jayesh's coterie had yet another member—Amrito's former girlfriend and Osho's legal secretary Anando, who, as a child was raised in a conservative Christian family in Australia. Anando exercised tight control on access to Osho in the final months of his life, going to the extent of turning down a request from Mataji to visit Osho, three to four days before his death. Mataji lived just a few paces from Lao Tzu House.

In an interview to the in-house *Osho Times* magazine in 1995, Anando spoke of her childhood in Australia where, after her education in a girls' school, she went on to study Law. She was also interested in dance and the performing arts and came from Australia to London to study Modern Dance. She was a bright, young achiever and was employed in a publishing firm for five years with a well-paying job, but felt an inner emptiness.

"I had everything—money, husband, a house, but something was missing deep within me which made me restless. I felt like a misfit in society," she said of her life to her interviewer and fellow sannyasin, Amrit Sadhana.

In the early 1970s, Shunyo had met Anando at the Rajneesh Meditation Centre at London, "sitting in the round white tunnel, knitting a multi-coloured, ethnic patterned scarf," and hiding the fact that she was a "successful businesswoman and lawyer."[3] Her presence at the centre every night indicated her attraction to Osho's philosophy. After one of her visits to India, she embraced the Rajneesh Movement, became a sannyasin, and since 1975, worked in various capacities in the Osho Commune till the years in Oregon when she was moved to Osho's legal department because of her background in Law. She qualified for the U.S. Bar and was part of the team that handled the legal cases against Osho. Anando was brought closer to the circle of Osho's top managers by Hasya.

The Jayesh-Amrito-Anando trio acquired a new aura of importance immediately after Osho's death: Amrito and Jayesh were the only two persons who had witnessed Osho's death and Amrito had claimed that just before dying, Osho had asked for Jayesh and whispered to him, "I leave you my dream." In almost that same breath, the doctor said that Osho had designated Anando as the "medium" through whom he would give "guidance" to the Commune after his death.

In the 'Don't Ask-Don't Tell' environment of the Commune, most of the senior sannyasins were unaware of the hectic, behind-the-scene activities around Osho during 1989. These activities and initiatives led by Jayesh were related to creating a legally sound, fool-proof mechanism for the running of the Commune after Osho's death. The 'stamp' of 1989 is also seen on many later developments, the most startling of which was Osho's Will, which was produced 23 years after his death as evidence by the Jayesh-controlled parent trust Osho International Foundation in Zürich. This Will bears the date and stamp paper of this period: June 16, 1989. It bears Osho's signature dated four months later, October 15, 1989.

Incidentally, 1989 was also the year when Jayesh and his associates began the groundwork for renaming the European trust, Rajneesh Foundation Europe as Osho International Foundation, registered at Bahnhofstrasse, 52, 80010 Zürich, Switzerland. In his Witness Statement before the European Union Intellectual Property Office (EUIPO), Klaus Steeg (Swami Pramod), Director and OIF board member cited the Witness Statement by Jayesh before the EUIPO and said it was Osho who had directed the name change and that the implementation of re-branding of all of Osho's intellectual properties such as meditations, meditative therapies, books, discourses and sound and video recordings began in September / October 1989. Steeg claimed that Osho was "very involved in this re-branding process in conjunction with OIF." According to him, the process of filing trademark applications to register OSHO in a number of European countries like Germany, UK, Benelux, France, Spain and Italy began in 1990, the very year that Osho died. There were also plans to move the publications headquarters to New York "to operate the international publishing licensing business and development" of brand OSHO, he told the European Union's trademark registration office.[4]

The name changeover from 'Bhagwan' to 'Osho' also happened in 1989, with some sannyasins stating that the suggestion for the name 'Osho' came from Anando. If this is true, then there are reasons to suspect that the change of name from 'Bhagwan' to 'Osho' was part of a larger strategy. In October 1989, the Osho Commune International Press Office released the 'Biography of Osho—Factsheet' and explained that during January-February 1989, the Master stopped using the name 'Bhagwan,' retaining only the name 'Rajneesh'. "However, his disciples asks *(sic)* to call him Osho and he accepts this form of address." The Commune explained that 'Osho' was derived from ancient Japanese: "'O' means *with great respect, love and gratitude* as well as *synchronicity* and *harmony*. 'SHO' means *multidimensional expansion of consciousness* and *existence showering from all directions.*" The factsheet stated that Osho dropped the name 'Rajneesh' in September 1989 "signifying his complete discontinuity from the past." He was now known simply as Osho "and the ashram is renamed 'Osho Commune International.'" While Osho himself spoke poetically about his name, it is abundantly clear that the name change was initiated by the Commune to break from the ignominy of the past associated with the name 'Rajneesh' and 'Bhagwan'.

Clearly, these strategies were aimed at moving the entire 'Osho business' out of India, with all the legal rights resting with a few trustees such as Jayesh, Amrito, Jayesh's brother D'Arcy O'Byrne, Steeg and a few others. The only Indian name that figured among these trustees was that of one of Jayesh's point-persons in India, the Gujarati sannyasin, Swami Mukesh Bharti, also known as Mukesh Kantilal Sarda. While Jayesh and Amrito take all the decisions and pull the strings from behind, he is the one who attends to all the legal and official formalities of the Commune in India.

The process of emptying the Commune of its residents, which was pursued aggressively after Osho's death, began in

1989 itself as is indicated in a blogpost titled 'Self-sufficiency in the Garden of the Beloved' by Antar Navjot. In her blog, *A Year in Lao Tzu—1989*, Navjot wrote that a meeting of all ashram workers was called on May 8, 1989 by Amrito, Anando and the Chief Ashram Administrator Nandan. Stating that they were delivering a message from Osho, Amrito and his co-convenors said that "people needed to support themselves, rather than be supported by the Commune." Navjot found the self-sufficiency message daunting. "The Commune could not afford to keep so many people rent-free in the ashram or give them food passes," the Commune residents were told. They were instructed "to go back to the West and find work, and when they had more money, then they could come back."

Since the message had come from Osho, everyone accepted it without complaint. Navjot realised that she would now be able to stay only for two months more instead of four if her food pass was cancelled.

A major initiative in 1989 was the introduction of a committee of top sannyasins called the Inner Circle for the running of the Commune. Created in the middle of 1989, the top three positions in the Inner Circle—a committee of 21 sannyasins—were held by Jayesh (Chairman), Amrito (Vice-Chairman) and Anando (Secretary). The other members were simply informed that this decision was taken by Osho. While Osho may have agreed to the formation of this committee, as with many such claims of decisions-taken-by-Osho, there was never any evidence in the form of audio / video recordings or documentation that Osho had approved the finer details. These were always worked out by Jayesh and communicated to the rest.

It was around June, 1989 that Anando informed a select group of top sannyasins about Osho's decision to form a secret committee to manage the Commune, with Jayesh, Amrito and Anando at the top. This was the 21-member 'Inner Circle' which the Commune claimed in a press note was formed by Osho on April 6, 1989. In his Witness Statement, Jayesh states that he played an important role in the formation of this body which was announced by Osho in May 1989 after having discussed with him "in private for two months." According to him, Osho made him Chairman of the Inner Circle which he created "as a body of individuals responsible for the continuation of his work in India, including operating the Osho International Meditation Resort, formerly known as Osho Commune International."[5]

Tathagat said he and Neelam were informed about the Inner Circle's formation and their inclusion, by Anando "in May-June 1989". The Inner Circle had the influential and well-connected Hollywood group of sannyasins including Hasya, Kaveesha, Yogi and Avirbhava as its members. It met for an hour on Sundays at 2 p.m. in the Lao Tzu library. Nothing substantial was achieved in these meetings, says Tathagat and gossip and mundane matters were discussed in a convivial atmosphere.

The existence of this group was revealed to other sannyasins and the press only after Osho's death. This was done through an undated Commune press note which quoted Osho as saying, "I am tired…I want to retire" while setting up the Inner Circle. The press note said this committee was formed "to reach unanimous decisions about the continued functioning and expansion of the Commune" and Osho's work.

The names of the 21 members were listed in alphabetical order preceded by those of Jayesh, Amrito and Anando. The remaining 18 members were: Amitabh, Anasha, Avirbhava, Chitten, Devageet, Garimo, Hasya, Jayantibhai, Kaveesha, Mukta the Greek, Neelam, Potinus, Prasad, Satya Vedant, Tathagat, Turiya, Yogi and Zareen. Revealed for the first time after Osho's death, the composition of the Inner Circle formalised the power structure inside the Commune. Nirvano's name was missing from this list as she had been replaced by Zareen after her death.

The Commune sought to create the impression through press notes that the Inner Circle was a mechanism created thoughtfully by Osho for the smooth functioning of the Commune after his death. According to the Commune, Osho finalised the committee chosen to represent his work and the Commune departments. "He stressed that the inner workings of the committee were to remain a secret. He also said that the committee is not to be involved in spiritual considerations, but should look to the mundane work, the practical problems of the Commune. The Inner Circle is not a club to discuss philosophy. It is a pragmatic and practical way to decide things," the press note issued by the Commune said.

Although the Commune claimed that Osho "kept a close watch" on the functioning of this committee, "giving guidance where necessary, and adding a few new members," the fact is that he did not address the Inner Circle even once. Anando was the person who communicated between this group and Osho, carrying messages back and forth, week after week.

When seats fell vacant in the Inner Circle because many top sannyasins such as those from the Hollywood group, Neelam and Tathagat left the Commune due to differences with Jayesh, they were quickly filled up with Jayesh's yes-men. One of them was his brother, D'Arcy. Chaitanya Keerti, who had served as the Osho Commune's spokesperson for many years recalled his conversation with Devendra Bharti, a newly inducted Inner Circle member who rose rapidly under Jayesh. "When I asked Devendra (Devendra Singh Dewal) what was the criteria for his selection, what was his role, he said, he was asked to support the chairman."

According to Neelam and Tathagat, their understanding of the Inner Circle was that the members were appointed for life and the post of Chairman was to be rotated every two years to convey that they were all equals. This was not honoured, they said, and this committee became a rubber-stamp exercise after Osho's death as many top functionaries either left the Commune voluntarily or were forced out.

In March 2016, when the author asked Amrit Sadhana for the latest list of members on the Inner Circle, she stonewalled the query as she had done with a few other queries. "The list is secret and cannot be disclosed," was the cryptic response of the OIF spokesperson, who was also an OIF-India trustee and a prominent member of the Osho International Meditation Resort's Management Team in Pune. When pointed out that the first list was released voluntarily by the Commune way back in 1990, she said that was in the past and had no bearing on the present.

According to Shunyo, eight months before forming the Inner Circle, Osho called her one night and dictated 13 names. She said this was in the middle of the night in August 1988 when she was serving as Osho's caretaker and the Master called her on the beeper. She hurried down the Lao Tzu corridor with the worrying thought that Osho may be having an asthma attack. "I unlocked the door, and saw that He was sitting up in the bed wide awake, the room in darkness except for a small bedside light." Osho asked her to bring a notepad and gave her 13 names to be written in a circle with 'Bhagwan' in the centre. The names around the circle in clockwise were: Jayesh, Avirbhava, Nitty (Nityamo), Nirvano, Kaveesha, Maneesha, Devageet, Neelam, David, Chetana (Shunyo's former sannyas name), Hasya, Anando and Amrito. He called it his "secret group of 13."

In April 2016, the author's request for an interview with Jayesh was turned down by Amrit Sadhana. "Jayesh doesn't talk to the press," was another of her cryptic responses. Since Jayesh has always sought to remain invisible by not giving press interviews, by staying away from cameras, by never revealing much about himself either through his own writings, write-ups or photographs, his Witness Statement of July 19, 2011 in the EUIPO in defence of the 'Community Trade Mark Registration No. 1224831 OSHO in Classes 41 & 42 in the name of Osho International Foundation' is a rare, first-hand account of his introduction to the Osho Movement and his interactions with Osho, especially in his last days.

In that statement, Jayesh said he had known Osho since 1984 and had worked with him closely since 1985. Osho had appointed him to many leadership positions within the Commune which included Head of Finance in 1985, Director, Osho International Foundation (1985), Chancellor of Osho Multiversity (1988), Chairman of Inner Circle (1989) and Chairman of Osho International Presidium (1989).

Jayesh said that nine months prior to his death, Osho asked Neelam and Hasya to stop attending his meetings with Jayesh, even as Jayesh continued to meet with Osho "alone on a regular basis" during the last three months of his life. (Not only is it strange that Osho asked his personal secretaries to stay away from important meetings but it seems that hectic developments were apace in the final months before Osho's death.)

Jayesh said that Osho rarely saw anyone in private other than "members of a very secretarial team," his caretaker, dentist and doctor, and in the last nine months of his life, Osho met only with four persons—Amrito, Anando, Ma Shantam, Avirbhava. As Osho's health continued to deteriorate, "Over this same nine-month period, my meetings with him increased to the point where we were meeting in the morning, in the evening, and often in the middle of the night," Jayesh said.

The first time that Jayesh came under the media's radar was in the U.S. when he along with Osho, Amrito and Nirvano had been arrested in October, 1985 when their private planes landed at a North Carolina airport. Jayesh came under the second round of sustained media coverage in later years. In February 1994, the *Los Angeles Times* described him as the "affable, polite and smooth-mannered son of a provincial judge from Edmonton, Canada." Jayesh, said the newspaper was "the real genius" behind the Osho Commune's transformation into a meditation resort, renamed the Osho International Meditation Resort. In February 1997, Canadian journalist Ric Dolphin published an exhaustive profile of Jayesh in *Saturday Night* magazine which mentioned that an Alberta court had issued a default judgement against Jayesh "for non-payment of a series of Bank of Montreal demand loans totalling $1,318,069.96." Dolphin reported that Jayesh (then known by his legal name Michael O'Byrne) could not be found till he was traced to Oregon "and the debt—like so many Edmonton debts then—

became derelict." Dolphin visited the Pune Commune to meet Jayesh, but as also happened with journalists from *LA Times* and *The New York Times*, Dolphin was not granted an interview.

Dolphin managed to speak to D'Arcy who confirmed that Jayesh resided at the Oberoi Hotel in Bombay. The Canadian journalist's interview with the Bollywood actor and sannyasin Vinod Khanna (Swami Vinod Bharati) was revealing. In that interview, Khanna said that Jayesh used to come over for dinner "to try and interest him in real estate deals, including an assemblage of farmlands outside booming Poona." The actor said that Jayesh was not much interested in meditation. "He used to come over for drinks and he'd say, 'Osho said this, Osho said that,' and I'd say, 'Jayesh, don't bullshit me. Osho never said that, ever. I knew Osho better than anyone.'" At no point has Jayesh or the Osho Commune challenged or contradicted any of these reports.

While Amrito was the Operational Head of the Commune and interacted with the press, visiting celebrities and bureaucrats when necessary, Jayesh was the person in the background who called the shots. Mention Jayesh and the senior-most sannyasins clamp up even today. The lead pall-bearer at Osho's funeral, Jayesh was the person issuing the orders for things to be rushed for a quick cremation.

Broadly, some common strains of thought emerged whenever Osho's followers discussed Jayesh with the author: They saw him as someone with a charming and pleasant personality, extremely efficient in his work, with an ability to handle and manage huge sums of money and to spot talent within the ashram. Jayesh was also hugely ambitious and at the same time highly secretive, with an obsessively low profile. For example, he never gave press interviews and his photographs appeared rarely in the Commune's literature and in-house magazines. He is of course, seen in videos seated at Osho's discourses, and most certainly in the video of Osho's funeral procession.

When asked for his impressions of Jayesh, Satya Vedant went into a deep pause. He seemed unwilling to take the risk of speaking even off the record about Jayesh. After much hesitation, he said: "Jayesh has a very brilliant mind and is a keen observer of the people he has been with. In his own way, he has certainly given a certain shape or direction to Osho's work—whether you agree or disagree is a different matter. He is on top of whatever has happened as far as I understand. Osho gave him responsibility, trusted him 100%. Jayesh's word was the last word for us as he was directly in touch with Osho. Whenever he came to our meetings, his word was the last word. He knew how to take help from different people."

Satya Vedant recalled that Jayesh had once told him that his father was a senior judge in Canada and he had big dreams for Jayesh—"that he should become Prime Minister of Canada." He obviously saw that Jayesh had some qualities and capabilities and even tried to get him interested in politics.

There was another aspect to Jayesh's personality: sannyasins were afraid of him. The 64-year-old landscaping specialist Swami Vedant Bharati (Mann Singh) had worked closely with Jayesh on the Osho Teerth (Nala Park) garden behind the Commune. Bharati had joined the Neo Sannyas Movement in 1976 and had seen all the ups and downs of the Movement. He was in Jayesh's good books till he was eased out of the Commune. "I was taken care of," he said, adding that Jayesh "had a carrot-and-stick approach." Vedant Bharati saw that there was nobody in the Commune who could stand up to Jayesh.

There were others who pointed out that many top sannyasins who were once close to Jayesh left the Commune to pursue their own, independent lives. This was a fact. Sannyasins were surprised at the suddenness with which his once right-hand-man, Chitten and his wife Ma Prem Amrita, left Pune and resettled in North India. Chitten who has since dropped his sannyas name and taken on a new name as 'Santosh Thomas Hoehne', runs a company in Almora, Uttarakhand, manufacturing natural cosmetics and organic health foods. There was no response from Chitten when the author reached out to him twice and asked him the reason for leaving the Pune Commune all of a sudden. Sannyasin Ma Anand Bhagwati's interview with Amrita, circulating on the Internet, mentioned that they founded SOS Organics in 2002 in village Pant, Chitai, in the Almora district of Uttarakhand and the firm became operational in 2007.[6]

Seniors at the Commune said Chitten had worked in the Finance Department of an Osho centre in Cologne and in the Pune Commune during Poona-I and that's how he had been roped in by Jayesh into the Accounts Department in Poona-II. Chitten was on the first Inner Circle list and as Jayesh's trusted lieutenant, he had played an important role in coordinating closely with him and Amrito at the time of Osho's death. Many sannyasins believe he is one of the key persons who knows the truth about Osho's death. Most were reluctant to speak about the circumstances in which he left the Commune.

"He was a beautiful man, a beautiful sannyasin. Totally dedicated. I came to learn that he left because, as I heard, he was asked—or forced or coerced—to do certain things—which things I don't know. He disagreed with that. So he voluntarily decided to get out. That, in a nutshell, is all that I know," said Satya Vedant.

In the Poona-II years, Jayesh was more like the CEO of an international business organisation rather than the head of a non-profit charitable trust specialising in meditation, meditative therapies and spiritualism. One of his strengths was his self-confidence to disagree with Osho. He became the centre of power and authority after Osho's death because he alone stood out as the custodian of Osho's dream. As Vedant Bharati said, "Jayesh had all the answers as he had Osho's dream. Even Osho was uncertain at times, but Jayesh had absolute clarity; he knew exactly what had to be done."

After Osho's death, Jayesh became firm and assertive about the path he had chosen for the Commune's future. He rewarded his supporters in the Commune handsomely but kept his cards close to his chest. Even D'Arcy who was later inducted into the Inner Circle in the mid-1990s may not have been privy to Jayesh's plans, said Vedant Bharati. "You cannot find one person who knows Jayesh; not even his brother. What is in his mind, what he is doing, why he is doing it, what is the motive...He is a mysterious man," said Vedant Bharati.

Mukesh Sarda emerged as one of the key Indian associates of Jayesh after Osho's death. He was the only Indian trustee on OIF-Zürich for many years even as he continued as a prominent trustee of OIF-India, Neo Sannyas Foundation, India and Director on the firm Osho Multimedia & Resorts Pvt. Ltd, along with other Indian sannyasins such as Devendra Bharti. Sarda represents the Trust in the various court cases, and hearings at the Charity

Commissionerate in Mumbai. Senior sannyasins such as Jyoti Ma remembered Sarda from his days as an LIC agent from Bombay who later functioned as the Pune-Bombay courier boy for the Commune. "He had a sudden rise in Poona-II; he was picked up by Jayesh," she said.

Now in his 80s, the U.S.-based Gujarati ENT surgeon, Dr. Gokul Gokani, had interacted with both Jayesh and Amrito, most closely when he was called urgently to issue Osho's Death Certificate in a secretive manner. Dr. Gokani offered voluntary services in the Medical Department of the Commune and also served as a tour guide at the Commune in the afternoons. During a lengthy interview, he vividly recalled one particular medical emergency when a German sannyasin had suffered 60-70% burns when his robe had caught fire during a therapy session with lighted candles all around. The sannyasin was first admitted to the Inlaks & Budhrani Hospital just outside the gates of the Commune and was then rushed to Bombay as he had to be flown to Germany. Dr. Gokani accompanied Jayesh and Amrito in a convoy of 3–4 cars to Bombay, with the injured German in an ambulance. "The ashram was very worried that if this sannyasin died, his next-of-kin might sue the ashram. They were so worried that they were prepared to do anything," he said. The ENT surgeon who did not know a word of German was asked by Amrito to carry his passport along and to be on stand-by in case he was required to fly to Germany from Bombay itself. That was the occasion when Dr. Gokani and Amrito were put up in Jayesh's well-appointed apartment in Bombay at Cuffe Parade. Eventually, Jayesh and Amrito found a German to accompany the patient who was airlifted by the Commune to his home country. At one point when

Amrito opened his briefcase, Dr. Gokani found that half of it was filled with the imported 555 cigarette packets and the other half with bundles of currency notes. "I was shocked, and wondered how Osho's personal physician could be a heavy smoker. Osho was so sensitive to smell!"

In keeping with the impressions and recollections of other sannyasins, Dr. Gokani too described Jayesh as always pleasant in his interactions which he kept to the minimum and did not discuss anything beyond work with the people around him. He remembered an incident from the mid-1990s when he was reprimanded over an innocuous comment he had made in an interview to *The Indian Express*: "I was asked by the journalist about the Commune's finances and I said, I have no information as I have neither asked them nor have they given me any information." The top managers at the Commune were furious when the interview appeared and Dr. Gokani was called and reprimanded by Devageet. His 'crime' was speaking to the press without the Commune's permission, and he was asked by Devageet to sign a pre-drafted apology. Hurt and offended, Dr. Gokani not only refused but also stopped going to the Commune, although his wife and daughter continued to be active in the ashram. "About nine months later, Jayesh called one day and said he wanted to come home for tea or coffee," Dr. Gokani recalled, saying this was extremely unusual. "I said, you are a busy man, I will come over. But instruct the guards at the gate not to insist on the AIDS test otherwise I will go back [a valid HIV–negative certificate was mandatory for all persons entering the Commune]," Dr. Gokani said. Later when they met in the Commune over coffee, Jayesh pretended he didn't know why Dr. Gokani had stopped visiting the Commune. When Dr. Gokani showed him the pre-drafted apology that

Devageet wanted him to sign, "He simply took the paper, tore it and throwing it in the dustbin, said, 'Swamiji, we want your energy from tomorrow.'" All was well once again.

Did Jayesh go out of the way to mend ties with Dr. Gokani because he felt a sense of obligation to the doctor who had signed Osho's Death Certificate in mysterious circumstances?

Premgeet said that since the Commune had regained its vitality during Poona-II, with lots of activity and funds pouring in with rising footfalls, the sannyasins were very happy with Jayesh's leadership. "Nobody was bothered whether he had a permanent suite at the Oberoi. Everybody wanted him around," said Premgeet.

The theory that Osho may have been poisoned, ultimately resulting in his death in 1990, first surfaced in the Commune in late 1987–88. With pathological hatred, Osho and his followers accused the Ronald Reagan administration of slow-poisoning him with thallium and harmful radiation. This theory became the official line of the Commune. According to Amrito, Osho had developed "a simple ear infection" (in November 1987, says Shunyo) which took nearly two-and-a-half months to resolve "with prolonged injections of antibiotics and local surgery by a Poona ear surgeon." Amrito says it was at this time that Osho's doctors "were alerted to the possibility that he had been poisoned." Samples of Osho's blood, hair, urine, X-ray prints and detailed medical history were then sent to the ISPS Laboratory in London for examination by pathologists and experts. "It was their opinion," said Amrito "that the symptoms from which Osho had been suffering since being incarcerated by the U.S. Government were consistent only with poisoning by a heavy metal such as thallium."[7]

The Commune did not have any evidence but linked this alleged poisoning to Osho's incarceration in the Oklahoma County Jail in October 1985. In a book that she wrote on Osho's alleged poisoning, *Was Bhagwan Shree Rajneesh Poisoned by Ronald Reagan's America*, Anando explained that there was no conclusive evidence of thallium poisoning as it had happened two years before the symptoms began showing. As she said: "Unfortunately, the test for thallium will only show its presence in quantities of more than one microgram per litre of fluid. So the test in Bhagwan's case made two years after his symptoms began and therefore long after the poison had left his body, could not provide any positive evidence."

Some sannyasins, such as the Britisher and London School of Economics alumnus, Swami Anand Parmartha, rejected this theory. Described as a "longtime faithful disciple" and member of the household around Osho, Parmartha said in one of his many, detailed posts (*Osho in the Dental Chair*) on sannyasnews.org, it was unlikely that Osho was poisoned with thallium. As he put it: "I do not think the evidence that Osho received thallium is very convincing; the symptoms really do not match those Osho was experiencing. The 'official' line is, and he himself seemed to believe that he had been poisoned by thallium. However, Osho seemed quite well between late 1985 and 1987, in Greece, and was in fairly good shape in the Himalayas, the world tour, and in Bombay for almost two years."

James S. Gordon, a teacher at The Georgetown University of Medicine, and a practitioner of Psychiatry and Holistic Medicine in Washington D.C. said in his paper, 'A Letter from Poona, November, 1989', that neither the two doctors—Amrito and Osho's dentist, Devageet—nor Anando, could present any hard evidence in support of their claim that Osho's deteriorating health was due to thallium poisoning and exposure to radiation in an American prison. "They refer me to several books and pamphlets that sannyasins have published on the subject. But neither they, nor the books, present any hard evidence for either of these charges," said Gordon in his paper which was presented at a conference and published in a book titled, *The Rajneesh Papers: Studies in a New Religious Movement*.[8] Gordon, who had authored a book on Osho, said, "The only certifiable poisonings in this group's story were those that Sheela and the previous leadership initiated against their opponents on and off the ranch." Gordon, who had experienced the Commune life as a participant in Oregon and later in Pune, said, while his request for an interview with Osho was declined, he received messages from Osho which "are delivered by Amrito and are most often responses to impressions of our conversations that he or Anando have conveyed to Osho." Gordon called it "a bizarre way to communicate..."[9]

The fact is that Osho had suffered from a troublesome ear infection around 1983 nearly two years before he had been jailed in Oklahoma. Shunyo has noted in her memoirs that while in Oregon, a specialist had been called to attend to a painful middle ear infection that Osho was suffering from for nearly six weeks. "Discourse and car rides were cancelled." Around this time, Osho also had trouble with his teeth and had about nine root canals. Due to his dental problems, a dentist's chair had been installed next to his bedroom. Besides, he had been suffering from a series of ailments which grew worse over time and this has been recorded right from the early 1970s. Osho suffered from chronic diabetes and severe backache which recurred from time to time. A year before his death, he had severe chest pains which were diagnosed as heart attack by the Pune cardiologist Dr. H.V. Sardesai. Besides him, the Pune doctors who were consulted for Osho included the orthopaedic surgeon Dr. Sharad Hardikar, ENT specialist Dr. Mohan Jog and dentist Dr. Darius Mody.

Two accounts of senior disciples help us understand Osho's routine during Poona-II. Satya Vedant records that in early 1988, around the time when Osho created the Mystic Rose Meditation, he followed his normal routine: he ate frugal meals, had a nap in the afternoon, met his secretary in the evening and stepped out to give a discourse at 7 p.m. in the Buddha Hall. This routine included "looking at new books, magazines and newspapers that his disciples were now producing in greater numbers than ever before," giving suggestions for the cover designs and titles reflecting "his love for beauty and aesthetics".[10]

Eight months before his death, Osho stopped speaking in public and ended his discourse on *The Zen Manifesto* on April 10, 1989. Saying, "Remember, you are a Buddha. *Sammasti* (right mindfulness)," he got up and left. This was his last discourse.

Osho, however, continued to come in the evenings to the Buddha Hall to attend the White Robe Brotherhood. By October 1989, he had become considerably weaker. "From here on, he would be sleeping most of the time," says Shunyo. She would wake him up at 6 p.m. and after taking a shower, Osho would come to the Buddha Hall and then "by 7.45 p.m. would be back in bed."[11]

In the last three months of his life—from mid-October 1989 onwards—Shunyo was asked to leave Lao Tzu House and stopped being his caretaker. She was replaced by Anando. After this, Shunyo saw him only in the Buddha Hall. From here on till Osho's death, Anando served as Osho's caretaker "while Amrito stayed close to Osho day and night."[12] According to Chaitanya Keerti, in the final months of his life, "It was mainly the doctor who was interacting with Osho." This account matches with that of Shunyo, Jayesh in his Witness Statement and Osho's cook, Ma Amrit Mukti, who spoke to the author in a telephonic interview.

Since 1974, it was mostly Mukti Ma, one of Osho's earliest Gujarati disciples, who cooked food for him. Also known by her legal name, Hemlata Adhia, she was among those arrested along with Osho on October 28, 1985 at Charlotte-Douglas International Airport, as soon as her plane landed before the arrival of Osho's jet. Mukti Ma was 44 years old then and her name in the U.S. records was mentioned as Hemlata Adhia DesRosiers. Over the years, Mukti Ma cooked simple, vegetarian, non-oily and non-spicy Gujarati meals for Osho. In the earlier days, he liked soups, *dalia* (broken wheat dish) and *khakra* (crunchy Gujarati snack made of flour and mat bean, usually served at breakfast) on some days, and the usual dal, rice, chapatis and vegetable preparations for his meals. In the last two months of Osho's life, Mukti Ma, who resided in Jesus House, would come to Lao Tzu House twice a day—in the mornings at 9 a.m. and then in the afternoons. In the previous months, she would come thrice—her first visit being early in the morning to make tea for Osho at around 6.30–7 a.m. However, that visit had to be dropped as Osho entirely stopped taking tea in the last stage of his life because of teeth extraction. (Shunyo records that as many as 10 teeth were extracted.)

"As per my routine, I would arrive at Lao Tzu by about 4 p.m. and prepare a milkshake for Osho. For almost a month-and-a-half, Osho had been having just milkshakes three to four times a day as he had difficulty in eating solid foods due to extraction of many teeth. I would make a variety of milkshakes—sometimes of fruits, sometimes of almonds—and keep it *(sic)* in the fridge as Osho would want it cold. Amrito would then take it to Osho's room. There was a small fridge in Osho's room too," she said in an interview on February 25, 2016. Even on the day Osho died, Mukti Ma was in Osho's kitchen in Lao Tzu and had prepared his evening milkshake.

In the last 18 months of her life, Nirvano who had first seen Osho when she was 21 years old in Bombay and had been physically and emotionally closest to him as his lover and personal caretaker since the early 1970s, was romantically involved with Jayesh. Osho's senior sannyasins recalled that in 1989, Nirvano, who had been extraordinarily protective of Osho in the previous decades, would now often be with Jayesh in Bombay or at his room in Krishna House, but not in Lao Tzu. One version had it that she was kept away from Lao Tzu "because of her mood swings" but this had made her extremely unhappy. She died in suspicious circumstances on December 9, 1989, barely 41 days before Osho passed away. The circumstances of her death were hushed up and she was cremated swiftly and unceremoniously.

If the story of Poona-II begins with Osho's reluctant return to Pune, it ends, not with Osho's death, but with the emergence of the elusive and obsessively secretive Jayesh who seized complete control over Osho's empire.

प्रमाणपत्र क्र. / Certificate No. N2016420-2896-000024-2/2-Aundh

नमुना - ६ / Form -6

महाराष्ट्र शासन
GOVERNMENT OF MAHARASHTRA
आरोग्य विभाग
HEALTH DEPARTMENT
पुणे महानगरपालिका
PUNE MUNICIPAL CORPORATION

सत्यमेव जयते

मृत्यु प्रमाणपत्र
DEATH CERTIFICATE

(जन्म व मृत्यु नोंदणी अधिनियम, १९६९ च्या कलम१२/१७ आणि महाराष्ट्र जन्म व मृत्यु नोंदणी नियम २००० चे नियम ८/१३ अन्वये देण्यात आले आहे.)

(Issued under section 12/17 of the Registration of Births & Deaths Act., 1969 and Rule 8/13 of the Maharashtra Registration of Births and Deaths Rules, 2000)

प्रमाणित करण्यात येत आहे की, खालील माहिती मृत्युच्या मुळ अभिलेखाच्या नोंदवहीतून घेण्यात आलेली आहे. जी की (स्थानिक क्षेत्र) पुणे तालुका: हवेली जिल्हा : पुणे महाराष्ट्र राज्याच्या नोंदवहीत उल्लेख आहे.

This is to certify that the following information has been taken from the original record of death which is the register for (Local area/Local body) Pune of tahsil / block : **Haveli** of District : **Pune** of Maharashtra State

मृताचे पूर्ण नाव : Full Name of Deceased : अलिशा एलेक्संडर ALISHA ALEXANDER

लिंग : Sex : स्त्री Female

मृत्यु दिनांक : **Date of Death** 09/12/1989

मृत्युचे ठिकाण : Place of Death : एन.एम.वाडीया हॉस्पिटल, पुणे N.M.WADIYA HOSPITAL, PUNE

आईचे/पत्नीचे पूर्ण नाव : Full Name of Mother / Wife :

वडिलांचे / पतीचे पूर्ण नाव : Full Name of Father / Husband :

मयत व्यक्तीचा मृत्यु समयीचा पत्ता : Address of deceased at the time of death : 17 कोरेगाव पार्क पुणे 1 17 KOREGAON PARK PUNE 1

मयत व्यक्तीचा कायमचा पत्ता : Parmanent address of deceased :

नोंदणी क्र. : Registration No. : 1989D0006081

नोंदणी दिनांक : Date of Registration : 11/12/1989

शेरा : Remarks (if any) :

निर्गमित करणाऱ्या प्राधिकाऱ्याची सही : Signature of the issuing authority : Dr.S.T.Pardeshi Registrar & Health Officer Birth Death Department

प्रमाणपत्र दिल्याचा दिनांक : Date of Issue : 20/04/2016

शिक्का / Seal

MUNICIPAL CORPORATION OF THE CITY OF POONA पुणे म्युनिसिपल कॉर्पोरेशन स्था. १९५० EST-1950

प्राधिकाऱ्याचा पत्ता : Address of the issuing authority : Pune Municipal Corporation

This Certificate Having Scan Signature And Therefore No Need Of Physical Signature.

प्रत्येक जन्म आणि मृत्युची घटना नोंदल्याची खात्री करा.

Ensure Registration of Every birth and death.

6

The Suspicious Death of Osho's Girlfriend

Christena Woolf Smith, an attractive Britisher known by her sannyas name Ma Prem Nirvano, had been Osho's caretaker for the most part of his life since 1974, and his lover for many years. At the time of her death, she was just three months away from her 41st birthday on March 19.

A search for her death records with the Pune Police resulted in some interesting findings: Recorded as 'Death No. 135' under the Bund Garden Police Station, her name was entered, rather strangely, as 'Alexa Alexander'; 41-year-old female "Rajneesh disciple," residing at 17 Koregaon Park, Lane No. 1. The police records stated that Nirvano was brought to the N.M. Wadia Hospital's Ward No. E/4 on December 9, 1989 at 6.15 a.m. and declared dead at 18.20 hrs (6.20 p.m.). The cause of her death was mentioned as "accidental." The details of her viscera report could not be ascertained immediately as the report could not be located. Investigations into her death were conducted by Constable G.V. Wani (Badge no. 2225) from Mangaldas Police Chowki. He made 11 entries in the

Case Diary and closed the investigations one year later, on December 13, 1990.

In the Pune Municipal Corporation (PMC) records, Nirvano's Death Certificate mentions her name as 'Alisha Alexander,' as against 'Alexa Alexander' (see p. 104) in the police records. All the details of her address, age at the time of death, date and name of the hospital where she died match with the police records. Under the column 'Cause of Death,' the PMC's Death Register states ominously, "opinion reserved."

Why the name variations? None of the senior-most sannyasins the author spoke to were able to identify Nirvano by the names that have assumed her identity in the PMC and Pune Police records.

Several questions arise from this record:

Why was Nirvano's name entered in the official death records as 'Alexa Alexander' and 'Alisha Alexander,' and not as per her known legal name Christine Woolf Smith, or as 'Christena' Woolf Smith which she spelt out, letter-by-letter, in her testimony before the Wasco County Grand Jury in Oregon on October 18, 1985?

Why was she brought to Wadia Hospital about two kilometres away from the Osho Commune and not taken to Inlaks & Budhrani Hospital, just outside the gates of the Commune?

Who was the person who admitted Nirvano in an unconscious state to the Wadia Hospital on the morning of December 9, 1989?

Was Nirvano residing in a Bombay hotel before being brought to the hospital in Pune as is stated almost emphatically by some sannyasins? Or was she residing in the Pune Commune?

Nirvano first met Osho in 1971 when he was 40 and she was 21 and there was instant attraction between the two. Osho described her as the reincarnation of his childhood sweetheart, Shashi Gudiya. Nirvano had unrestricted access to him, going to the extent of even locking Osho once in his own room in the early 1970s. She did this when she felt that Osho was too unwell to step out to give a discourse. Nirvano spoke about this incident in a rare interview with Ma Yoga Sudha in December 1978.[1]

When she died suddenly on Saturday, December 9, 1989, many in the Commune were shocked that Nirvano was cremated hurriedly that same night in the presence of a quickly assembled group of sannyasins at the Tulsiram burning ghats in Koregaon Park.

The Commune informed its senior-most members that Nirvano had committed suicide with an overdose of sleeping pills as she had been suffering from depression. Neither was the press informed about her death nor was the news leaked out.

During an interview with the author at his Osho Nisarga base at Dharamsala, Tathagat who was the Commune In-charge then, said when he came to the Commune at around 6 a.m. on the morning of Saturday, December 9, he was told by the guards that "somebody had gone sick in the night and a car had been driven out of the Commune to the hospital." When Tathagat checked, he found it was Nirvano.

"She was admitted sometime in the night," said Tathagat, adding that she had been brought in an unconscious state to Wadia Hospital, off Bund Garden Road, about two kilometres from the Commune. Nirvano was declared dead at around 6 p.m., Tathagat said. Her body was then taken to the government's Sassoon General Hospital for the post-mortem which he termed as "the medico-legal, viscera inspection," and then, after the autopsy, it was brought to the burning ghats for cremation.

Tathagat was not aware of the precise cause of Nirvano's death. "She might have over-dosed herself as she was suffering from depression and taking treatment from a hospital in England," he said.

Tathagat was emphatic that Nirvano had been found unconscious inside her room in the Commune itself and had not been brought from Bombay as was being stated by some former sannyasins on the Internet, and during interviews with the author.

Tathagat and the Front Gate Guard Coordinator, Premgeet said they did not know when Nirvano was moved out of the Commune in the night. Since she had been frequently travelling to Bombay with Jayesh and coming to the Commune on the weekends, was she then taken directly to the Wadia Hospital on her return from Bombay? Who was the person who admitted her to Wadia Hospital? Tathagat did not have this information even though he was the Commune In-charge at that time.

Death at the Osho Commune would always be a celebration. Whenever someone died at the Commune, Osho's followers would try to live up to their Master's philosophical approach to death and organise a celebration. A funeral procession at the Commune would be an occasion to sing and dance with drums and other musical instruments as it proceeded to the burning ghats just a few lanes away. They would stop-and-proceed as they sang and danced, presenting an interesting spectacle. This was how Osho's father, Babu Lal, addressed affectionately as Daddaji, was taken on his final journey on

September 8, 1979, and so was 33-year-old Swami Anand Vimalkirti on January 9, 1981.

In sharp contrast, Nirvano's death was a hush-hush affair and there was no "death celebration" at her funeral. This shocked many sannyasins as it was not in keeping with the norm at the Commune. This was doubly shocking because Nirvano was no ordinary sannyasin but someone who had been extremely close to Osho.

Nirvano's sudden death was kept hidden from the press and public and discussion was not encouraged even within the Commune which was in the midst of preparing for Osho's 58th birthday celebrations on December 11. Since Neelam, and Tathagat were also unaware—or unwilling—to disclose the circumstances of her death, it meant that the facts were known only to the top-most rung at the Commune—Jayesh, Amrito and Anando. The official line was that Nirvano was suffering from chronic depression and had died accidentally due to an overdose of sleeping pills. According to the Commune, she was denied the "death celebration" on Osho's instructions as she had not died a natural death. [2]

This simplistic explanation did not satisfy the sannyasins who were not just shocked by her death, but also stunned by the secrecy around it. They have been speculating intensely for the last 26 years—among themselves, privately and publicly on online networks such as sannyasnews.org—on the real circumstances of her death.

The author asked Tathagat about the secrecy around her death, the absence of the usual "death celebration" and the few people at the cremation. To this, he said that these decisions were taken by Jayesh and Amrito and that her personal friends and "the Lao Tzu people" were there at her cremation, but not the general crowd of sannyasins.

"After autopsy, we never thought of bringing her to the Commune. We took her straight to the burning ghats and the people came there." The top sannyasins in attendance at her cremation were her boyfriend Jayesh, Anando, Amrito, and Shunyo, who fainted at the cremation, he said.

About the hush-hush manner of her cremation, he said it was done according to the instructions received from the top. He had been shuttling between the hospital and the Commune to give updates on Nirvano's condition and had simply been informed about what had been decided after she died.

"When I went to Lao Tzu, I could only find Anando. Anando informed Amrito and I briefed him too. I then went to the hospital, and when I came back, there was this message for me (about taking Nirvano's body directly to the burning ghats)," he said.

Tathagat was not sure who took the decision but he was certain that "Jayesh, Amrito and Anando were a party to the decision" to take Nirvano directly to the burning ghats and cremate her without any fanfare in the presence of a small group of people. He said since Nirvano was married (on paper) to an Indian based in Pune, the husband from that sham marriage may have been a party to the decision. It was possible that the cremation was done quietly as "there was some function at the Commune that night relating to Osho's birthday celebrations," he said.

It was extremely odd that Tathagat drew a complete blank when his attention was drawn to the 'Alisha Alexander' and 'Alexa Alexander' names under which the details of Nirvano's death had been entered in the PMC and police records.

Assuming that Nirvano had committed suicide as a result of depression, did she not deserve a decent send-off? Was it so very important to continue with Osho's birthday celebrations while cremating Nirvano without the love and respect she deserved? Why was Nirvano denied a fitting farewell by the Commune, knowing her extraordinary significance in Osho's life?

Or was her death not a case of suicide in the first place?

If Nirvano did commit suicide, what were the circumstances? Was her suicide intentional or accidental?

Was there abetment to suicide in any way?

Why was the possibility of murder ruled out?

Why was the news of her death hushed up?

At the hospital, Tathagat said, the Parsi sannyasin Zareen and her husband, Dr. Mody were actively engaged in handling Nirvano's case. What was the nature of their engagement?

On the day Nirvano died, Premgeet was on guard duty at the Commune and was asked to be present at Nirvano's funeral. He recalled that episode vividly. "On that day," said Premgeet, "I could not go to the evening darshan as I was sitting in Hotel Dreamland with my friends Rajani and Samarpan who had come from Surat. Whenever I would go out of the Commune, I would call the front gate to check if all was okay. When I called the guards at around 8 p.m., they sounded alarmed and said, "Where are you? Tathagat is searching for you frantically." So I left the party and came to the ashram."

On reaching the Commune, Premgeet met Tathagat who asked him to rush to the Tulsiram burning ghats. He did not give any details and said, "You will know once you reach. You may be required there."

"So I reached the burning ghats and saw 10–15 people there. It came as a shock to me when they brought out Nirvano's body. Till that point, I didn't know that Nirvano was dead. Very few people were informed that Nirvano was dead."

Apart from the death, he was shocked by the hurried cremation. As he put it, even when an "ordinary person" would die at the Commune, Osho would come to the Buddha Hall, offer flowers and then the body would be taken for cremation. Here was a person who had been Osho's lover and caretaker for so many years, "who was like a shadow to Osho all his life," who had died. "A person of that importance, and nobody even comes to know of her death? Why?" wondered a shocked and puzzled Premgeet.

It all seemed very strange, mysterious and suspicious to him.

He and many other sannyasins could not figure out why Nirvano would commit suicide. "Even if we asked about it, the seniors would be evasive. I was told by Tathagat, 'Focus on your tasks. Don't bother about other things.'"

Premgeet recalled that the talk in the Commune in those days was that Nirvano was Jayesh's girlfriend and their relationship had turned rocky "with a number of fights between them." He was himself a witness to one such fight during guard duty one night, almost a year before Nirvano's death. Premgeet said he had heard some screaming, shouting and hurling of abuses in the Blue Room kitchen in Krishna House where Jayesh and Nirvano lived. "They had fought so badly that all the crockery was smashed on the floor. I just saw that they had had a big quarrel, but don't know what it was about. I left, saying to myself, why bother about these fights of big people. I have come here to be with Osho."

Satya Vedant said he did not have any details about what had happened and added, "I know that before that (her death) she was in Bombay. Why she was in Bombay I don't know."

How close was Nirvano to Osho?

In her rare interview with Sudha on December 17, 1978, Nirvano said she met Rajneesh in 1971 when she was drawn to India as a tourist and attended one of his Hindi lectures in Bombay at Chowpatty Beach, without understanding the language. She later attended a meditation camp at Mount Abu where Osho "called me over and he put his arm around my shoulder and said, 'You're going to come and live with me. Come to Bombay and you'll live with me.'" Nirvano said, she leaned against his chest and "it felt like a continuation of something that I had forgotten...that just came right back." She ignored a warning from a Western participant who said, "You know, the Acharya has his eye on you."

It was in 1973, a year before the Pune Commune was born, that Nirvano started looking after Osho "sort of permanently".

Osho publically called Nirvano the reincarnate of his childhood girlfriend who had died as a teenager. As he said in a discourse (*The Path of Love*): "I had a girlfriend when I was young. Then she died. But on her deathbed, she promised me she would came back. And she has come back. The name of the girlfriend was Shashi. She died in '47. She was the daughter of a certain doctor in my village, Dr. Sharma. He is also dead now. And now she has come as Vivek to take care of me. Vivek cannot remember it. I used to call her Shashi Gudiya, and I started calling Vivek Gudiya also, just to give a continuity. Life is a great drama, a great play—it goes on from one life to another to another."

The various books on Osho's life written by his followers and those published by the Osho Commune restrict themselves to this romantic and mystical account of Nirvano's relationship with Osho. They go a step further and refer to Nirvano simply as "his caretaker". The fact was that during the peak of her relationship with Osho, Nirvano was more like Osho's devoted and possessive wife who loved him, cared for him and nagged him whenever she felt necessary.

On his *Sannyas Wiki* website, Swami Anand Rudra, (Ruddy Vogelsang), one of Osho's followers since 1977, has described Nirvano as "Osho's lover and the only friend he had." Osho's former secretary Sheela was direct about this and wrote in her memoirs that Nirvano lived with Osho as his wife and had sex with him. According to her, Osho always insisted on the use of contraceptives by Nirvano as he never wanted children. Sheela has presented an elaborate account of an incident from 1978 when Nirvano became pregnant and underwent abortion "supervised by Dr. Saraswati," who, she said was a prominent Pune gynaecologist.[3]

There are other accounts of Nirvano's proximity to Osho. "She was like his shadow," said Premgeet. An image that has stuck with Premgeet is that of Nirvano picking food particles from Osho's beard during one lunch session when she was sitting by his side. Premgeet caught a glimpse of this during his guard duties outside Lao Tzu House.

In the earlier years, said Premgeet, "No one could touch Osho without Nirvano's permission. Even if Amrito wanted to give him an injection, he had to go through her." Nirvano was always around and extremely protective of Osho.

In her October 1985 testimony before the Wasco County Grand Jury (Oregon), Nirvano described herself as Osho's "friend," not as his disciple or follower. "…I'm his caretaker. I look after his needs. If he falls sick, I get the doctor for him. I look…I oversee his food, his clothes, his rooms; just things like that," she said. Nirvano said Sheela had been extremely jealous of her proximity to Osho and had tried to have her removed from the Lao Tzu residence in Oregon, going to the extent of even spiking her tea with drugs that made her extremely sick. She said she was the only person authorised to have the keys to Osho's room and Lao Tzu House.[4]

This was true of Pune also where, sannyasins said, the practice was to lock the door leading to Osho in his part of the house for the sake of safety.

During her last three years in Poona-II, Nirvano left the Commune many times on short visits abroad and every time she returned, Osho welcomed her back and gave her complete freedom to do whatever she liked. "It was an exception he made for her that applied to no one else," Shunyo recalled.

Nirvano was that one person who could never be stopped from meeting Osho whenever she desired, even though she did not live in Lao Tzu House and was not his caretaker at the time of her death. Such was her legendary attachment to Osho that there is intense speculation among his followers even today that she may have been eliminated to get her out of the way for the grand finale of Osho's elimination itself, 41 days later.

According to the written accounts of a number of senior sannyasins, Nirvano had been suffering from depression for many years. She had been under treatment in the U.K. and had been known to take prescription drugs to calm herself. Sheela, in her memoirs, said Nirvano, who lived in Osho's house "received a morphine preparation as a sleeping aid, and for migraine, and for no apparent reason, larger quantities of sodium pentothal, a narcotic which is usually used only in surgical operations." Nirvano was also consuming the mood-enhancing drug Ecstasy which had then newly arrived in the U.S. market.[5]

On paper, Nirvano was married to an Indian, a Pune-based disciple of Osho to enable her and others to stay in India without a periodic renewal of visa. This was one of the nearly dozen "paper marriages" between Indians and foreigners in Pune. Sham marriages were one of the immigration frauds that Osho had been held guilty of in the U.S. where many of his Indian disciples had entered into "contract marriages" with Americans for the sake of gaining permanent residency there.

Since Osho encouraged free love and was against the institution of marriage, Nirvano had had many boyfriends throughout her stay in India. Since 1988–89 she had been Jayesh's girlfriend, right till her death. "She had been staying for a long time with him. Every week, Jayesh used to stay at the Oberoi and come to the Commune on Saturdays, Sundays. So similarly, she was also flying out with him every week," Tathagat said.

Shunyo wrote that Nirvano had been working with Jayesh and Chitten for about 18 months and travelling to Bombay each week for a couple of days. "Nirvano said she enjoyed the work, even as she suffered from overpowering depression from time to time." Shunyo, however, could not figure out the reason for her death and found her "desperately unhappy" in the last few months of her life.[6]

Antar Navjot has written about Nirvano's tragic situation due to heavy medication or drug overdose that occurred on May 10, 1989. Navjot's blog is about her experiences of working in Lao Tzu House under Maneesha, the Australia-born editor of many of Osho's books. As Navjot recalled, on the afternoon of May 10, Nityamo (medical assistant to Devageet) brought her to Krishna House and led her upstairs to a room that "was large by ashram standards, big enough to fit in a double bed and cupboard." She and another lady sannyasin were then asked "to give the room a good clean and change the bed linen." Just as they were finishing this task, Nityamo came in along with Ma Krishna Priya, both of whom were helping support Nirvano. "Nirvano was incoherent, and was helped into the freshly prepared bed. She appeared to be on heavy tranquillisers or some other strong drug." Nirvano's speech was slurred. "Krishna Priya was stroking her forehead and settling her down. Nityamo gestured to me and the other cleaner, and hustled us out of the room, closing the door quietly behind her."[7]

Navjot, who was extremely disturbed by what she saw, was told not to talk about it. "I didn't actually know what had happened, except that Nirvano did not seem to be very well, or drugged, and had to be put to bed in the middle of the day."

Earlier that year, there had been another incident witnessed by Navjot, in which Nirvano had called the Lao Tzu library "sounding either drunk or drugged, and asking for Shunyam." Navjot who had answered the phone gave the message to Maneesha and was told to be discreet about it. Navjot could never figure out what was wrong with Nirvano.

Jyoti Ma, 74, who had been with Osho since 1968, said the relations between Jayesh and Nirvano were indeed strained. She recalled that they would mostly stay in Bombay and come to Pune over the weekends for the White Robe Brotherhood. On one occasion, Nirvano was sitting in the front row in the Buddha Hall and Osho was looking intently at her. "But she was sitting without any emotions, like a statue. I wondered what had happened to her."

On December 7, 2015, the Osho sannyasin Shantam Prem, a prolific writer and commentator on the Osho sannyasins' discussion forum sannyasnews.org posted the details of his telephonic talk with Tathagat about Nirvano's death. As Shantam noted: "I asked Tathagat had he sensed some foul play in her death, that she took overdose herself or someone forced her or gave her the wrong dose as it happens in many cases?" His reply was, 'Many things became clear during the later years. At that time, Osho was present and we were covering each other. Surely because of Nirvano's death, these people got complete access to Osho. She was a hindrance in their plan.'"

From "these people", he mentioned the names Jayesh, Amrito, Shunyo, Anando, Devageet. That these people created a smoke wall around Osho.

At this point, Shantam told Tathagat, "I won't mention your name but say a reliable source."

He insisted, "No, you write my name."[8]

7

January 19, 1990: 'Osho Has Left His Body'

The author distinctly remembers springing to his feet and quietly exiting from a Marathi literary meet in Pune when a fellow journalist whispered that there was talk of Osho having died.

It was around 6–6.15 p.m. and much before the era of mobile phones or breaking news on TV. There was no point rushing blindly to the Osho Commune International at Koregaon Park; some phone calls had to be made as the news had to be confirmed and the author's newspaper headquarters in Bombay informed. The next priority was to be at the Commune, about 6 kms away.

According to the official account, Osho died at 5 p.m. The news of his death was first announced to the members of the Inner Circle at an emergency meeting at around 5.30 p.m. by Jayesh and Amrito. Osho's mother and the press were the next to be informed. By 6.30 p.m., Osho's sannyasins dressed in white robes had begun to gather in the Buddha Hall for the White Robe Brotherhood, the evening routine of discourse and meditation where Osho would arrive to give darshan, when in good health. On January 19, however, it was Amrito who arrived at 7 p.m., took centre-stage and shocked the gathering of a few thousand sannyasins with his announcement of Osho's death. Amrito said Osho had desired that his body be kept in the Buddha Hall for darshan for "just 10 minutes" and then be taken to the burning ghats.

The gathering of an estimated 10,000 sannyasins, was stunned by this announcement, with many breaking down in grief. At around 8 p.m., Osho's body, dressed in a black velvet gown with silver stripes and a matching winter cap, hands resting across the chest and black socks on the feet was brought to the Buddha Hall. Jayesh and Amrito were the lead pall-bearers, the others being Anando, Avirbhava, Mukta and Satya Vedant. Sprinkled with rose petals, the body was placed on the podium for the last darshan of 10–15 minutes.

Amidst loud music, sannyasins were seen 'celebrating' with tears, swaying bodies, and some dancing. The imagery of the bier being carried a few feet from the ground to give the sannyasins a glimpse of Osho, as it made its way from the Buddha Hall to the Commune's exit, with sannyasins lining the path on both sides, is still vivid. The funeral procession was headed for the Tulsiram burning ghats where Osho's younger brother Vijay Bharati lit the pyre at around 10 p.m. As the cremation proceeded through the night, there was the accompaniment of music, the strumming of guitars and singing. Many sannyasins such as Vedant Bharati, Tathagat, Jyoti Ma and others said their mind "went blank" from the time they heard the news of Osho's death, and performed their tasks at the funeral mechanically. Satya Vedant described it as a "no-mind" state.

Within about two hours of Osho's death, Amrito read out a brief statement before the assembled sannyasins in the Buddha Hall and followed it up the next evening, on January 20, with an extended statement. The 1,400-word statement was read out by Amrito in 11½ minutes, and a transcript was provided to the press. (See pp. 122–124.)

ANNOUNCEMENT IN BUDDHA HALL JANUARY 20TH, 1990

As you know, over these last few days, Osho's body has been becoming noticeably weaker. What you may not know is that He has also been in considerable pain. By the night of 18th, the pain in His legs was so severe that He was not able even to come and stand on the podium with us.

Over that night He became weaker and weaker. Every movement of the body was obviously agonizing. Yesterday morning I noticed that His pulse was also weak and slightly irregular. I said I thought He was dying. He nodded. I asked Him if we could call in the cardiologists and prepare for cardiac resuscitation. He said, "No, just let me go. Existence decides its timing."

I was helping him to the bathroom when He said, "And you put wall-to-wall carpet in here, just like this bath mat." Then He insisted on walking over to His chair. He sat down and made arrangements for the few items that He has in His room. "Who should this go to?" He said, pointing to His small stereo. It is audio? Nirupa would like it?" He asked. Nirupa has cleaned His room for so many years.

And then He went carefully around the room and left instructions for every item. "Those you take out," He said, pointing to the dehumidifiers which He had found too noisy recently. "And always make sure one air conditioner is on," He continued.

It was incredible. Very simply, in a very matter-of-fact and precise way, He looked at everything. He was so relaxed, as if He were going for the weekend.

He sat on the bed and I asked what we should do for His samadhi. "You just put my ashes in Chuang Tzu, under the bed. And then people can come in and meditate there, "He said

"And what about this room?"I asked.

"This would be good for the samadhi?" He asked.

"No," I said, "Chuang Tzu will be beautiful."

I said we would like to keep His present bedroom as it is. "So you make it nice," He said. And then He said He would like it marbled.

"And what about the celebration?" I asked.

"Just take me to Buddha Hall for ten minutes," He said, "and then take me to the burning ghats - and put my hat and socks on me before you take my body."

I asked Him what I should say to you all. He said to tell you that since His days in the marshal's cell in Charlotte, North Carolina, in America, His body has been deteriorating. He said that in Oklahoma jail they poisoned him with thallium and exposed Him to radiation, which we only came to know when the medical experts were consulted. He said they had poisoned Him in such a way that would leave no proof. "My crippled body is the work of the Christian fundamentalists in the United States government," He said. He said that He had kept His pain to Himself, but living in this body has become a hell.

He lay down and rested again. I went and told Jayesh what was happening and that Osho was obviously leaving His body. When Osho called again, I told Him Jayesh was here and He said for Jayesh to come in. We sat on the bed and He gave us His final words.

"Never speak of me in the past tense," He said. "My presence here will be many times greater without the burden of my tortured body. Remind my people that they will feel much more – they will know immediately."

At one point I was holding His hand and I started to cry. He looked at me, almost sternly. "No, no," He said, "That is not the way." I immediately stopped and just smiled beautifully.

Osho then spoke to Jayesh and talked about how He wanted the expansion of the work to continue. He said that now that He was leaving His body, many more people would come; many more people's interest would show, and His work would expand incredibly beyond our ideas.

Then He said, "I leave you my dream."

Then He whispered so quietly that Jayesh had to put His ear very close to Him, and Osho said, "And remember, Anando is my messenger." Then He paused, and said, "No, Anando will be my medium."

At that point Jayesh moved to one side, and Osho said to me, "'medium' will be the right word?"

I hadn't heard what had preceded it, so I didn't understand.

"Meeting?" I said.

"No," He replied, "For Anando, medium – she will be my medium."

He lay back quietly and we sat with Him while I held His pulse. Slowly it faded. When I could hardly feel it, I said, "Osho, I think this is it."

He just nodded gently, and closed His eyes for the last time.

Osho has given some very specific guidance for His work.

About nine months ago, Osho formed "The Inner Circle," a group of sannyasins now numbering twenty. Osho said He would have no successor, the Inner Circle would be His successor. The function of the Inner Circle is – in Osho's words – "to reach unanimous decisions about the continued functioning and expansion of the commune and Osho's work." Anando is preparing a full account of Osho's guidance on the workings of this group and who is in it. It will be available for you all to read tomorrow.

We are preparing in the next *Osho Times* all that Osho has said about what will happen when He leaves His body. I have two of these beautiful pieces for you.

Ten years ago, in answer to the question: What happens when you leave your body?

He replied:

I will be dissolved in my people. Just as you can taste the sea from any place and it is salty, you will be able to taste any of my sannyasins and you will find the same taste: the taste of the Blessed One.

I am preparing my people to live joyously, ecstatically. So when I am not in my body, it won't make any difference to them. They will still live the same way – and maybe my death will bring them more intensity .

About six months ago, He responded to a question from Italian T.V. about what would happen after His death, by saying,

"I believe and trust absolutely in existence. If there is any truth in what I am saying, it will survive. The people who remain interested in my work will be simply carrying the torch, but not imposing anything on anyone,

either by sword or bread. I will remain a source of inspiration to my people, and that is what most sannyasins will feel. I want them to grow on their own. Qualities like love, around which no church can be created, like awareness, qualities which are nobody's monopoly, like celebration, rejoicing, and maintaining childlike, fresh eyes. I want people to know themselves, not be according to someone else, and the way is in.

I hope I have conveyed to you what, throughout all these months of ill health and impending death, has been most striking about what Osho has been saying. And that is that when His work continues without His having to be in the body, then this is the flowering of His dream. Let me repeat His exact words in reference to His leaving the body: "My presence here will be many times greater...." "Remind my people that they will feel much more, they will know immediately."

He said, "My work is going really well, the commune is running beautifully, and after my death, many many more people will be coming here."

One of the things Osho always said is: "Always make room for sannyasins to contribute to my work."

I think you can take it that there is going to be a lot for us all to do.

In some inexplicable way it feels, not that His work is over, but that it has just begun.

It feels that His whole life has been a preparation for the moment when His people can sit in silence and feel His presence without His having to do the work of carrying His body. He always says He is a lazy man. Two nights ago, for the very first time, that happened. For the first time, we ALL sat together in silent communion without His physical presence.

It is already gone 7 o'clock. He will be waiting for us now, for that to happen again.

8

Behind the Scene: Securing Osho's Death Certificate

To the outside world, everything from the time of the announcement of Osho's death to his swift cremation seemed to have proceeded with clockwork precision, without any hitch. However, what had happened at the Commune that day was quite different.

On the morning of Friday, January 19, 1990, a frantic search began at the Osho Commune to locate an intensely devoted disciple of Osho, the soft-spoken ENT surgeon Swami Anand Krishna, also known by his legal name, Dr. Gokul Gokani. A well-established and much-travelled doctor, Dr. Gokani's wife Kumud, elder daughter Devapriya and younger daughter Chetna, were ardent Osho devotees.

Dr. Gokani had relocated to Pune from Mombasa (Kenya) in 1989 to be close to his Master. He had lived in Kenya for 12 years and had risen in his career to become the vice-chairman of the Kenya Medical Association. In Pune, he had a flourishing practice and was attached to three prominent hospitals, besides having his own clinic in Aurora Towers, Camp, and a consulting room at Medinova Diagnostic Services, a newly-established diagnostic centre in the city. At the Osho Commune, he volunteered at the ashram's medical centre and as a tour guide, while his wife Kumud and daughters Chetna and Devapriya were also active as volunteers and Osho's followers.

On that crisp January morning, Tathagat, was taken by surprise when, at around 9.30 a.m., the German sannyasin Chitten walked into his office in Krishna House. Chitten wanted help to locate Dr. Gokani.

Chitten was a confidant of the Commune commander Jayesh and if there was something that the Chairman of the Inner Circle wanted to be done, the task had to be done without unnecessary questions being asked. Administrative efficiency of Western standards was always a high point at the Commune where Germans, Americans and the British were in top positions.

Since Chitten could not locate Dr. Gokani on his own, he reached out to Tathagat. The only way to locate Dr. Gokani was through landline telephones and Tathagat tapped into his network. He soon learnt that Dr. Gokani had come in the morning at his consulting room at Medinova on Jangli Maharaj Road, about 6 km from his residence in Koregaon Park, but had returned home as he was not feeling well. According to Tathagat, a car with Chitten, driven by a sannyasin, Akhil Saraswati was then sent to Dr. Gokani's residence at Devnagri Apartments, next to the popular Prem's Restaurant on North Main Road, a few lanes away from the Commune.

Dr. Gokani was lying on his settee in the living room when Chitten came and said the Commune needed his help and that "Jayesh wants to see you." Was he in a position to come?

This was most unusual and it had never happened that the top man Jayesh had sent his emissary asking Dr. Gokani to come urgently to the ashram. Assuring Chitten that he was perfectly alright to go to the Commune, especially as Jayesh had called him, Dr. Gokani agreed. Without giving any details, Chitten asked him specifically to carry along his emergency medical bag and prescription letterheads and said Jayesh would explain on arrival. Dr. Gokani could now sense that "someone important" was not well at the ashram.

Both Tathagat and Akhil clearly remembered that Dr. Gokani was picked up well before lunch and was at the Commune by around 11 a.m.

On arrival at the Commune, Dr. Gokani said, he was brought to Jayesh's office in Krishna House. When Tathagat met him "after about half-an-hour to 45 minutes," Dr. Gokani looked nervous and disturbed. He did not utter a word—and was neither asked—about his meeting with Jayesh.

While it became well-known later that it was Dr. Gokani who had issued Osho's Death Certificate, what has remained under the wraps are the details and the circumstances in which he did this. Dr Gokani never spoke about this in the years after Osho's death and in October 1998 he left Pune and emigrated to the U.S. as his Green Card had been processed. Almost everyone at the Osho Commune knew that Dr. Gokani was privy to the secrets of Osho's death and he only needed the courage to speak out to satisfy the curiosity of Osho's followers the world over, and in India, in particular, to bring about a closure. Neelam recalled that over the years, rumours were rife that Dr. Gokani had spoken privately to his close friends (she mentioned the Bollywood music director Kalyanji Virji Shah, of the Kalyanji-Anandji fame, being one of them).

For 23 years after Osho's death, there was nothing on paper in terms of hard evidence and for nearly two decades, Dr. Gokani only spoke privately despite the enormous pressure on him to reveal the truth. He began opening up only after 2011, as he said, to unburden his conscience. First came a video interview by Satsang TV in Cologne at a gathering of Osho's followers. What received greater publicity was the doctor's letter to Swami Rajneesh, an Indian disciple settled in Argentina which made a presence on Facebook in 2013 and soon disappeared from the Internet. The same year, he spoke to a small group of Osho's followers at the Madhavpur (Ghed) ashram near Porbandar, established by senior Osho follower, Swami Brahma Vedanta.

In November 2015, Dr. Gokani agreed to be interviewed by the author on video during his visit to India, and on that day, also signed an affidavit on a Rs. 100 stamp paper in front of two witnesses, one of whom was the author (affidavit on pp. 140–143).

Born on November 1, 1935, Dr. Gokani was now 80 years old and the burden of suppressing the facts relating to his role in issuing Osho's Death Certificate had been weighing heavily on his mind. And he said so in as many words in his affidavit.

He explained in the affidavit that he kept silent about the facts of Osho's death, known to "only a few intimate people," in the hope that he would be able to "suppress the controversy about Osho's demise." However, what had troubled him was the "serious mismatch" in the statements made by Amrito and Jayesh relating to the time of Osho's death. He was also disturbed by the fact that on the day Osho died, he was "locked in a room"—very precisely, latched from the outside—to prevent him from leaking the information about Osho's death. Something else that bothered him was that he was called only to issue Osho's Death Certificate and, not attend to the Master when he was in his final moments on his deathbed.

Dr. Gokani says in the affidavit he was unhappy that Amrito and Jayesh did not feel it necessary to reach out to "many other doctors also present in the Osho Commune" or seek the assistance of hospitals nearby. He says that he felt compelled to execute the affidavit in view of his passing age and his heart ailments. "I do find it necessary to bring out the truth on record. Hence, this affidavit is executed by me," he wrote.

Recounting the events of January 19, 1990, Dr. Gokani gives the time of Chitten's arrival at his residence, in the Commune car, before lunch at around 12.30 p.m. His wife Kumud who was inside the Commune that morning doing voluntary service "in the tape department" had escorted Chitten to their residence as the German didn't know the location. In fact, on his way home from Medinova, Dr. Gokani had stopped by at the ashram where he had told his wife not to expect him for lunch at the Commune as he was going home to rest. "That's how she knew that I was at home and she brought Chitten with her," he said.

On arrival at the Commune, Dr Gokani was taken straight to Jayesh's office in Krishna House. "I asked why I was called and what can I do. He (Jayesh) said Dr. Amrito will come soon and explain."

Amrito arrived after 5–7 minutes "and after short, usual preliminaries he said, 'He is leaving the body'."

It was not clear to Dr. Gokani who was dying and so he asked specifically, "Who?"

Amrito hugged him and said, "Osho."

On hearing this, Dr. Gokani had tears in his eyes, to which Amrito said, "This is not the way to give a send-off to our Master. Just gather yourself and do your routine work in the ashram…"

Dr. Gokani was told to keep Osho's critical condition a secret—even from his own family—and was then asked about the nature of the voluntary work he did in the ashram. "I said I do work as a tour guide in the ashram from 2 p.m. to 4 p.m." Amrito and Jayesh then told him "to be a normal tour guide" and not show any emotions or disclose anything to anyone.

After he finished his tour guide duty at 4 p.m., he went back to Jayesh's office and was then asked to go and rest in Chitten's room, on the first floor of Krishna House, "till Amrito and Jayesh need you…"

He recalled that Chitten latched the door from the outside and also unplugged the telephone from his room "to ensure that I was not disturbed." Dr. Gokani recalled his reply to this: "I said I would not be able to sleep but I may lie down till you call me."

Chitten returned at around 5 p.m. saying, "Amrito wants you."

Dr. Gokani was then taken to Osho's bedroom in Lao Tzu House where he was plainly told by Amrito that Osho had "just left the body" and that he should write the Death Certificate needed for cremation.

In his video interviews to Satsang TV on August 15, 2011, and to the author on December 14, 2015, Dr. Gokani said he followed the standard procedure and examined Osho's vital signs such as pulse, blood pressure, pupil reflexes, and other reflexes to confirm his death. On his insistence, he was allowed to lift Osho's robe "up and down" to identify three birth marks or scars to validate that the body was indeed Osho's and not otherwise. While doing this, he saw that there was "some spillage of food or a bit of vomit on his robe," which he found unusual, but did not ask or write about. Later, in the Satsang TV interview he wondered whether Osho had been given some injection which had a reaction. He could not arrive at a conclusion, he said, because "as a doctor I can give you so many possibilities..."

Having ascertained that Osho was dead, Dr. Gokani then asked Amrito what he should write as the cause of death as he had not seen Osho when he was alive. He was then instructed by Amrito and Jayesh "to write myocardial infarction, which in layman's term is heart attack." During his interview in multiple sittings with the author at Baroda on December 14, 2015, Dr. Gokani said there was a discussion between him, Jayesh and Amrito "in front of Osho's dead body" on what should be written as the cause of death which would be accepted as natural death and not arouse any suspicion or need for post-mortem. "They discussed if we write 'myocardial infarction, then there won't be any need for further investigations and it would be easy to get the government certificate (cremation pass—the permit to cremate a body)." It was after this discussion that he was asked to write "myocardial infarction" as the cause of death.

"So, I entered 'myocardial infarction'. I trusted Amrito because he was Osho's personal physician and had treated him for years; he was literally with him for 24 hours," Dr. Gokani said. (The cause of Osho's death in the Pune Municipal Corporation's Death Register has been mentioned as "Cardio-respiratory arrest, diabetes, coronary thrombosis." The name of the person who provided the information is mentioned as

Dhyanesh Bharati who had rushed to the Sassoon Hospital to get the cremation pass.)

After Dr. Gokani wrote the Death Certificate on his letterhead, Jayesh took the hand-written certificate and brought a typed copy on another of Dr. Gokani's letterheads for signature. Such was the hurry in being done with the certificate that when some typing errors were pointed out, Jayesh asked the ENT surgeon to correct them by hand rather than lose time in retyping.

Dr. Gokani also mentions in his affidavit that very strangely, the lower part of the letterhead where his clinic address was printed was neatly cut and snipped off with a paper cutter. As he noted: "A little later, I saw that Jayesh had torn a portion of the Death Certificate where my address was printed."

Why was this done? Was it to put hurdles in the path of someone wanting to confirm and cross-check with the doctor?

Wanting to ensure that there were no hurdles in obtaining the cremation pass from the Pune Municipal Corporation, Dr. Gokani was sent along with three others to an office, under the Births and Deaths Registration Department, in the Sassoon General Hospital premises near Pune Railway Station. Osho sannyasins Dhyanesh, Prem Anadi and Dr. Narayan Kshirsagar from Joshi Hospital, left the Commune at around 6.15–6.30 p.m. and accompanied Dr. Gokani to get the cremation pass.

Anadi told the author in an interview: "Dhyanesh was furious about something and was driving the car quite recklessly. I had to warn him to be careful or else we would end up in a mess of our own." He remembered clearly that all four were dressed in white robes as they were ready for the evening meditation, and had gone in the Fiat car of the Commune. Once they reached the Sassoon office, Anadi said, "Dhyanesh kept Dr. Gokani's Death Certificate on the clerk's table along with two currency notes of Rs. 500. That man immediately made the cremation pass and we left in 10 minutes."

The Commune's insistence on sending the doctor who signed the Death Certificate to the municipal office to get the cremation pass was unusual. Why was a second doctor sent to accompany Dr. Gokani to get the cremation pass? Anadi surmises that this was perhaps a back-up arrangement in case some problems arose over Dr. Gokani's authority in issuing the Death Certificate as he was an ENT surgeon and not a general physician. Also, Dr. Gokani was relatively ncw to Punc.

On returning to the Commune, the ENT surgeon was instructed by Jayesh to be present alongside Amrito at the "World Press Conference" the next day in the Commune. "I was told by Jayesh, 'You have to be present but Amrito will answer the questions.'"

Although Dr. Gokani has now revealed that he could not ascertain the cause of Osho's death, the press note released by the Commune on January 20 stated: "An Indian physician, Dr. Gokul Gokani, gave the clinical cause of death as heart disease." The next day Dr. Gokani was given a crystal artifact by Jayesh saying, "Osho has left it for you."

Did Dr. Gokani feel that he was in any way used by Jayesh and Amrito and tricked into issuing Osho's Death Certificate without as much as giving him an opportunity to examine Osho when he was alive and ascertain the cause of death? The short-statured Gujarati doctor leaves behind a very strong impression that he was manipulated by the Commune into doing something that he would not have done in the normal course of his professional life. Osho sannyasins who have known him over the decades said he kept silent about the Death Certificate episode as he was afraid of losing his medical licence if the truth were to emerge.

For more than 20 years, Dr. Gokani spoke in whispers about the circumstances in which he issued Osho's Death Certificate, till the "burden on his conscience" troubled him and he began making revelations before small groups of Osho's followers. Was he afraid of incriminating himself in any way? Did Dr. Gokani know more than what he had revealed about Osho's death? There is intense speculation among Osho's senior disciples that Dr. Gokani was not allowed to even touch Osho's body and was asked to trust Amrito completely and quickly issue the Death Certificate.

For Dr. Gokani, worshipping Osho was all that mattered, and not the politics around him. Osho, and the joy of cooking delicious vegetarian meals along with his wife, Kumud, were the two passions of this doctor. Well-known inside the ashram for his and his wife's culinary skills, often, high profile guests at the Commune, such as top musicians and performers would be treated to a dinner at Dr. Gokani's residence where he and his wife would cook some special dishes. The Bollywood music director Kalyanji was among his close friends anda frequent guest at such dinners whenever he visited the Commune.

As a doctor, Dr. Gokani had never attended to Osho, although he had offered to do so when he had heard that the Commune was looking for an ENT specialist to treat a severe ear ache that Osho was suffering from on his return from the U.S. He had spoken to Amrito who had told him that they were consulting Dr. Mohan Jog from Pune. The only live contact that Dr. Gokani had with Osho was at the time of his sannyas in 1973 and later at an "energy darshan" in 1980 when Osho touched him on the forehead and he felt "a flow of transcendental energy" in him. "I was floating in the air for three days," he said of the experience.

Originally from Jamnagar, it was Dr. Gokani's elder brother, also a doctor, who had mentioned to him in the late 1960s about a guru called 'Acharya Rajneesh'. The young doctor had then refused to be drawn into hearing audio tapes of this person who his brother said was "revolutionary" in his thinking. Dr. Gokani had returned from his post-graduation in ENT surgery from England and whenever his brother mentioned Rajneesh to him, the doctor would become furious. "I would say, fuck off, I don't want to see any of your sadhus or babas. Their only idea is to rip you off..."

In 1972, while attending a nephew's wedding in South Bombay, Dr. Gokani was whiling away time with some relatives near Cross Maidan when the group saw huge crowds assembled to hear someone speak. Initially, they thought it was a political rally either by Indira Gandhi or Morarji Desai and with nothing better to do in the hours intervening between the wedding ceremony and reception, they sat in. Soon a bearded man in a white *lungi*-shawl took the stage, did a *namaste* and began speaking on the last *shloka* of the 13th chapter of the *Bhagavad Gita*. Dr. Gokani remembers that day vividly. "Since I was seated along with the others, I decided to hear him and was soon transfixed for one, one and a half hours. My elder brother was also there and I said to him, this is enlightening (to hear this man speak)." Dr. Gokani was stunned that it was the same Rajneesh his brother had spoken of. After the lecture, he bought all the 19 Osho titles in English, Hindi and Gujarati that were on sale at the makeshift bookstall at the maidan and read them one by one.

The obsession with Osho was now unstoppable and the next year, Dr. Gokani went to Mount Abu to attend a 10-day meditation camp where Osho was delivering talks on the *Kathopanishad*. Dr. Gokani shocked those around him by taking sannyas. The day was October 6, 1973 and he was given the name Swami Anand Krishna by Osho. Back home in Jamnagar, his family was shocked when they saw him in an orange attire with a *mala* and wondered how he would run his professional life as a doctor in such an attire.

In 1977, he rushed to Mombasa on hearing about the accidental death of his sister and young niece in a car accident and eventually emigrated to Kenya with his family, staying there till 1988. The fascination with Osho continued through the years and in 1983, Dr. Gokani made a trip to Oregon to stay for a week at Rajneeshpuram. He was thoroughly impressed with the "magnificent city that Osho was creating" and on returning to Kenya, applied for a Green Card in 1984. Meanwhile, he continued to do well in his career and rose to become the vice-chairman of the Kenya Medical Association. In 1988, however, he decided to relocate to Pune to be close to his Master and arrived in India in 1989 and rented a flat on North Main Road, Koregaon Park.

In 1998, Dr. Gokani's application for the Green Card matured and he decided to proceed to the U.S., although he and his family were well-settled in Pune. He felt he would return after a few months, but ended up emigrating to the U.S., although he continued to maintain his flat in Pune and visit India every other year.

In the U.S., Dr. Gokani settled at Ashland, Oregon, where he founded the Aum Awakening Center, where he began conducting meditation classes and workshops and undertook spiritual counselling. The Gokani husband-and-wife team produce television programmes on meditation, health and Indian Ayurvedic cooking for the Rogue Valley Community Television, and two of Dr. Gokani's videos on meditation—'Meditation' and 'Meditation—the Art of Living' have won awards.

Looking back at the entire episode, Dr. Gokani said, he felt that since he was specially called in to issue Osho's Death Certificate, Jayesh and Amrito should have at least let him see Osho's condition when he was dying. "That way, I would have known what was the cause of death."

The author asked Dr. Gokani, whether he endorsed the time of Osho's death as 5 p.m.

He replied: "Actually if you ask me, his body was still warm and there was no *rigor mortis*. I can say that he must have left his body at least, not earlier than one hour or half-an-hour." He could not say with certainty that Osho died at 5 p.m. as claimed by the Commune.

When asked why the Osho Commune was so very secretive about Osho's death that even he was not allowed to see Osho in his last moments, the ENT surgeon said: "That is a question that only they (Jayesh and Amrito) can answer." He was unwilling to speculate on the motive for the secrecy.

Did he at any point feel that something was wrong in what was happening? To this, Dr. Gokani said that he was so overwhelmed and overcome with emotions on hearing that Osho had died that everything went blank. "There were no thoughts...I even carried out my tour guide duties like a zombie…" Dr. Gokani broke down at this point and his voice choked.

Although he continued to maintain a flat at Sukhwani Classic Apartments on South Main Road close to the Commune, he stopped visiting the ashram since 2012. "I was no longer experiencing the energy that Osho had created," he said. Clearly unhappy with reports of what was happening at the Commune, Dr. Gokani said he wanted to appeal to all who love Osho to come forward and help "in bringing out the truth;" the truth about the mystery around Osho's death, the manner in which the ashram was being run, the removal of Osho's pictures from publications and Commune premises and the controversy around Osho's Samadhi…

प्रमाणपत्र क्र. / Certificate No. N20131028-0951-00038-1/5 ORIGINAL नमुना – ६ / Form - 6

महाराष्ट्र शासन
GOVERNMENT OF MAHARASHTRA

आरोग्य विभाग
HEALTH DEPARTMENT

पुणे महानगरपालिका
PUNE MUNICIPAL CORPORATION

मृत्यू प्रमाणपत्र
DEATH CERTIFICATE

(जन्म व मृत्यू नोंदणी अधिनियम, १९६९ च्या कलम १२/१७ आणि महाराष्ट्र जन्म व मृत्यू नोंदणी नियम २००० चे नियम ८/१३ अन्वये देण्यात आले आहे.)

(Issued under section 12/17 of the Registration of Births & Deaths Act., 1969 and Rule 8/13 of the Maharashtra Registration of Births and Deaths Rules, 2000)

प्रमाणित करण्यात येत आहे की, खालील माहिती मृत्यूच्या मूळ अभिलेखाच्या नोंदवहीतून घेण्यात आलेली आहे. जी की (स्थानिक क्षेत्र)– पुणे तालुका : हवेली जिल्हा : पुणे महाराष्ट्र राज्याच्या नोंदवहीत उल्लेख आहे.

This is to certify that the following information has been taken from the original record of death which is the register for (local area/local body) Pune -of tahsil / block : Haveli of District : Pune of Maharashtra State

मृताचे पूर्ण नाव : भगवान श्री रजनीश
Full Name of Deceased : BHAGWAN SHREE RAJNEESH

लिंग : पुरुष
Sex : Male

मृत्यू दिनांक : 19/01/1990
Date of Death : 19/01/1990

मृत्यूचे ठिकाण : 33 कोरेगाव पार्क पुणे 1
Place of Death :

आईचे पूर्ण नाव :
Full Name of Mother :

वडिलांचे / पतीचे पूर्ण नाव :
Full Name of Father / husband :

मयत व्यक्तीचा मृत्यू समयीचा पत्ता : 33 कोरेगाव पार्क पुणे 1
33 KOREGAON PARK PUNE 1
Address of deceased at the time of death :

मयत व्यक्तीचा कायमचा पत्ता :
Parmanent address of deceased :

नोंदणी क्र. : 1990D0005225
Registration No. :

नोंदणी दिनांक : 19/01/1990
Date of Registration :

शेरा :
Remarks (if any) :

निर्गमित करणाऱ्या प्राधिकाऱ्याची सही : Tokeun
Signature of the issuing authority :

प्रमाणपत्र दिल्याचा दिनांक : 28/10/2013
Date of Issue :

शिक्का/Seal : MUNICIPAL CORPORATION OF THE CITY — पुणे म्युनिसिपल कॉर्पोरेशन स्थापना १९५० — ESTD 1950

प्राधिकाऱ्याचा पत्ता :
Address of the issuing authority : Pune Municipal Corporation

प्रत्येक जन्म आणि मृत्यूची घटना नोंदल्याची खात्री करा. **Ensure Registration of Every birth and death.**

मुमादामु. (१९३०) १,००,०००-२-१३ आ/जन्म-मृत्यू

भारतीय गैर न्यायिक

एक सौ रुपये Rs. 100

रु. 100 ONE HUNDRED RUPEES

सत्यमेव जयते

भारत INDIA

INDIA NON JUDICIAL

ગુજરાત गुजरात GUJARAT

14 DEC 2015

AR 620645

અનુક્રમ નંબર: ૨૭૩૧૭ તા: ૧૪/૧૨ -૨૦૧૫ રૂ. ૧૦૦

ખરીદનારનું નામ:- DR. GOKUL GOKANI

સરનામું:- Nr. Flour Rest. Akashwani Rd, Makarpura, Vadodara

સ્ટેમ્પ વેન્ડરની સહી: [illegible] [illegible] સહી: [illegible]

(શ્રીમતી ભાવનાબેન [illegible]) લા.નં. [illegible]

(ઓ.) ૧૪૪, સરસ્વતી કોમ્પલેક્ષ, માંજલપુર અતિથિગૃહ સામે, વડોદરા-૧૧. | (રહે.) ૨૬/બી, જનકપુરી સોસા. માંજલપુર નાકા, વડોદરા-૧૧

NOTARY GORAKH VITTHAL KIRVE Reg. No. 5511 DISTRICT PUNE EXPRIED DT. 12/3/201[illegible] GOVERNMENT OF INDIA

Affidavit

I the undersigned Dr. Gokul Gokani, Age: 80 Years, Occupation Doctor ENT Surgeon residing at Ashland, Oregon, 97520, USA Today at Vadodara (Baroda) Gujarat, India

DO HEREBY STATE, SUBMIT AND DECLARE ON SOLEMN AS FOLLOWS:

I am disciple of Osho formally known as Bhagwan Shree Rajneesh since1973. I am practicing as medical practitioner/ E. N. T. surgeon since

1970 in Jamnagar and from 1989 to 1998 in Pune attached with 3 Hospitals – Inlak and Budhrani Hospital situated at Koregaon Park, Pune, Ruby and Jehangir Hospitals Pune - and few years during that time worked in medical center of Osho Commune International Koregaon Park, Pune.

I remember that unfortunate day of 19th January 1990 as on the day my beloved Master Osho died. I have been the witness on the events which took place on 19th January 1990. As, I had signed Osho's death certificate, I am witness to the events which took place around Osho. The details of which follow hereunder.

At around 1:00 pm (13.00 hours) on January, 19, 1990;

Swami Chitten – German sannyasin, who was very active with Michael Byrne's (Jayesh's) right hand or assistant. Chiten came to my residence with my wife Kumud (Ma Yoga Kumud,) as Chiten did not know, where our residence was. As I was not feeling well, I was lying on a Setee (bed) in our living room. As I was not feeling well on that day I had left my consulting room in Medinova on Jungli Maharaj road, Poona. Chitten first asked me how I was as he saw me resting.

I sat on the bed and told Chiten, that I was just resting, as something was not right inside, but I told him for not to worry and asked him, what was the purpose of his visit and what can I do! He asked again that are you alright then we need your help and to go with him.

Specifically, He said that take your (Dr.'s) emergency bag and your letter head and Mr. Michael Byrne (O'Byrne) aka Swami Jayesh needs you.

I asked, is anyone serious or passed away, as requesting me to take my letter head book specifically. He answered that Jayesh will talk to you, but you come now with me and I have got Ashram's car and you need not to drive, as you are not feeling well!

Around 1.30 pm Chiten took me to Jayesh's room in Krishna house in Ashram and Jayesh asked me what I would like to drink any hot or cold drink and to have a seat. I asked, why I was called and what can I do. He said Dr. Amrito (Dr. John Andrew alias Dr. Geroge Meredith) will come soon and he will explain to you about it.

Soon, within 5-7 mintues, Amrito appeared and after short usual preliminaries, he said," HE IS LEAVING THE BODY," But it was not clear to me who?

So I asked him, who? He said Osho and hugged me, then I had tears and he said, this is not the way to give send off to our Master, just gather yourself and do your routine work in the ashram and not to tell this news to anyone including my immediate family – Kumud, Devapria and Chetana – and then asked, what work do I do in the ashram and I said I do work as tour guide in the ashram from 2 to 4 pm. So he and Jayesh told me to be normal tour guide and without showing any emotions and sharing this news at all.

So I carried out my tour guide work in the ashram without any real energy or interest and showing ashram to visitors.

As told earlier by Jayesh, to meet him in his office after I finish my guide work, so just after 4 pm I went to his office in Krishna House and he said, I should go with Chiten and Chiten took me to his room in Krishna House and said you just rest or sleep till Amrito and Jayesh need you and I thought, they will call me, when Osho is still in the body.

Chiten unplugged the telephone in his room, so he said, while you are resting, you don't get disturbed. I said, I would not be able to sleep, but I may lie down till you call me.

Around 5 pm: Chiten came to his room and told me Amrito and Jayesh wants me, so he took me and emergency bag also to Osho's room, where Amrito told me that he just left the body and you write death certificate, needed for cremation.

So I asked him, what is the cause of death, as I have not seen him alive, before he left the body. So Amrito and Jayesh decided to write MYOCARDIAL INFARCTION, Which in layman's term is heart attack.

Though I was resting there in Chitten's room in the Ashram, I was not called for and did not see Osho till He left body (demise).When Chitten took me to Osho's room and saw his body, where Jayesh and Amrito were present. I did not know whether I was called for the death certificate, as many Indian and western Drs. Were there in the Ashram very much known to Amrito and Jayesh!

I asked Amrito that I will need Osho's passport, to write exactly his name as in his passport. He said his passport is expired and I said it does not matter I just need to write his name as in his passport, so he brought his passport and I copy it in his death certificate. I insisted them that I will have to see 3 identity marks on Osho's body to validate that it is HIS BODY and not otherwise, so he said you can search those signs and so I found on his body 3 identifying birth marks or scars pulling his robe up and down.

Then Jayesh took that hand-written certificate and brought typed copy on another of my printed letterhead and asked me to sign! I found, couple of typo errors, but he said you can correct those spelling mistakes rather than retyping it again. Little later I saw that Jayesh had torn portion of the death certificate whereby my address was printed. And then Jayesh asked me to go to Sasson- Govt. – Hospital and to get government cremation papers, which I did go with Swami Dhaynesh (Mr. Dhanesh Joshi) and others and brought it to him.

Then I asked him, can I go home now, as my family was not to come to Ashram for white robe (Evening Meditation) and I did not want them to miss the death celebration and we did not have phone at home. SO JAYESH SAID HE WILL SEND SOMEONE TO MY HOME AND BRING MY WIFE KUMUD AND DAUGHTER. I requested them not to mention them about Osho and why I am calling them to ashram, but just to bring them for me.

All these years, I have been keeping these facts known to only few intimate people. I thought that I will be able to suppress the controversy about Osho's demise. But during past few years while talking to other persons I found serious mismatch / controversy in the statements made by Amrito and Jayesh, such as timings on which Osho left His body (demised), locking me in the room so that I cannot speak to anyone on Osho's demise and calling me only for the purpose to issue a certificate. However, on 19th January there were many other doctors also present in the Osho Commune, Poona. In spite of all these assistance and hospitals available, Amrito and Jayesh did not felt necessary to call for the same.

At the end, Osho's body was taken for cremation / funeral within almost 60 minutes of the public announcement.

Having regard to my passing age and having heart problems knowing the mortality of life, I do find it necessary to bring out the truth on record. Hence, this affidavit is executed by me.

In Witness whereof I had affirmed on this 14th Day of December 2015 at Vadodara, Gujarat India

Executant

Dr. Gokul Gokani (Sw. Anand Krishna)

In Witness: K. Gokani

1) Mrs. KUMUD GOKUL GOKANI
47 Garfield st.
Ashland, Oregon 97520, USA
(Today at Baroda)

2) ABHAY PREM VAIDYA

9

Osho's Death: A Fabricated Account?

If Osho did die a natural death as claimed by Amrito, where was the need for the extreme secrecy at the time of his death?

Why was Dr. Gokani who was hurriedly brought to the Commune on January 19, 1990 to issue Osho's Death Certificate not allowed to see Osho in his last moments?

Why did Amrito wait for Osho to die before allowing Dr. Gokani to see the body?

Why was Osho cremated in a tearing hurry?

There are three critical aspects to Osho's death which demand close scrutiny. The first is the extraordinary secrecy around Osho at the time of his death. This was followed by his speedy cremation, and then came the elaborate, almost minute-to-minute official account of his death as presented by Amrito through a statement that he read out. When read carefully and dispassionately, this account appears theatrical and contrived, inspired, most likely, by the account of the final hours of the 4th century BC Greek philosopher Socrates whom Osho admired immensely. Since the Indian guru was hailed and worshipped as an 'Enlightened Master' and a mystic by his followers, it only seemed appropriate that he could not be allowed to die an ordinary death, without an element of mysticism.

Was the account of Osho's death a factual account? Or was it drafted by a scriptwriter after careful thought and multiple revisions?

If Amrito's account is to be believed, it would seem before dying, Osho said all the right things and pressed all the right buttons. He began by taking a shower and putting on a robe in the morning (Satya Vedant's version[1]). After that, Osho instructed that many of his personal effects be given as gifts to his sannyasins, including to the Indian doctor who issued his Death Certificate. Osho then asked for Jayesh and left him his dream to be fulfilled. He named Anando as his "medium" through whom he would communicate after death and issue guidance to the Commune. He gave elaborate instructions for his Samadhi to be beautified with marble. In addition to saying all this to Amrito in the last conversation of his life, Osho did not forget to accuse the American government and "Christian fundamentalists"—very precisely—of poisoning him during his incarceration in an Oklahoma jail. He turned down Amrito's suggestion for emergency medical assistance and preferred natural death. Finally, he asked for a quick cremation, wanting his body not to be kept in the Buddha Hall for more than 10 minutes. When Amrito felt his pulse fading rapidly, he said to the Master, "Osho, I think this is it," and Osho closed his eyes, and bravely embraced death.

If Amrito's account is to be believed, one would have to accept that Osho did all this amidst rapidly deteriorating health parameters, physical and mental disorientation and intense pain.

According to the official account, Osho's death was witnessed by just two persons: Jayesh and Amrito. Both were at the helm of affairs at the Commune and enjoyed the complete trust of all the sannyasins. They however, did not deem it fit to inform anyone that Osho was critical and could die ('leave the body' in the Commune's parlance) within hours. They did not deem it fit to consult other senior sannyasins and seek their opinion on the best course to follow. Clearly, Jayesh and Amrito were not just controlling the show but also being extremely secretive about it. All that Amrito did after Osho's death, was to make an announcement that Osho had handed over his dream to Jayesh for fulfillment! According to the testimonies of senior sannyasins inside the Commune on that day, Jayesh then issued orders for Osho's speedy cremation, stating that was Osho's last wish.

Even Anando who was otherwise closest to Jayesh and Amrito among all the other sannyasins, was kept in the dark. She was told later that Osho had remembered her in his dying moments, but, by her own admission, was not called to see him although she was in Lao Tzu House on that day.

The 1995 annual issue of *Osho Times*, an official publication of the Osho Commune, published an interview with Anando which proved to be revealing on two counts: the approximate time of Osho's death and the anointing of Anando as Osho's "medium"—the person through whom Osho would communicate with his followers after his death. The interview was conducted five years after Osho's death when the controversy around his death had not just subsided but been forgotten. The interviewer, Amrit Sadhana, asked Anando the significance of Osho's words at the time of dying: "Anando will be my medium". Sadhana notes in her interview in Hindi titled

'Aakashganga ke tat par' (On the edge of the galaxy): "As I asked this question, Anando suddenly became silent. She closed her eyes, became introspective and then said, 'I don't know. Osho never told me anything. He said this to Swami Jayesh and Amrito and then merged with the infinite sky.'"

When Anando was asked to recall the moment when she first heard of Osho's death, she shared this anecdote: "On the morning of January 19, I did Osho's work as per the routine and then Amrito took charge. In the afternoon, something strange happened. I normally take my plate and have lunch while sitting outside Lao Tzu. That day, however, I left my plate and went on the Lao Tzu terrace, right above Osho's room and was enjoying the sight of trees swaying in the breeze under the open sky. How could I know that downstairs Osho was slowly leaving the body? When I came down the stairs, I saw Jayesh standing there. And he said in a low voice, 'Osho has left the body.'"

Did Osho actually say "Anando will be my medium"? As Osho's caretaker in his final days, Anando was present in Lao Tzu House as Osho lay dying. She could easily have been called at a moment's notice and heard it from Osho himself. Why was she not called and why couldn't she hear it from his own mouth?

Such was the thick veil of secrecy around Osho at the time of his death that even Dr. Gokani who had been brought to the Commune with the sole purpose of issuing his Death Certificate, was not allowed to see Osho when he was alive.

The Commune knew that Osho was not well, but no one even had an inkling that he was critical. Neelam, whose room was next to Anando's in Lao Tzu House, said Anando was in bed that morning when she left for her office in Krishna

House. When she returned to her room briefly in the afternoon, according to her routine, everything inside Osho's residence appeared normal. Every effort was made to project a picture of normalcy, right to the point of having his cook prepare his evening milkshake.

The announcement made by Amrito in the Buddha Hall did not mention a word about Dr. Gokani examining Osho's body and declaring him dead before issuing the Death Certificate. Amrito's statement made no mention of Osho having taken a shower on the morning of January 19 and putting on his robe, as claimed by Satya Vedant in his account of Osho's last day. In an interview reproduced in *Allah to Zen* by Ma Chetan Unmani and Swami Chaitanya Keerti, Satya Vedant has said: "And you will not believe this, but He went into the bathroom, took a shower, came out and put on His robe by Himself. He said: 'You do only one thing, you just put my socks on and my cap; you take me to Buddha Hall for 10 minutes and then take me to the burning ghat."

Satya Vedant's version that Osho took a shower in the morning and then put on his robe himself, finds no mention in Amrito's account. Amrito begins his carefully-prepared statement on Osho's death by saying that Osho was in considerable pain and his body was becoming noticeably weaker over the past few days. By the night of the 18th, the pain in his legs was so severe that he could not come to the Buddha Hall. Over that night, Osho became still weaker "and every movement of the body was obviously agonizing." By 19th morning, his pulse had become weak and irregular.

Why was Satya Vedant then claiming that on the morning of the 19th, Osho had taken a shower by himself and put on his robe? Vedant provides an explanation in the interview by saying that Osho left his body in a very conscious manner, as was done by "Zen masters" about whom he spoke often. Reinforcing the story presented by Amrito, Vedant says, that until the last breath, Osho was conscious. "This is what the death of a master is: to die consciously, with full awareness, aware at the last moment that death is coming."

On March 18, 2016, the author interviewed Satya Vedant during his visit to Pune, drawing attention to his statement: "And you will not believe this, but He went into the bathroom, took a shower, came out and put on His robe by Himself." When asked for the source of this information as there was no mention of it in Amrito's account, Satya Vedant drew a blank. He said, "I don't remember who told me that." He could not explain the reason for the extreme secrecy around Osho's death. "Lots of things are said and heard but I have no way to figure out, to check or to find out," he said. The former Chancellor of Osho Multiversity, however, remembered clearly that it was Jayesh who had made the announcement of Osho's death at the emergency Inner Circle meeting.

On the very day that Osho died, the Commune released what is known as "the Shirley MacLaine Press Note" criticising the American actress and her brand of meditation. The Commune then clumsily and hastily sought to have it withdrawn from newspaper offices in Pune. This strongly indicated that the person issuing press notes on Osho's behalf was not aware that he was either already dead or on his deathbed and could not possibly have released the press note. The press release dated January 19, 1990 read:

PRESS RELEASE

FOR IMMEDIATE RELEASE

WARNING: SHIRLEY MACLAINE IS DANGEROUS TO YOUR SPIRITUAL HEALTH, SAYS OSHO

"Just as cigarettes are damaging to your physical health, Shirley Maclaine's so-called `Inner Workout' exercises are harmful to your spiritual health," warned the enlightened Indian mystic Osho, in a statement from his international commune in Poona, India.

Osho was responding to questions from his American disciples about the dangers of visualization exercises that work with the body's seven energy centers, known in India as "chakras." In Shirley Maclaine's `Inner Workout' video the centers are said to be located at the sex organs, belly, solar plexus, heart, throat, forehead, and crown.

But Osho cautioned: "These centers differ in both manner and location with each individual. Theoretical visualization exercises like Shirley Maclaine's can be very destructive, because you begin to mentally project a fictional experience over the reality. If someone like Shirley Maclaine says that `Here is the chakra, here is the energy center,' then you hypnotically begin to see the chakra at that spot and it may not be there at all."

The mystic added: "Exercises like this slowly create in you a false world of dreams, illusions and projections. Shirley Maclaine should put a warning on her videotapes like those found on American cigarettes, informing people of the dangers. Otherwise, she is unconsciously doing tremendous damage to spiritual seekers wishing to go into meditation."

END

For further information contact:

Swami Chaitanya Keerti

Swami Chaitanya Keerti
January 19, 1990

Osho Commune International Press Office
17 Koregaon Park, Poona 411 001 (MS), India
Tel.: 0091-212-660963, FAX: 0091-212-664181, Telex: 81-0145-474, Gram: Tathata

The release of this press note and the clumsy attempt to withdraw it was perplexing as Amrito had stated that Osho was "in intense pain for three days preceding his death." Did Osho then, still have the humour to issue silly statements?

Osho had skipped the evening darshan on January 18, and on January 17, when he had arrived on the podium in Buddha Hall, he was clearly disoriented and had difficulty in maintaining balance while walking. This footage has been captured in the video, '*The Last Namaste*'. "He greeted everybody and sat in his chair. Got up, greeted everybody and left. That's when everybody saw his body had become frail. For the first time, we saw that he was taking the support of the wall to even walk," Tathagat recalled.

Osho's physical weakness and his unsteadiness as witnessed by his followers and recorded in this video sought to suggest that his death, two days later, was the result of a natural deterioration of his health. Given this condition of Osho, and Amrito's statement that he was in intense pain for three days, the question arose: who was it that was issuing statements on Osho's behalf, right on the day of his death?

As a journalist in Pune, the author repeatedly sought an explanation from Chaitanya Keerti, the spokesperson of the Commune, about the issuing of that press note, followed by an attempt to withdraw it. Finally, Keerti said in an interview that "the text for the press release came from Lao Tzu House." He said that it was either Amrito or Anando who routinely provided the text for the Commune's press notes which were then released by the spokesperson through his network. Keerti suggested that the words attributed to Osho "may have been a few days old" and the issuing of the press release "could have got delayed" in the routine course. This was hard to believe given the enormous pride that the Commune took in the high degree of efficiency and professionalism in all its operations.

About the withdrawal of the press note, he said the Commune did not want Osho's criticism of the American actress "to be construed as his last words" and it, therefore, decided to withdraw it. Among the hundreds of press statements and press notes issued in Osho's name over the years, the one on Shirley MacLaine appeared one of the silliest because the "Enlightened Master" was on his deathbed and seemed to have nothing better to think about. More importantly, it raised questions of credibility about claims made by Jayesh and Amrito about the instructions left behind by Osho as he lay dying on January 19, 1990. It also suggested that statements were being manufactured in Osho's name which he did not make in the first place.

Amrito's statement on Osho's death suggests that just before dying, Osho was precise and cogent in blaming the U.S. government for killing him with poison.

Did Osho actually say all this? Or was it part of a conspiracy to promote the Osho-poisoned-by-U.S.-government theory? The fact is that without any hard evidence, the Commune invested considerable energy in building this theory.

In October 1989, the Commune's International Press Office released a biographical statement which said that "It is probable that he (Osho) was poisoned with the heavy metal thallium while in that jail (Oklahoma County Jail) and the El Reno Federal Penitentiary." On February 8, 1990, Amrito released a detailed medical history of Osho from 1987 to 1990 to state emphatically that Osho's death "was clearly the result of damage to His body, caused by poisoning in America." He felt the need to release this statement to refute the allegations that "Osho's death was sudden, and that the stated cause of death—heart disease—was unrelated to the poisoning by the U.S. government."

The thallium poisoning allegation was repeated once again the same day in a statement by Osho's attorney Prem Niren headlined: 'U.S. politicians killed Osho, says his attorney.' The Osho-poisoned-by-U.S.-government theory also sits very well with the attempt by the Commune to compare Osho to Socrates, who was accused of corrupting the youth in ancient Athens and was sentenced to death by poison. A much-celebrated part of the philosoper's life is the conversation that he had with his followers and the account of how he fearlessly sipped hemlock and embraced death. Socrates was a favourite of Osho along with the Buddha, Lao Tzu and Chuang Tzu, and Osho's talks on Socrates while in Greece in early 1986 have been transcribed under the title *Socrates Poisoned Again After 25 Centuries.* Osho then speaks extensively about why he likes Socrates.

In Amrito's elaborate announcement in the Buddha Hall on the day after Osho died, he had said that Anando "is preparing a full account of Osho's guidance on the workings of this group (Inner Circle) and who is in it. It will be available for you all to read tomorrow." That promise was not kept and Anando's "full account" was never presented before Osho's followers.

In June 2000, when the Osho Commune released a full-page advertisement in *The Indian Express* to reply to allegations in the media against the Commune, Anando revealed that she had stopped being a member of the Inner Circle for nearly a year and was no longer associated with any trust or foundation associated with Osho. She said she had decided to move on,

10 years after Osho left his body. In March 2015, an Osho disciple, Shantam Prem posted an update on sannyasnews.com stating that Anando had "reverted back to Susan Hefley". "It says much," said Shantam, "when the third top-most person in the Osho Commune hierarchy who, 'as per the story,' was remembered by Osho till his last breath, chooses to drop sannyas and reclaim her Christian name."

Indeed, Anando moved away from the Osho Commune in Pune and her bio-sketch on her website lifetrainings.com (http://lifetrainings.com/About-Anando-and-Shunyo.html) on January 2016 made no mention of her exalted status as "Osho's medium". Settled in Italy, she, along with Shunyo, and Shunyo's boyfriend Marco, conducted a series of personal development programmes. Anando also ran a paid online course on meditation.

Immediately after Osho's death, Jayesh, as Chairman of the Inner Circle, and Amrito, as his deputy, took complete control over the Osho Commune, its trusts and properties. They took extraordinary decisions and exercised their authority over everyone in the Commune by claiming that Osho had given the two of them a set of instructions before dying. There was a new halo of power around Jayesh as he was now the custodian of Osho's dream. Was the 'I Leave You My Dream' and the rest of Osho's purported instructions to Jayesh and Amrito from his deathbed, a fabricated story? Many of Osho's followers believe so in the absence of hard evidence presented by the Commune.

Dr. Gokani is one such disciple who insisted that he wanted to see a video before he could believe the 'I Leave You My Dream' story. He stressed that every small moment of Osho's life had been video-taped by the Commune—"even when he went to the bathroom"—Dr Gokani said angrily, for effect. How come Osho was not video-taped or even audio-taped at a time when he was giving the message of his life—that someone will be his medium and that he is leaving his dream with Jayesh, to be fulfilled by his followers, asks Dr. Gokani.

He found it hard to accept that Osho could have said any such thing. "Can an enlightened person who is shaking everyone out of their dreams say to someone, 'I Leave You My Dream'?" Dr Gokani had serious doubts about this claim on the very day it was made in the Buddha Hall by Amrito.

In the days following Osho's death, the author had asked Keerti for evidence in the form of a Will or an audio / video recording to support the claims and assertions made by the Commune about Osho's last instructions. Echoing the Commune's official position, Keerti said there was no Will left behind by Osho. He was furious when asked for audio / video recordings and said: "Our Master is dying and you expect us to video-tape him? Hold a microphone in front of his mouth?"

Dr. Gokani did not find this outburst rational. If Osho was indeed making the 'I Leave You My Dream' statement and leaving behind other instructions, "it means he was totally conscious and fit enough to be videoed," was the doctor's opinion.

As one of the two persons who witnessed Osho's death and as the only person who spent the longest time with Osho in the days leading to his death, a detailed investigation into Amrito's role is necessary. It is all the more necessary as Amrito was Osho's personal physician and the second-in-command at the Commune since the beginning of Poona-II in 1987. In addition to being the vice-chairman of the Inner Circle and trustee of Osho International Foundation, Zürich, he is also a signatory as a 'witness' to Osho's Will which is suspected to be a forged document.

In April 2016, the author's request for an interview with Amrito, whom he had met on a few occasions in previous years, was turned down by Amrit Sadhana.

10

Did Drug Overdose Kill Osho?

There are far too many inconsistencies in the official version of Osho's death, too many contradictions and damning eye-witness accounts which demand that Osho's death needs to be re-opened for investigations.

Did Osho die of drug overdose? Was his death the result of euthanasia or assisted suicide?

In August 2011, Dr. Gokani was interviewed on video for nearly two hours at a gathering of Osho's German followers in Cologne. The interview was conducted by Englishman John David, also known as Premananda, a structural engineer and architect by training who had become an Osho disciple at age 28 and had spent many years in Pune and Oregon. Several probing questions were asked of Dr. Gokani who made some fantastic revelations at this interview recorded by Satsang TV ('Sat TV'; Premananda's TV station on the Internet). In that interview, Premananda is seen persistently probing into the final hours of Osho's life, seeking answers to the circumstances of his death. After the preliminaries and several questions, he begins to probe deeper and explore whether Osho chose to commit suicide and was assisted by Amrito. As Premananda says to Dr. Gokani in the interview: "What I receive from your story is some kind of strong possibility that Osho could sense his body becoming weaker and he had been in pain already for a long time; maybe for two years, and basically he chose a time to go and perhaps it was assisted by something from Amrito..."

To this Dr. Gokani replied, "That is my first doubt."

When Premananda suggests that this could be the reason Osho's mother was not allowed to meet him a few days before his death and he was cremated in a hurry, Dr. Gokani nods in agreement without saying anything.

As mentioned previously, a secretly taped conversation between Osho and Amrito discussing euthanasia was the provocation for the murder attempt on Amrito by Sheela's aide Shanti Bhadra. David Knapp, Mayor of Rajneeshpuram, testified that he "listened to a copy of a tape from a bug in Bhagwan's room where he (Devaraj) and Bhagwan discussed him assisting Bhagwan in committing suicide."

Did Osho die at 5 p.m.? Or earlier in the day?

History has recorded Osho's death as having occurred naturally at 5 p.m. Several testimonies and the chain of events on January 19, 1990, strongly suggest that Osho died well before 5 p.m.—most probably by late morning or early afternoon. Is it then possible that Dr. Gokani wrote the Death Certificate on arrival in the afternoon itself and not after the first announcement was made at the Inner Circle emergency meeting at around 5.30 p.m.?

Tathagat said that about four to five years after Osho's death, he urged Chitten to confide in him and tell him what exactly had happened. It was Chitten who had come to Tathagat seeking help to locate Dr. Gokani on the morning of January 19, 1990. What happened after Dr. Gokani arrived at the Commune? "Chitten was not ready to speak," Tathagat said in his interview to the author. "I questioned Chitten and told him, 'Tell me the truth.'" According to Tathagat, Chitten said that after Dr. Gokani's arrival, he took him to the Lao Tzu gate where Jayesh came out and the three of them went inside. On the basis of what he was told, Tathagat believes that Osho's Death Certificate was signed by Dr. Gokani in the afternoon itself—that too, without examining the body. Neelam said she believes that Osho died before noon and not at 5 p.m.

How did news of Osho's death reach England and Cologne in the morning?

The precise time of Osho's death became a matter of intense speculation among Osho's followers much before the contradictions in Dr. Gokani's account began to surface. One reason for this was the assertion of some of Osho's international followers in England and Cologne, Germany, that they had learnt of Osho's death on the morning of January 19 itself, which translates into afternoon, Indian Standard Time (IST).

Chaitanya Keerti draws attention to the written account of Osho's British sannyasin, Ma Shivam Suvarna who was in Devon, England when she heard of Osho's death. Suvarna was at the Osho Ko Hsuan School for Kids, participating in an intensive cleaning activity at the school that Friday morning when the phone rang at around 10 a.m.

(3.30 p.m. IST). According to her written account: "I was in the kitchen with several others scrubbing away, the music blaring when Nisheetha picked up the phone. I saw her crying and wondered what had happened. 'Osho's dead,' she said. Just two words to blow my world apart. The music stopped and we all stood in shock."[1]

Keerti says if Suvarna got the news of Osho's death in the morning (mid-afternoon in Pune), it is possible that the news leaked out internationally hours before Osho's followers were informed in Pune. Could it be possible that news of Osho's death was leaked out of the Commune to some contacts in Europe in the afternoon itself?

Tathagat also has a parallel account: "Three-four days later, when the German crowd came in, the sannyasins from the Cologne Centre started whispering. How come you came to know at 5 o'clock that he left the body? We came to know at the time of breakfast." The time range from 9 a.m. to 11 a.m. in Cologne would translate to 12.30 p.m. to 3.30 p.m. IST and 8 a.m. to 10 a.m. in England, matching perfectly with Suvarna's account in England and the hectic activity around Dr. Gokani's arrival at the Commune.

"I feel they (Jayesh and Amrito) did not tell us earlier because they had to prepare the statement for the public. If the Inner Circle meeting was called in at around 5 p.m., then definitely Osho died much earlier. If Dr. Gokani was called at around lunchtime, then it means that some story has happened before," said Keerti.

He felt that Jayesh and Amrito "may have had their own reasons to withhold the information from Osho's sannyasins. They may be wanting to discuss things amongst themselves, take the opinion of experts...there can be anything."

Even if this is true, it still does not explain the tearing hurry with which Osho was cremated and why the actual time of Osho's death was stated as 5 p.m., if indeed, he had died much earlier.

It is hard to believe that Osho died at 5 p.m., also because a lot happened on multiple fronts between 5 p.m. and 6 p.m. inside the ashram. The Commune's version leads one to believe that within moments of Osho's death in Lao Tzu House, Jayesh and Amrito called an emergency meeting of the members of the Inner Circle. This is most unlikely.

Tathagat recalled that the message for an emergency meeting of the Inner Circle came in at 5 p.m. and by 5.30 p.m., the members had begun assembling in the Blue Room on the first floor of Krishna House. "The Inner Circle had been formed in May-June 1989 and normally we met in Lao Tzu House, but that day, our meeting was at Krishna House, right above my office, in what we called the Blue Room," Tathagat said. He recalled that all were there barring three persons—Amrito, Anando and Jayesh. "Jayesh walked in at 5.30-5.45 p.m. Normally when we meet, it is *ha ha, he he.*" The moment Jayesh announced that Osho had left his body, "all people started howling, crying, especially the women. It took us time to settle them."

Jayesh then gave out the instructions and on the point that Osho was to be cremated that evening itself, some Inner Circle members protested, why not the next day. "Then again, came no, no; this is what he (Osho) wanted and we should do it. So obviously, we all surrendered and said, okay, this is what we do."

Tasks were distributed at this meeting: Neelam was told to inform Osho's family which included his mother and brothers; Tathagat was asked to make preparations for the cremation and

Satya Vedant was asked to inform the press. Amrito took upon himself the task of reading out a statement at 7 p.m. before those who would gather for the White Robe Brotherhood meditation by 6.30 p.m.

Immediately after the Inner Circle meeting concluded, a profusely sobbing Neelam rushed out at around 6 p.m. to Osho's bedroom to get a glimpse of her Master. A resident of Lao Tzu House, she had no inkling throughout the day that Osho was dying in his bedroom.

"I stood there in the room. His body looked so fresh. He had a cap on his head and socks on his feet. His hands were folded like this (shows hands folded on the chest) and somehow, it felt, as if he would just open his eyes…After three-four minutes, I came out and I went to tell Mataji."

Tathagat recalled: "Osho's body was all ready. He had been dressed in a robe, a cap and his beard was well combed—maybe they may have blow-dried his beard. It was like another photograph." Tathagat found it incredulous that Osho died at 5 p.m. and within 45 minutes or so, he was all dressed up and prepared to picture-postcard perfection.

A question was posed by the author to Tathagat and Neelam: When he would be inside Lao Tzu, would he be dressed like that? In his ceremonial robes? Neelam said, "No. He wore another kind of a robe—that was also a robe, but without wings (the specially-tailored stiff shoulder flanks). We called it 'Nightie.'"

What explains the tearing hurry to dispose Osho's body?

Tathagat was assigned the task of organising the funeral pyre and it had to be done with speed. By the time the Inner Circle emergency meeting ended, it was 6 p.m. Tathagat recalls, "I said, it can't be done so fast. It will take some 2–3 hours." He was, however, told to rush with the cremation arrangements at the burning ghats.

As planned, Amrito arrived at the Buddha Hall at 7 p.m. to make a statement on Osho's death. The music had begun playing from 6.30 p.m. onwards according to the routine at the daily White Robe Brotherhood meditation. Dressed in a white robe, Osho's disciples had started arriving for the meditation, unaware of the shocking news that awaited them. The music was now playing at full blast. The Inner Circle members were there; Dr. Gokani was sitting in the Buddha Hall like one of Osho's disciples. (Since he had not gone home to change, he had borrowed the robe from the Robe Department, where Jyoti Ma and Mukesh Sarda quipped that since Dr. Gokani was borrowing a robe for the evening meditation, it was likely that Osho would make an appearance.) At the Commune's press office, however, Chaitanya Keerti was attending to phone calls, one after the other, literally, from all around the world. Osho's body was brought in for darshan at the Buddha Hall by 8 p.m.

"By 8.15–8.30 p.m. we left the place for the burning ghats," recalled Tathagat. He had reached out to the Pune Police for security cover for the procession to prevent any desecration of Osho's body and any untoward incidents, triggered by fanatics.

"The burning pyre was not ready and there was a communication going on between me and Jayesh through a runner." Tathagat wanted the procession to take a longer route to the burning ghats by proceeding on North Main Road and then take a right turn at the junction of the two gasoline stations. "But Jayesh insisted on taking the inside road. I said there is no wood. The material has not come."

Vedant Bharati, one of the sannyasins in the funeral procession who was coordinating with Tathagat's team making the funeral arrangements, had been asked by Jayesh not to lose eye contact with him. "Jayesh was asking us to hurry up at the burning ghats. He would say, 'Tell them to hurry up,'" recalled Vedant.

Clearly, there was confusion, but it was not visible to those not in the know. Once Osho's funeral procession reached the lane adjoining the German Bakery restaurant in Koregaon Park, there was confusion over whether the short route was to be taken to the cremation grounds through the German Bakery lane or the longer route from the junction at the gasoline stations to give Tathagat's team enough time to make the funeral arrangements. Vedant remembers that there were some tension-filled exchanges with Jayesh on this score and finally, the procession proceeded on the longer route.

At the burning ghats, the crowds arriving for Osho's funeral had begun to swell and Tathagat was facing difficulty in organising the pyre. Wood was being brought in autorickshaws and they could not reach inside the crematorium because of the crowds. They were stopped at the Popular Heights Apartments adjoining the crematorium, and "some 15–20 sannyasins were stationed there so they could pick up a log and rush in." Tathagat is convinced that Jayesh and his confidants were in a hurry to proceed with the cremation. He is unwilling to speculate why they were in such a great hurry to cremate Osho.

The pyre was lit by Osho's younger brother Vijay Bharati amidst a lot of singing and dancing, the beating of drums and the strumming of guitars, to keep up the spirit of the 'celebration' of Osho's death. Midway through the cremation, kerosene was poured on the pyre from a few canisters kept handy. "Not a small amount of kerosene," recalled Vedant Bharati. Dr. Gokani, who was present at Osho's funeral, was also shocked at the use of kerosene in the funeral pyre. "I can't understand what was that hurry," he said in his interview to Premananda, and to the author.

Laxmi, who used to reside in Bombay and could not attend Osho's funeral was furious when she arrived at the Commune. "She was of the firm opinion that Osho had been killed. She wanted an investigation," said Tathagat. The editor of *Blitz*, R.K. Karanjia, who knew Laxmi and had carried a story based on her interview, supported the call for an investigation into Osho's death.

"Suddenly, the whole Commune management, including me, became defensive. We felt we had to protect ourselves. We didn't want to get into the hands of the police for the purpose of an investigation," said Tathagat.

Were early cremations really the norm in the Commune?

The fact that Osho's body was kept in state for just 10 minutes and then taken out hurriedly for cremation, without giving thousands of his followers the opportunity of a 'last darshan,' raised a storm in the press and among his followers. Some were outspoken, like Laxmi. On January 25, 1990, the Commune issued a pressnote defending Osho's early cremation and attacked a report filed by the author for *The Times of India* from Pune. The press note issued by Chaitanya Keerti said, "An implication that close family members of Osho were unhappy with the speed with which the mystic's body was cremated, made by a *Times of India* reporter, has been strongly refuted by Swami Shailendra Saraswati, one of Osho's brothers."

Reacting to the report, 'Row over Rajneesh Cremation' (*The Times of India*, dated January 24, 1990), the press note carried extracts from a letter by Shailendra Saraswati to *The Times of India* editor stating that early cremations was the norm in the Commune. Quoting Shailendra Saraswati, the press note said:

"Many sannyasins have died in the ashram in the last 15 years, and every time Osho's clear instruction was to cremate the body as soon as possible. When my father died, his body was burnt within two hours after death. The same thing happened in the case of Swami Vimalkirti, who was the Prince of Hanover, Germany. Osho did not make any exception of himself. There are deep spiritual and esoteric meanings and implications in doing so, but I will not talk about those at present, because most of your readers won't understand it."

In January, 1990, Neelam was among those who had issued a statement that early cremations were the norm at the Commune. When asked about this in October 2015, her memory of issuing a signed statement was hazy[2] and she said, "I don't remember." However, she contradicted Osho's younger brother Shailendra Saraswati and said that neither the cremations of Daddaji or Mataji were done in a tearing hurry.

"Even in the case of Vimalkirti, there was no urgency to cremate the body as happened in Osho's case. Osho's father, Swami Devateerth Bharti (Daddaji) and Vimalkirti had died in Pune hospitals and their deaths were not sudden."

Why was a special effort made to get Dr. Gokani to issue the Death Certificate?

To this day, Dr. Gokani is perplexed why he was picked out that day from a host of available doctors from within and outside the Commune to issue the Death Certificate, especially as he had never treated Osho. Dr. Gokani and other Osho disciples who were in the Commune on that day recalled that Osho's younger brother, Shailendra Saraswati ("Shailendra bhaiya," as he was called) was a qualified doctor present in the Commune on January 19. But he was not informed either. Prominent Pune doctors who had treated Osho in the past included the well-known cardiologist Dr. H.V. Sardesai who had visited Osho in 1989, the ENT specialist Dr. Mohan Jog and the orthopaedic surgeon Dr. Sharad Hardikar whose clinic Osho had visited in Poona-I days. None of them were reached out to. Why was Dr. Gokani picked out for the task of issuing the Death Certificate? Was it because the Gujarati doctor was seen by Jayesh and Amrito as someone pliable who could be easily manipulated because of his deep and unquestioning devotion to Osho and who could be trusted with keeping the secret of Osho's death?

Why did Osho complain of being harassed by "black magic"?

For all their brilliance, 'enlightened awakening' and illustrious professional careers, none of the top sannyasins of the Osho Commune could explain what was the "knocking on the doors" in the middle of the night and the "black magic" that Osho complained of in the last months of his life.

Osho complained of some "spirit" or some person disturbing his sleep. He complained of "knocking on the doors" in the middle of the night and of "black magic". Was this the result of mental disorientation and hallucination caused by heavy medication which also weakened him day after day? According to Shunyo, in the last three months of his life, Amrito was looking after Osho full-time and she used to wake up Osho at 6 p.m. till she was his caretaker.

Shunyo was called a few times by Osho to his room and he complained that someone was knocking on the doors in the middle of the night. He had previously complained to Nirvano that he had heard knocking on his door at 2 a.m. "She went around to everyone's room in the house (Lao Tzu) to ask if we had been up and knocking on Osho's door. Nobody had and the guards at the gate were not aware that anyone had entered the house. It happened many times since but the mystery was never solved."[3]

In the very month that he died, Osho complained that he had heard "someone chanting a *mantra*, and it had disturbed the silence." Shunyo writes about this episode in her memoirs: "Despite announcements asking whoever it was to cease, it continued. The chant began to cause pain in Osho's stomach." He said "it was being done deliberately" and blamed "the same people who had destroyed the Commune in the U.S.A." He later accused the C.I.A. of using black magic. Osho's top sannyasins then took the help of a psychic to try and find "the person or persons" responsible for this. People were moved from their usual sitting areas in the Buddha Hall, all the electrical appliances were checked and a search was also conducted "for a machine of new invention that could maybe send out a death ray, or sound that was above the usual human hearing level."[4]

Nothing was found and Osho said the man responsible was sitting in the Buddha Hall during the evening meditation "in the fourth row." Shunyo recalled: "That night we videotaped the fourth row of people and watched the film looking for a suspect." Nothing was found and the search was dropped.

Premgeet corroborated this incident and said the German group had undertaken this video recording secretly and some suspects were filmed closely. The film was watched carefully later but nothing could be established.

11

"They Have Killed You… Killed You, My Son"

An anecdote related by Neelam is revealing. Three to four days before Osho died, Mataji, had requested Neelam that she wanted to meet Osho. Neelam told her to speak to Anando as she was his caretaker. When approached, Anando denied permission to Mataji to meet Osho. Mataji was extremely bitter about this after Osho's death.

On the evening of January 19, 1990, the news of Osho's death came like a bolt from the blue for Mataji who resided in Francis House, less than 300 metres away from Lao Tzu House where Osho lived. Neelam had been given the task of informing his family—especially his mother—about his death. At the time of Osho's death, Jyoti Ma was serving as Mataji's caretaker apart from doing other duties in the Commune. She recalled that evening when a sobbing Neelam, with tears running down her cheeks, came inside Francis House looking for Mataji. Jyoti Ma was alarmed. On hearing of Osho's death, she also began crying and soon Mataji stepped out of the bathroom, wanting to know what was the crisis.

"Neelam was unable to speak and so I informed Mataji and she broke out into a loud wail," said Jyoti Ma. "Neelam got up and closed the doors because Osho's death had still not been announced and nobody knew that Osho had gone." When Mataji was taken by Neelam inside Lao Tzu House along with other family members, she once again wailed as she stood near Osho's body: "*Beta tujhe maar dala inhone, maar dala…*" (They have killed you…killed you, my son). She kept saying, "*Maar dala! Maar dala! Mere bete ko unhone maar diya!*" (He has been killed! He has been killed! They have killed my son!) When asked why Mataji was alleging that Osho had been killed, Neelam said, "I don't know, but she felt that the medicines that Amrito was giving Osho were not good." *(sic)*

Neelam reiterated this account in a television interview to the Indian news channel ABP News on August 11, 2016.

Why did Mataji suspect that her son's death was an internal conspiracy? Was it mere hysteria that he did not die naturally, but had been killed by some form of drug overdose? Why was it so important to deny Mataji permission to meet her 58-year old ailing son when she had gone to Lao Tzu House a few days before his death?

Almost everyone at the Osho Commune knew that Dr. Gokani was privy to the secrets of Osho's death. Osho's family members, especially his brother Vijay Bharati and his wife Shashi bhabi, had persisted with Dr. Gokani to tell the truth about the strange and secret manner in which Osho had died. Every time he visited Pune from the U.S., someone from Osho's family would meet him and ask him to share the details about Osho's death. Dr. Gokani felt that Osho's family members did not trust the official version of his death. "They didn't take the story," he said. Dr. Gokani took the names of a few family members who persisted with him about the death. "They ask me, 'Can you tell us what happened?' I tell them, 'I have nothing new. I've told you before so many times,'" Dr. Gokani said in his Satsang TV interview in Cologne. He maintained this in an interview with the author too.

Mataji did not pursue the issue of Osho's death any further.

According to Jyoti Ma, Shailendra Saraswati who was a qualified medical doctor believed that Osho's diabetes was not handled well by Amrito. He had told Jyoti Ma that he was unhappy with the discontinuation of Osho's diabetes medication by Amrito. She remembered Shailendra telling her that Amrito had stopped Osho's diabetes medication and had said that he would manage his blood sugar through calorie control. Shailendra did not like the idea and at the same time had no access to reach out to his own elder brother. He then wrote in large letters in Hindi on a big sheet of paper urging Osho not to discontinue his diabetes medication. He held this sheet in front of Osho during an evening discourse in the hope that Osho would see it and follow his suggestion," Jyoti Ma said. Swami Shailendra Saraswati denied this during his interview to the author and said what Jyoti Ma had said was not true.

With an age difference of 24 years between them, Shailendra Saraswati never had a normal, brotherly relationship with Osho. Like the other family members, he too did not have any unrestricted access to Osho. "We never had a *bhai-bhai ka rishta* (normal brotherly relationship). I was born three-four years after Osho attained enlightenment and was eight-ten years old when Osho was 34-35 and a professor in a college in Jabalpur. He would come home to Gadarwara about three to four times a year for festivals such as Diwali, Holi,

Rakshabandhan and then stay for just three days or so. There would be a crowd accompanying him from the railway station itself and even at home, there was a constant flow of people wanting to meet him. He was always surrounded by people, and being a voracious reader, he would be immersed in his books whenever he had some time to himself. He would use a red and blue pencil to underline sentences or make notations. The elders in the family treated him with considerable respect and I grew up with the same attitude. I always treated him as my guru and saw myself as his *shishya* (disciple)," Shailendra Saraswati said in his interview to the author.

Unlike Mataji who was informed of Osho's death by Neelam, Shailendra Saraswati, who was also residing inside the Commune, came to know of it only during the announcement in the evening discourse. "We knew that he was in weak health, but none of us had any inkling throughout the day that he was critical. We were taken completely by surprise by the news of Osho's death." He had no recollection of anything dramatic that Mataji said about Osho's death. "There was a lot of crying all around," was all that he recalled.

He felt there was nothing unusual in Mataji being denied permission to meet Osho a few days before his death. "This would happen sometimes. When Osho was not well, he would not meet anyone. He would not even come for his discourse. It was known that his doctor and caretakers would isolate him to protect him from infections. So, there's nothing wrong in what Anando did. We assume that she did so on his instructions," he said in an interview.

Osho's brother was most reluctant to go into the circumstances around Osho's death. Asked if he and the other family members had discussed Osho's death with Dr. Gokani,

Shailendra Saraswati said, "I don't have any interest in the past. We cannot undo anything. There's no point in digging the past. I have no interest in that. I live in the present. That is Osho's central teaching. I did not even go to the cremation ghat because I felt it served no purpose. Instead, I focused on my sorrow and looked at it deeply."

Like most other sannyasins, Osho's family too have let things pass by and have reconciled themselves with the past.

12

Disbanding Osho's Commune

The first clash in the Commune after Osho's death was not between the Western and Indian sannyasins but within the Western group itself as Jayesh began to assert himself firmly and diplomatically as the chief decision-maker. He had authority; he had been anointed 'custodian of Osho's dream' and he had the full support of Amrito and Anando, who held top positions in the Commune. Unknown to the five Indian sannyasins of the Inner Circle—Neelam, Tathagat, Satya Vedant, Jayantibhai and Zareen—differences and disagreements between 'the coterie' and the 'Hollywood group' were approaching boiling point. This set of people from Hollywood was led by Hasya, one of Osho's wealthiest, most ardent, and well-known followers. In the very first year after Osho's death, Hasya and some key members of this group got up one day and headed back to the United States.

Slowly a pattern of drastic changes in the Commune started emerging: Western and Indian sannyasins were being told that they would no longer be supported by the Commune with free food passes and accommodation. Sannyasin-publishers—who were publishing Osho's discourses and running small Osho

Centres across India and the world—were being harassed with demands for royalty for the first time. Unknown to most sannyasins, the strategy to transform the Commune into a resort had been unrolled and for this, it was necessary to get rid of the large number of Commune residents—almost 600 to 800.

Tathagat recalled how very diplomatically, sannyasins who had been with the Commune for decades, many of them, since the inception of Poona-I and many who had seen the birth of the Neo Sannyas Movement firsthand, were now being asked to move on. Citing "Guidance from Osho," the top coterie at the Commune instructed: "Now that Osho has left his body, everyone should take care of themselves. The Commune will not take care of them."

The Hollywood group was well settled in the Pune ashram during Poona-II when Kaveesha headed the immensely popular Mystery School which conducted many therapies. However, in the last year of Osho's life, Hasya's influence stood diminished by Jayesh, Amrito and Anando who held the top three positions in the Inner Circle. Jayesh's romantic relationship with Hasya had ended almost two years ago and he was now in a relationship with Nirvano.

No one seemed to know why the Hollywood group left abruptly in the very first year after Osho's death. Even if some knew, they were not talking about it. There was smoke but no fire and this generated considerable gossip. By 1994, the entire Hollywood set had left the Pune Commune and re-settled at Sedona, Arizona, where they established the Osho Academy.

Tathagat shared his vivid memories of the day when Hasya and her group informed him and other members of the Inner Circle about their decision to leave the Commune. According to him, after Osho's death, disagreements and differences were simmering between the Hollywood people and Jayesh, Amrito and Anando. There was tension and a cold war between the two groups, but nothing on the surface, to the extent that none of the five Indians in the Inner Circle knew about it. Hasya and her friends took everyone by surprise during a meeting of this core committee when—literally out of the blue—they gave a statement that "they were not being supported, their work was not being respected and supported and so they had decided to quit the Commune."

Tathagat recalled: "They spoke just three or four lines, got up, went to their departments which included the Mystery School, called a meeting, read a statement and the next day, they packed and left." The Indian members of the Inner Circle were shocked and stunned by this sudden development as none of them had any inkling of the extent to which the Hollywood group and Jayesh's faction were at loggerheads. They could not imagine that things had reached a breaking point. "Nothing was known to us five Indians," said Tathagat. Since he knew everyone from Hasya's group personally, he went up to them to know what was wrong.

"I felt humiliated and hurt and I said, 'How can you say that you are not being supported by the Inner Circle?'" To this, one of them said, "Tathagat, it is too late and we don't want to discuss anything. We have taken a very thoughtful decision. You will realise it when your time will come." Hasya, Kaveesha, John and David first went to Bombay by the Deccan Queen and Tathagat and Neelam were the only persons from the entire Commune who went to see them off.

Wouldn't it have helped the Movement if Hasya and her group had opened up to the rest of the Commune about the nature of their differences with the coterie? To this, Tathagat said they remained tight-lipped throughout. Some of the key members such as Hasya and Kaveesha are now no more.

"Within six months or so of Osho's death, the Hollywood group left. We sensed a rift. They were the main people in Oregon before Jayesh came into the picture," said Keerti.

It was with enormous courage and self-sacrifice that many young men and women had abandoned their families, forsaken jobs and careers and silently withstood public ridicule and contempt to be with Osho. Over the years, they had served Osho selflessly, worked in the Commune in various capacities and turned it into a beautiful place, be it Poona-I, Rajneeshpuram or Poona-II. They were the ones who had recorded and transcribed Osho's words into hundreds of books, produced hundreds of audio and video recordings, conducted meditation camps after learning and imbibing the technique from Osho and did everything necessary to run the Commune efficiently. The sannyasins contributed with their sweat, money and ideas in whichever way they felt most capable and were willing to work hard at any task assigned to them. Keerti worked in the press office, Jyoti Ma worked in the Accounts Department, and later in the Robe Department, Dispatch Department and Publications Department as a Hindi-English translator. Without any formal training, Vedant Bharati had emerged as a landscaping expert and a favourite of Jayesh. He had played a stellar role in transforming a stinking, running sewer into a beautiful garden. Prem Anadi, a talented singer and musician, was with the Commune's singing group. Tathagat had good administrative skills and served as the ashram In-charge besides serving as the Commune's interface with government officials and the police. What the sannyasins got in return was the joy of being in Osho's vicinity, the freedom to live life on their terms, a monthly food pass which entitled them to free food in the Commune, and accommodation.

As related by Antar Navjot, Western followers were told from the middle of 1989 itself that the Commune won't be able to support them with free food pass and accommodation.[1] Swami Surendra (Surendra Mohan Singh), who had quit his Punjab State Electricity Board job and taken sannyas in 1976, was among the Indian disciples who had been told to leave in 1990. Engaged in the press and publication work of translating and transcribing Osho's Hindi discourses, Surendra was told by Anando in August 1990: "You are no more required." Amrit Sadhana, however, needed his services as tour guide and he was engaged till 1993. He finally left in 1993.

"The Commune started asking sannyasins to leave one month after Osho's death. There were about 1,500 to 2,000 sannyasins supported by the Commune with either food pass or accommodation or both," Surendra said. Sannyasins were given three to six months' time to leave and people began leaving in droves.

Jyoti Ma, like many others, felt betrayed and believed Osho's vision stood compromised by the Commune's leadership after Osho's death. Her resentment towards the Commune's managers kept accumulating over the years and after a few clashes, she left the Commune in 2000, 10 years after Osho's death.

Having worked in the Accounts Department at Rajneeshpuram, Jyoti Ma had told Osho after returning to India about five deposits of $1 million each being moved from a bank in Portland to Chicago. She spoke of how she had been relieved of her duties because she had suggested that one of these deposits be liquidated to pay sannyasins who wanted to return to India and their home countries after the collapse of Rajneeshpuram. Jyoti Ma had donated her life's savings of $5,000 to the Commune in Rajneeshpuram and "had tears in her eyes" when she was given just $100 and asked to organise her own plane ticket to return to India. "Finally, they gave me $500 and a plane ticket," she said.

According to her, it was after she related the story of the high-value bank deposits to Osho that he instructed Jayesh to purchase properties in Koregaon Park for the expansion of the Commune.

She recounted the controversial changes that were introduced in Poona-II, two to three years after Osho's death. One was the stamping of the identity cards of the Commune's residents with "CG",—Commune Guest. For the first time, the residents were being told that no one was a permanent resident of the Commune. This came as a shock, but more was to follow. "We thought that this is our home and the message we got was 'This is nobody's home,'" said Jyoti Ma.

Then came the categorisation of the work done by the sannyasins as "essential" and "non-essential." Sannyasins who were important for the Commune because of the positions they held or because of the revenue they generated came under the essential category. Those who did 'menial' jobs and could be replaced easily came under the "non-essential" category. This categorisation came with further instructions that those in non-essential roles and duties would no longer be entitled to free food pass and accommodation at the Commune's expense. They were, however, welcome to continue to work in the Commune and be associated with it while supporting themselves. This came as another rude shock to the sannyasins, aggravating their insecurities further.

As Jyoti Ma noted, "When Osho was in the body, the work was not important, the person was important. Now, the person was not important, his function was important." Thus, if someone was a coordinator, he or she was entitled to a food pass and accommodation. "As a result, those with essential jobs started clinging to their jobs. They still felt insecure because they could lose their jobs to someone who said 'I'll do the same job; I don't want a food pass." She was among the many who was shocked by this change and wondered what was happening. In her understanding, "Osho's vision of a Commune was quite something else."

This senior sannyasin had greater freedom than others in terms of choosing her work. As one of Osho's earliest disciples, she was among the sannyasins who had made a one-time payment of Rs. 60,000 for her permanent accommodation inside the Commune when it was set up in the early 1970s. She also did not avail of the free food pass as she could pay for food from her own savings. Due to a sneezing allergy from the air-conditioned and carpeted confines of the Accounts Department, she decided to seek a transfer to the Robe Department which managed the maroon and white robes for the sannyasins. This department was open and airy. Her change of role was approved, but she was told that she would no longer be entitled to free accommodation.

Jyoti Ma remembers Zareen joking with her: "Robes are essential, but your job is non-essential." When she protested and told the Commune management that she had, in fact, paid for her room, she was asked to produce proof. There was now a complete atmosphere of distrust. Finally, the matter was resolved and the room episode over. But not without leaving behind a painful scar on her mind. She was among those who simply wanted to focus on her work and her meditation. But what was happening now was different. "It could be seen that those who were in power were mistreating others. They went around hurting people."

At one point, Jyoti Ma was told to start conducting out-station meditation camps. When not conducting camps, she would work in the Publications Department, helping translate Osho's discourses from Hindi to English. "The translation work was such that it was not necessary for me to do it while sitting in the office. I would work from my room, sometimes work at night or early morning; or work in the garden." However, this became an issue, with the Commune management insisting that she should sit in the Publications Office from 9 a.m. to 4 p.m., which were the working hours. This led to another round of arguments and it was clear to her that the management simply wanted to assert its authority. "I felt humiliated; I felt there was no freedom in the Commune."

The unfriendly pokes and pinpricks continued. Once she was pulled up for conducting a meditation camp without authorisation while on a holiday in Australia. On another occasion, meditation camp leaders were told that they would no longer be free to accept direct invitations for meditation camps; this would be decided by the Management Team. When Jyoti Ma received an invitation from friends in Nairobi to visit them and conduct a camp, the Commune informed her that instead of her, Devendra Bharti would be sent. "When the Nairobi people learnt of this, they cancelled the camp saying they wanted me and not Devendra," said Jyoti Ma. The last straw was when an invitation came from Japan for conducting a meditation camp and the Management Team once again prepared to prevent her from going on that visit.

"I then decided that the Commune environment had become suffocating and I wanted to move out. I didn't know where to go and where to stay, but it was certain that I wanted to move out." She decided that she would move out after the Millennium Festival at the Commune in 2000 when she would get to meet her friends from across the world who would be coming for the celebrations. Her message to the Commune administration that she would soon be leaving was not passed on to the Inner Circle. "I packed quietly and left. Not a single person from the Commune came to see me off," she recalled.

Jyoti Ma went and stayed on with a friend in Pune and her friends from Japan reached out to her once again. Her visit to Japan was very successful and instead of two weeks, she stayed on for two months, visiting many cities and conducting meditation camps. "I felt such freedom! A new phase had begun in my life and friends from all over the world started sending me invitations and calling me for camps."

She realised that "Osho is everywhere" while she was being confined to the small world of the Commune. "People would ask me about my leaving the Commune and I would say, 'I have been cooked enough. I did not want to get burnt there.' In 1994, Jyoti Ma wrote her memoirs, *One Hundred Tales for Ten Thousand Buddhas* about her interactions and experiences with Osho and this immensely popular book was translated into several languages, including Chinese and Russian.

Chaitanya Keerti, who was the Osho Commune's spokesperson till the year 2000 also left with a heavy heart after the Millennium Festival. He felt that Jayesh was uncomfortable with the older sannyasins who had been close to Osho in the earlier years and had been in the Commune for many years. They could question Jayesh any time and tell him that the new policies and initiatives he was introducing "were not in keeping with Osho's vision."

Keerti felt that such opposition was bothering Jayesh who began creating a situation whereby these sannyasins either left on their own or were compelled to do so. It was in 1999 that Keerti began questioning the management on things that rankled him. He found that Indian sannyasins were being discriminated against and were not getting access to the Basho Health Club and swimming pool with the same swiftness that foreigners were getting.

He also noticed that unlike in the past, sannyasin-publishers were being harassed; they were not receiving the same cooperation from the Commune as in the past. He cited the example of an Indian sannyasin based in France who published Osho's books in French. "They were sitting on his agreement and he was not receiving any cooperation." The same was happening with another Indian sannyasin in Japan who was also doing good work, but not getting any cooperation from the Commune "because suddenly, things were changing. The Commune was demanding royalty, putting conditions…" Till then, the understanding was that the sannyasin-publishers won't be harassed and they would spend the equivalent of the royalty amount on promotional work.

A sannyasin-publisher from an ashram in Bangalore complained that Devendra Bharti, a newly-inducted member of the Inner Circle, was coming and asking for royalty. The sannyasin was bitter that apart from the burden of repaying loans for publishing Osho's books, there was now this additional demand for royalty. "He was literally crying in front of me," Keerti said. The same was happening with the supply of video footage to TV stations interested in showing Osho's discourses and publications printing extracts from Osho's discourses. In previous years, Keerti would make copies from the Master tapes and provide them to stations like Jain TV. He recalled that in 1999, "I was suddenly told that 'New York will decide.'"

"I said, why New York? Who is this New York person? In 1999, I saw that I could no longer freely do the work of publicity for Osho that I was doing before. My hands were being tied." It was in 1999 that Keerti discovered on his own, that the Commune had set up its "publishing headquarters" in New York, headed by Klaus Steeg. Keerti was soon told that all his press notes and all decisions relating to press relations would have to be cleared by New York before these could be issued by him. He felt undervalued and offended by this and wondered how a person sitting in New York could give directions on press notes to be issued in India? "I said, what does he know about Indian press notes?"

On a few occasions, Keerti found that Steeg would keep the press notes pending till they would go stale.

This was extremely insulting for Keerti who had been assigned the work of dealing with the press way back in 1987 after the death of Swami Anand Maitreya who had been in charge of the press office. Keerti used to assist Maitreya, and after his death, the work was assigned to him directly by Osho. Till Osho was alive, Keerti had complete freedom to do his work. "Everyone was happy with my work and no one interfered with my work—what I was getting published, who I was communicating with, who I was sending press notes to…" As he pointed out, there was tremendous hostility in the media and society towards Osho and his sannyasins after they returned from the U.S. It was not easy dealing with the press. There was much negativity because of the Sheela scam, the 'sex guru' tag... Osho's guidance had helped Keerti in dealing with the press in such a situation: "Whenever something negative is written about me, don't freak out. They are writing like this about me because they don't know me; they don't know how I am functioning. Your job is to inform them with the facts. They don't know, you know. You already are around me, so you know it. Second, when they publish something about me, thank them. Be grateful. You have to do two things: do not freak out on the media, and give them the facts."

Keerti followed these instructions and within two to three years, everyone could see the results. Journalists liked him as he was affable and always accessible. "The press knew I was available 24 hours." He did not restrict himself to the 9 a.m. to 4 p.m. routine of the Commune as he was aware that the media began its work only after 4 p.m. He skipped Osho's discourses if necessary, but made himself available to the media. "With Osho's guidance, I could see things change 180 degrees," he said. As a part of his interactions with the media, Keerti used to give Osho's books and videos generously to journalists "so that they could see, read and hear things directly." But after 1999, there was resistance to doing this also.

When an extract from Osho's discourse appeared in *The Times of India*'s immensely popular 'Speaking Tree' column, the reaction from the top managers in the Commune was: "Why have they not mentioned our copyright?" Keerti was flummoxed and wondered what was more important? The mention of copyright or getting Osho published in a widely-read newspaper?

He was surprised when Amrito was once upset that he was introduced as 'Swami Amrito' before some visiting journalists. "I realised that things were changing. If I introduced him as 'Swami Amrito', he would object in front of the journalists. He would say, 'Just say Dr. Amrito, not Swami Amrito.' But I said, 'So far you have been known as Swami Prem Amrito, now you are correcting me. What is your problem with 'Swami'?' For almost everything, there was displeasure, taunting and pointing of mistakes."

Several people had told Keerti about these changes and he had seen sannyasins, including Neelam and Tathagat, who were Inner Circle members, leaving the Commune. However, he had decided that he would see things for himself and leave if necessary, but not before questioning the Commune authorities. As he put it, "I did not come to Osho on someone's recommendation and I had decided that I won't leave on someone's recommendation. I will decide for myself. And I have to question them first. I won't leave without questioning."

Finally, he decided to leave after the 2000 Millennium celebrations and informed the Commune to appoint his replacement. He decided not to avail of the free food pass six months before his date of leaving and asked the Commune to purchase a one-way ticket to Delhi where he was headed to attend and manage the Osho Commune's pavilion at the annual World Book Fair.

"Jayesh would tell someone to go and explain things to me. They would be speechless when I would raise questions. I would say 'If you are not able to convince me on these points, then it means something is wrong.'" Finally, when he left, no one really cared. "They thought, maybe I will come back. I found them a bit heartless. They didn't care."

The Indian-American scholar Satya Vedant who had been with the Commune since mid-1970s and had served as Chancellor of Osho Multiversity began to feel unwelcome in 1999 when he returned after a three-year teaching stint in the U.S. Satya Vedant, who had snapped his ties with Sheela as her brother-in-law long back, had continued to serve as Chancellor of the multiversity but unlike in the past, was not provided with accommodation inside the Commune. He, therefore, rented a flat in a building opposite Prem's Restaurant on North Main Road and would cycle to the Commune in the mornings and evenings. This continued for two years. "I got a hint that I was not welcome as before," he said. An offer to teach at Nirma University, Ahmedabad proved handy and he left in 2002, never to visit again for the next 14 years till March 2016 when this author met him for an interview at Koregaon Park, less than a kilometre away from the Commune. He had no plans or the desire to visit his former home.

This mild mannered, soft-speaking sannyasin was never among those who had challenged the authority at the Commune; why then, was he also made to feel unwelcome and insecure and left with no option but to quit the Commune? Was it because fresh plans were being drafted for the Commune and there was no room for people who had been with Osho and who cherished his vision?

Satya Vedant said when he was inside the Commune, his "dedication and surrender to Osho was so total" that it simply didn't matter to him whether the headquarters were being shifted to Zürich or Afghanistan. "Our trust in Jayesh was such that we felt he was working under Osho's guidance. Jayesh's word was the last word, and that's how it was."

Now, however, he felt that things had definitely gone wrong somewhere. He was unable to understand why in Osho's name, the oldest of sannyasins were being insulted, hurt, humiliated and punished by Jayesh and his associates. He felt that the Commune in Pune had been reduced to a business enterprise and it was moving in a direction where the valuable properties of the Commune would be sold off one day.

In 1985, when it became evident that Osho would be deported to India after Sheela's flight and the messy court cases in the U.S., Neelam was picked up by Hasya to prepare her for the role of Osho's caretaker and secretary. Hasya had approached Neelam as she anticipated that the nearly two dozen members of Osho's staff, including his secretaries, cook, laundry-woman, caretaker and the seamstresses who stitched his robes, could face visa denials from the Indian government. "I was taken to his Lao Tzu residence (at Rancho Rajneesh, Oregon) to meet his caretaker, laundry person, his doctor. I made my notes and came back with him to Kulu Manali." This was November 1985 and Osho had appointed Neelam as his India Secretary and In-charge of his personal staff. Neelam also joined him when he left for Nepal and was with him during a part of the world tour. Her responsibilities as his secretary and caretaker increased when he returned to Bombay in July 1986 and stayed for five months at *Sumila* before returning to the Pune Commune in January, 1987. By now, Neelam was among the disciples closest to Osho and was among those living at his Lao Tzu residence. Nirvano had returned to Pune to serve Osho as his caretaker, but when she left for a two-week holiday to Thailand, it was Neelam who filled in for her as Osho's caretaker.

Neelam was inducted into the Inner Circle in 1989 and on December 23, 1989, she was informed by Jayesh that she had been additionally appointed as the "East West Connection" in the Presidium established to expand Osho's work internationally. This was less than a month before Osho died and it had been a few weeks since Neelam had unrestricted access to Osho which was controlled by the troika. Like most other sannyasins, Neelam did not seem to mind this at all and it was well accepted that Osho would meet someone only if he sent a message and called for that person. Her last direct contact with Osho was a chance meeting in December-end when, on his drive back from the Buddha Hall, Osho had called Neelam and asked her to include Zareen in the Inner Circle.

Soon after Osho's death, Neelam became a strong defender of the Commune's functioning and administration. She, like Tathagat, Vedant and Keerti, vociferously defended Osho's quick cremation while interacting with the press, although there had been internal differences on this in the Inner Circle. Neelam rejected all suggestions of a conspiracy and foul play in Osho's death, although, on hindsight, she found several discrepancies in the official story of Osho's death.

As in the case with Keerti, her differences with Jayesh and Amrito began building up towards the middle of the 1990s and came to a head in 1999 when she and Tathagat, with whom she had a close relationship, were asked to leave the Commune. This unpleasant task was not performed by anyone from the troika, but was assigned to Satya Vedant who told Neelam and Tathagat they were no longer welcome in the Commune.

"Vedant later apologised for his conduct," Tathagat said in an interview to the author.

"I was asked to talk to them and I did it over the phone. I was told what was to be told to them. I was told to do it and I did it," Satya Vedant said in an interview to the author on March 18, 2016. "Later, I apologised to Neelam and Tathagat and touched their feet for hurting them. But at that time, I was told to do that job and that is how it happened."

The Hollywood group's departure was the first big flashpoint in the Commune, although it went unnoticed by the press. Neelam's exit was acrimonious and was reported by the press as the first sign of an intense factional fight since Osho's death. Her 'Open Letter' of July 11, 2000 to Jayesh, Amrito and Anando was made available to the press and ignited a fresh controversy.

In her letter, Neelam accused the troika of showing "arrogance, disrespect and dishonesty" and defended her reference to them in press interviews as "the three dictators". She said their behaviour had changed after Osho's death. "In the name of Osho's guidance, you three started dictating your decisions, asking other [Inner Circle] members' opinions simply to implement them. When some of the members started raising their voice against it, you started undermining their work, highlighting their weak points to humiliate them. As a result, after one year, members of the Inner Circle started leaving."

Neelam said in her letter they were leaving because of "a certain hierarchy within the Inner Circle." She said that Jayesh and Amrito could no longer be trusted with their interpretation "of what Osho reportedly said in private and the policies created out of that."

These words from Neelam were extremely significant as she was the first senior sannyasin—no less than Osho's last secretary—to launch a direct assault on the authority of Jayesh and Amrito and accuse them of misleading the entire Commune in the name of Osho.

Neelam said by the time she left, 15 of the 21 original members of the Inner Circle had been replaced, when in fact, "the members of the Inner Circle were for life, only to be replaced after death."

She was extremely unhappy that Osho's pictures had been removed from the front gate and the Buddha Hall, his chair had been removed from the Buddha Hall and the wearing of maroon and white robes during meditation camps in India had been prohibited by the Commune. She objected to the moving of the trust headquarters to Zürich, the secretive manner in which Osho's works had been copyrighted and trademarked in the U.S. and the setting up of Osho's publishing headquarters in New York, which the sannyasins learnt about only in 1997. Neelam upheld Keerti's charge that sannyasin publishers were being harassed with legal notices and demands for royalty which was unprecedented.

On June 20, 2000, Neelam was denied entry into the Osho Commune. She told *The Times of India* on that day that since the Osho Commune was a public charitable trust, she would approach the government and ask it to look into its affairs.

On June 28, 2000, the Osho Commune International hit back at the Neelam faction with a full-page advertisement in all editions of the *The Indian Express* and in the *Times of India* editions of Ahmedabad and Bangalore. In that advertisement, the Commune said Osho did not want copyrights to his works to be returned to India. "Osho assigned them to a foundation in the USA, and later asked that they be transferred to a

Swiss-based foundation. He directed that they remain there," the Commune said, stating that all he wanted back in India were his 50,000 books.

The Commune said that collecting royalties from publishers of Osho's books was a standard practice and the only brief period when they were not collected was from 1987 to 1989.

The top management refuted the suggestion that Osho wanted his headquarters in India. "His specific request was for an international publishing headquarters, to be situated wherever was best for making his vision available around the world. At present, New York is the world centre for providing content to publishers—all the world's biggest media companies are there—and so it is the best location for Osho's publishing, and that's where it is," the Commune explained in its advertisement. It said the international publishing office at New York "is a wholly owned subsidiary of the Swiss foundation."

About the Osho trademark controversy, it said that applications to register the trademark 'Rajneesh' and 'Bhagwan' had been initiated in India and the U.S. since the mid-1970s and that the 'Osho' trademark was a continuation of that process.

Rejecting the charge that the "Osho Commune is being commercialised as a resort against Osho's wishes," the Commune said it was Osho's wish that "we create here the biggest and the most beautiful spiritual health club in the world. A kind of spiritual Club Med—as in 'meditation.'" (A visit to the Osho Resort today would show that it has hardly fulfilled this vision and gives the impression of being dead and deserted.)

About the allegation that old timers were being "thrown out", the Commune responded in its advertisement that Neelam herself had announced that "his sannyasins come and go and not be economically dependent on the Commune because this takes away people's dignity and grace."

On December 11, 1999, the Commune embarked on the "Osho Tribute 2000" Millennium Festival to mark the turn of the millennium. Coinciding with the 10th death anniversary of Osho, this was the last of the big events at the Commune with a series of recitals and concerts by eminent artistes such as Kelucharan Mohapatra, Pandit Hariprasad Chaurasia, Pandit Vishwamohan Bhatt, Japanese musician Kitaro; and meditation camps and group therapies.

After this, the Commune would never be the same again.

13

It's All About Money, Honey

Osho International Foundation is being run like a multinational corporation today rather than a public charitable trust to promote Osho and his philosophy of Neo Sannyas. In Osho's final months in 1989–90, his top administrators led by Jayesh saw to it that their creation, 'Brand Osho' replaced Bhagwan Rajneesh of the past. Their actions since then suggest that they want to promote and monetise Brand Osho with all their might.

The fortunes of this brand are controlled by a small clique who run the OIF headquartered in Zürich, and its publications headquarters in New York. All legal rights to 'Osho' now rest with these bodies outside India who are the sole beneficiaries of huge revenues generated on an international scale through the sale of brand 'Osho' licence and products such as audio-video discourses, meditation techniques, meditative therapies, music, books and publication rights.

The OIF owns and maintains the original archive of 6,500 audio discourse recordings of Osho, 1,870 video recordings and approximately 600 original book publications of Osho's daily talks. Since 1985, the OIF has been licensing and sublicensing publication rights in all media formats to publishers, TV stations and website operators around the world.[1]

On July 6, 2011, Klaus Steeg, Director and board member, OIF, informed the European Union's Intellectual Property Office (EUIPO) through his Witness Statement that more than 220 publishing houses in more than 80 countries were granted publishing licences by OIF. This resulted in more than 2,000 publishing contracts in 53 languages around the world. The total annual sales of OSHO branded items were around two million of which one million related to sales in the European Union alone. According to Steeg, after the Indian guru's name was changed from Rajneesh to Osho in 1989, OIF undertook "enormous investment" to promote the OSHO trademark and make it "the most well-known trademark in the EU in relation to meditation services in the field of mind, body and spirit." Presenting some figures, he said, in the first year after the re-branding, the annual turnover from books, audio and video royalties alone was €24,000. By 2010, this had increased to €820,000 annually. Defending the "OSHO" community trademark registration owned by OIF and challenged by the Osho Lotus Commune e.V. Cologne, Steeg said, "Whilst alive, Osho was perceived as a mystic and philosopher but since his death, OIF built up the OSHO name to become a well-known brand name for meditations and related goods and services."[2]

In a related submission in the same court, Ursula Hoess, also known as Vatayana, Coordinator of Osho Global Connections, a part of OIF-Zürich said that "policing" of the OSHO trademark usage was an ongoing process, and includes, among other activities, regular visits to OSHO branded centres in the EU and across the world.[3]

Thus, OIF-Zürich and Osho International, New York, headed by Steeg, operates with the zeal of a police department, not allowing anyone to use Osho's name or his pictures freely, or teach his meditation techniques without licence and permission from Osho Global Connections—the arm that monitors and coordinates with Osho Centres worldwide. One informed estimate placed the number of affiliated centres at more than 550.

Almost all OIF directors have established independent businesses around Osho. Thus, Steeg also held the position of President of American Multimedia Corporation, "trading as Osho International, responsible for developing international publishing programmes for OIF."[4]

A number of Osho's followers in India and Europe have been seeking greater clarity on a slew of private companies engaged in Osho's work, which host a number of OIF-India and OIF-Zürich trustees as their directors. These have raised conflict of interest issues. For example, the proceeds from the business at the hotel called Osho Guesthouse in Pune with 60 rooms, are credited to Osho Multimedia & Resorts Pvt. Ltd., a company that has OIF-India trustees Mukesh Sarda, Vidya Khubchandani, Devendra Singh Dewal and Lal Pratap Singh as its directors. Should the proceeds not go directly to Osho's trusts?

Such is also the case with the sale of some products in the Osho Commune's bookshop such as the introductory video on the Osho International Meditation Resort. While the copyright for this video is held by OIF, the video was produced by America Multimedia Corporation, which has OIF-Zürich trustees Klaus Steeg and D'Arcy as its directors. Are the proceeds from such sales flowing into private companies created by Osho trustees instead of flowing into the accounts of the charitable trust?

The OIF spokesperson Amrit Sadhana failed to respond when asked for clarifications relating to these private companies with OIF trustees as their directors. For example, OIF trustees Jayesh, D'Arcy and Klaus Steeg were directors in firms such as Mayfair Media International Ltd; Rebel Films Ltd, Mayfair Consultants International Ltd and Osho Digital Rights Ltd, registered in Ireland and London.

D'Arcy and Steeg were directors in Osho Foundation America Inc. and Osho International Corporation, both registered in New York. Jayesh and Amrito figured as directors in Osho Digital Media Ltd. and O International Digital Media Ltd. registered in Hong Kong. Jayesh and D'Arcy were directors in Adaptive Neural Biometrics Holdings Ltd. and Adaptive Neural Biometrics Ltd, both firms registered in Cork, Ireland.

Indian trustees of OIF such as Mukesh Sarda, Devendra Singh Dewal and Vidya Khubchandani figured as directors in firms such as Ami Industrial Leasing and Holding Pvt. Ltd, Zen Foundation, Zen Agro Pvt. Ltd. and Adaptive Neural Biometrics India Pvt Ltd, all registered in Mumbai. Steeg and D'Arcy were directors in Master Zone Ltd, a firm registered at 410 Park Avenue, New York, with another firm, Osho International Corporation, registered at the same address. Premgeet and Prem Anadi who are at the forefront of many legal battles against the trustees and managers of OIF and the Pune Commune, have raised serious questions about these companies.

One example of strong action by the OIF against an 'errant' centre was posted on sannyasnews.com on July 4, 2015 by Osho disciples Anand Arun and the Osho Sandesh Team from Osho Tapoban, Nepal. Arun said that YouTube had terminated the Osho Sandesh Magazine channel and had deleted the entire archive following a trademark complaint received from OIF signed by Steeg.

On the morning of March 8, 2016, a picture of Osho had been removed by Facebook from Chaitanya Keerti's account with a message that OIF had complained that the photo used was their copyright. Keerti wrote to Facebook saying that he was a disciple of Osho since 1971 and it was ridiculous to see OIF claim ownership of Osho's photos, "which are actually the contributions of hundreds of his known and unknown photographer disciples from around the world." He pointed out that these disciples have made these photos available on the net for thousands of other Osho lovers, free of cost. Keerti got no reply from Facebook. He said the social networking site generally asks that the matter be sorted between the parties concerned. It was unlikely that OIF would have liked to resolve the issue for Keerti.

In 2011, Steeg issued a sternly-worded copyright infringement notice on behalf of OIF to OSHORAJNEESH.COM saying "OIF is a public non-profit organisation of Switzerland and the estate owner of all intellectual property of an author named Osho." His legal notice read: "The copyrighted works are various textbooks and photos, all copyrights which are owned by OIF. All such copyrights are registered with the U.S. Copyright Office. The website is being used to offer these files of OIF's copyrighted works without license."

Thus, if a person feels inspired by Osho and decides to put the guru's picture on his Facebook account or, create an Osho website, or open an 'Osho Centre' in, say, Nepal, Mauritius or Timbuktu, the OIF is likely to serve him with a legal notice of trademark and copyright infringement. It will then demand that the centre or the website either shut down or comply with the licence fees and conditions put forth by Osho Global Connections. 'Osho' has thus been reduced to a brand and a business run by the parent charitable trust itself.

What is the genesis of this brand?

The ghost of 1989 returns: It was on January 7, 1989, that Osho dropped 'Bhagwan' from his name and left it at 'Shree Rajneesh'. According to Swami Anand Parmartha, he accepted 'Osho' (Zen Master) as his 'designation' from Anando in February and finally, in September 1989—less than four months before his death—his name was officially shortened from 'Osho Rajneesh' to simply 'Osho', with the process initiated to change all copyrights to this name. Right from the late 1960s, when Rajneesh launched his Neo Sannyas Movement, he had initiated hundreds of followers from India and abroad with new names that had Sanskrit and Indian origins. Was there a hidden agenda in changing his name, whereby, in one swift stroke, the new, four-letter name completely erased Osho's Indian origins? The new name 'Osho' was far removed from 'Rajneesh' or 'Bhagwan' which had a ring of notoriety to it. 'Osho' was also eminently suitable for branding purposes on an international scale.

Three months before his death, as Osho's health progressively deteriorated, Jayesh was working on registering 'OSHO' as a trademark in Europe to sell products and services around Osho's videos, meditations and therapies. The change of name from Osho 'Commune' to Osho International Meditation Resort, and the removal of his pictures from the premises of around 30 acres, the Osho website, books and DVDs on sale which happened in subsequent years was a part of this exercise. Brand Osho was created and Osho's pictures were wiped out from books, audio tapes and website and the meditation resort to get rid of the 'baggage' from the past and give a fresh start to the Osho business. The change of name from Osho Commune International to Osho International Meditation Resort (OIMR) was clearly yet another step towards breaking from the past and creating a new brand identity and image after Osho's death.

From the time Osho returned to Pune in January 1987 till the start of the new millennium 13 years later, the Osho Commune International in Pune thrived as the world headquarters of the Neo Sannyas Movement. Osho lived in the Commune till his death in 1990; the Inner Circle and the Presidium (for the expansion of his work internationally) had been created less than six months before his death and all the top functionaries of the Commune lived in Pune. There was the charming but elusive Jayesh shuttling between the Commune and his suite at the Oberoi Hotel, Bombay while Amrito, Anando and the rest of the top rung ran the Commune which had witnessed an expansion in Poona-II.

There was no reason for anyone to believe that Pune was not the world headquarters of the Movement. However, it was only towards the end of the 1990s that Neelam, Keerti and other senior sannyasins discovered with shock and alacrity that Osho's world headquarters had been registered—without their knowledge—as a post-box address at Bahnhofstrasse 52, 8001 Zürich, Switzerland, and a publications headquarters had been created in New York.

While this was being done on the one hand, on the other, the Pune Commune was introducing new policies which compelled many of the Commune residents to vacate the premises.

The removal of Osho's pictures from the premises; minimising and downsizing of Osho's pictures from various publications and the transformation of the Commune into the OIMR—Osho International Meditation Resort—were underway. Finally, in the first decade of the new millennium, the Commune stopped acknowledging that Osho's Samadhi existed on its premises.

Satya Vedant and others speculated that this was to facilitate the smooth sale of the Commune's properties when the time was ripe for it. Even as the Osho International Commune was renamed OIMR, and its character changed completely through the 1990s, the Pune establishment, controlled by OIF, India (registered at 608 Maker Chambers, Nariman Point, Mumbai) stood subservient to OIF-Zürich.

For more than a decade now, the 'Osho' trademark and copyrights have been fiercely guarded and administered by OIF-Zürich which is controlled by its trustees who include Jayesh (Chairman) and D'Arcy, Amrito (Vice-Chairman) Mukesh Sarda, Klaus Steeg and Rudolf Kocher.

The five trustees of OIF-India, namely Mukesh Sarda, Devendra Singh Dewal, Sadhana Belapurkar (Amrit Sadhana), Lal Pratap Singh and Vidya Khubchandani were more like puppets of the Zürich-based body, subservient as they have always been to Jayesh and Amrito.

When, in 2002, Osho's pictures were removed from the Pune Commune and no longer carried in *Osho Times*, D'Arcy was candid in his explanation to *The New York Times*.[5] He justified the "de-Oshoisation" of the Osho Commune, as the newspaper put it, by saying that young people coming to the Commune were put off by Osho's pictures all around. "Someone comes in and there are like 1,000 pictures of this dead guy, and they're like 'Whoa, get me out of here.'" From the year 2000 onwards, the Commune decided to reduce references to Osho and his life to the barest minimum and completely rejected the traditional celebrations around his birth anniversary, Day of Enlightenment, Guru Purnima and his death anniversary.

What was clearly visible was the concerted effort to minimise the use of Osho's pictures and write or speak as little as possible about him. Thus, the 27-minute introductory video *The Silent Explosion,* sold by the Osho International Meditation Resort at Pune with 'Amazing India' in large font on its cover (obviously to score points with the Indian government), does not carry a single image of Osho. It only talks about the various types of meditations developed by him which can be experienced for a price at the resort.

Books published by the Commune present biographical information on Osho in a very sketchy manner without any details of his early years. For example, the inside jacket at the end of the book *The Path of Yoga* published by Osho Media International describes Osho as "a contemporary mystic whose life and teaching influences millions of people of all ages, and from all walks of life. Osho was described by the UK's *Sunday Times* as one of the '1000 Makers of the 20th century. His internationally bestselling works are available in 58 languages around the world." Thus, unless a special effort is made to know more about Osho, visitors to the resort will never know much about the mystic.

The first time that Jayesh had met Osho was in the mid-1980s in Oregaon, in the last six years of Osho's life. He was always an ambitious businessman and a real estate developer and his interests in business far exceeded his interest in meditation and spiritualism. Even during Poona-II, he preferred to reside at the five star Oberoi Hotel in Bombay rather than spend his days in the Pune Commune. Given this background, it is not at all surprising that Jayesh is at the helm of affairs at the OIF and is running an international business enterprise rather than a public charitable trust engaged in promoting spiritualism in the unique manner that Osho did. To those like Jayesh who could see it, 'Osho' in his totality was nothing less than a magnificent business opportunity on an international scale, a gold mine, which could yield considerable wealth to someone who could manage some deft manoeuvering.

Osho Friends International, New Delhi, an association of Osho's followers opposed to the Jayesh-Amrito faction, and the Osho Lotus Commune in Cologne, have been in the forefront of the battle against the OIF which sought to trademark the name 'Osho' and exercise control on Osho Centres in Europe and other countries by demanding legal compliance, affiliation and use of the word 'Osho' under licence.

According to Osho Friends International, the groundwork for creating the 'Osho' brand began three months after Osho's death when the Rajneesh Foundation, Pune, changed its name to Osho International Foundation, with a registered address in Bombay. Rajneesh Foundation, Europe also did likewise and changed its name to Osho International Foundation, registered in Zürich. The first trademark application for 'Osho' was filed by OIF in the U.S. in July 1992 under the category of books and printed materials, followed by two more applications in March, 1997 for pre-recorded audio and video tapes in the field of Education, Religion, Philosophy and Science. Another eight trademark applications were filed between December 1997 and 2001.

In September 2010, the senior German sannyasin Ramateertha, (Robert Doetsch) from the Cologne Centre wrote an 'open letter' to the members of the Inner Circle asking them to oppose attempts by the OIF to trademark the name 'Osho'.[6] He said an attempt was made by the OIF soon after Osho's death "to establish control over the Osho Centres in Europe." Centre leaders were asked to sign a Letter of Understanding, which was seen as the start of a process to create a legal bond between the centres and the OIF by using the Osho trademark. "It became more and more obvious," said Ramateertha, "that the Osho trademark, was not so much to control the outside world but to control the Osho Centres and the meditation techniques to make money."

He said that the 'Osho trademark' initiative became an issue in 1997–98, nearly seven years after Osho's death when the OIF described it as a protective measure against the misuse of the name 'Osho'. Ramateertha emphasised that Osho had never ever mentioned the need to trademark his 'name'; on the contrary, he had always "opposed any kind of organisation that would create a legal bond amongst sannyasins in any form whatsoever."

Ramateertha said that Osho had made it very clear to him that he wanted the centres to be totally independent and at the most "spiritually affiliated". Osho never wanted "any centrally organised form of structure that would allow sannyasins to control or dominate other sannyasins." He cited Osho's words that "The world headquarters will be publishing my books, will be releasing my tapes, will be doing every kind of work. But it has no domination over anybody. All Communes of the world are independent. All centres are absolutely free. They are under nobody's guidance."

Ramateertha cited a declaration from Vatayana from 2004 to a court in the U.S. in which she said, "OIF-Zürich monitors Osho Centers without its licensees' knowledge by conducting Internet searches to confirm the licensees are not engaging in unapproved activities, and by communicating directly with its licensees' customers when those customers visit the Osho Commune." They testify, he said, "that they have been visiting Osho Centers in order to police, supervise, monitor or inspect the licensees' use of the term 'Osho'."

In her 'Open Letter' of January 18, 2010, Neelam accused Jayesh of betraying the trust that the Commune had reposed in him. Neelam said that in January 1987, Osho had made Pune his world headquarters and after the bitter experience in the U.S., had insisted that everything be done according to Indian law. "Jayesh, you know it," said Neelam, "because you were fully involved with all the aspects of this work and you spent a lot of money and energy to legalise all the assets of the Commune." Neelam said that Osho, being an Indian citizen, could not have given or transferred the copyrights of his work to a European trust. She said that would have been anyway illegal as he had already given his copyrights to a trust in India and "Sheela must have managed this transfer illegally." That was the reason Osho wanted everything transferred back to India.

Neelam said it came as a shock to know that instead of doing this, "you (Jayesh) started the whole process of getting everything secretly registered and copyrighted in Zürich, 18 months after Osho left his body."

Neelam said in her 'Open Letter' that she and others learnt of this much later in 1997 that Jayesh had copyrighted and trademarked Osho's works in the U.S. According to her, of the 880 signature paintings of Osho, only 40 remained in his Lao Tzu library and the rest were in a warehouse in London. The same happened with the thousands of photographs of Osho.

In connection with all this, some very striking revelations—of doubtful authenticity—were made by Jayesh in his Witness Statement on July 19, 2011 before the EUIPO. Jayesh testified that while leaving the U.S. in November 1985, Osho instructed him that his intellectual property rights; copyrights to his work, "to his name and image" be transferred from a U.S. foundation to the Swiss Foundation, known today as Osho International Foundation.

"Osho personally asked me to ensure the workings of the Swiss Foundation, to operate as his international headquarters as he wanted his work to be international in scope. OIF assumed this mantle," Jayesh said. According to him, in addition to his appointment as Chairman of the Inner Circle, Osho appointed him Chairman of the Osho International Presidium a few months before his death. Jayesh explained that the Presidium worked closely with the OIF overlooking "all areas related to Osho's and the foundation's intellectual property, international publishing and licensing activities, the maintaining of Osho Archives of documents and thousands of audio recordings, video recordings, art and music." In addition, the Presidium also oversaw Osho Meditation Center activities "and licensing in accordance with Osho's express instructions."[7]

He claimed that after changing his name from Rajneesh to Osho in 1989, the Master directed him to protect his name. Accordingly, all the meditation services, group and therapy programmes were changed and re-branded. "Osho was very much aware and involved in the use of OSHO as a brand and personally initiated the re-branding to OSHO on everything that had once been branded Rajneesh," Jayesh said in his Witness Statement. He said it was because of the efforts of the OIF, Inner Circle and the Presidium, along with a network of hundreds of Osho Centres and licensees in Europe and worldwide, "the Osho brand has become widely recognised for meditation services."

On January 13, 2009, responding to a petition filed by Osho Friends International, New Delhi, the United States Patent and Trademark Office (USPTO) cancelled a series of trademarks with the word 'Osho' registered by Osho International Foundation, Zürich. The trademarks that stood cancelled included Osho Active Meditations, Osho Multiversity, Osho Times, Osho Rebalancing, Osho Zen Tarot, Osho Kundalini Meditation, Osho Nadbrahma Meditation and Osho Meditation Resort.

The ruling by administrative trademark judges Charles Grendel, Peter W. Cataldo and Tom Wellington said, "The primary significance of Osho is as a religious or meditative Movement, and not as a source identifier for goods and services."

Amrit Sadhana, a member of the Osho Commune's Management Team expressed disappointment over this ruling in January, 2009 and lamented that by describing 'Osho' as "generic", the USPTO had put him "in the same category as computers and tissues." She stressed that the OIF "had always acted on Osho's request to protect his name, his copyright and his work, and would continue to do so." According to Amrit Sadhana, the 'Osho' trademark owned by OIF continued to be protected in more than 40 countries.

Prior to that, in March 2000, OIF, New York initiated legal action against the biggest Osho Centre in North India, the

Osho Dhyan Mandir, New Delhi to prevent them from using the word 'Osho' in the domain name www.oshoworld.com. A number of Osho sannyasins opposed to the Jayesh-Amrito regime in Pune rallied together and fought that case with all their might. The verdict in the case delivered by Arbitrator M. Kellery Tillery Esquire on July 28, 2000 went in favour of 'Osho Dhyan Mandir and Atul Anand'.[8]

In May 2001, the National Arbitration Forum of the United States rejected a plea by Osho International Foundation, New York for the denial of the domain name "Oshoworld.com" to Osho Dhyan Mandir and one of its chief patrons and Osho sannyasin, Atul Anand. The single member panelist of the forum who issued the order said there was no evidence that Bhagwan Shree Rajneesh (Osho) ever commercially exploited the name or mark 'Osho' or authorised someone to do so. "The record also reflects that Osho himself had little regard for or concern with intellectual property rights, including any related to the use of his chosen name," the order said. As of March 2016, after concerted legal battles, the OIF could not secure rights to the Osho trademark and Osho domain name in the U.S. but secured rights to the Osho trademark in Europe. The legal battle in Europe, however, is far from over.

On its website Osho.com, the OIF has laid out its policy and ownership claims to the trademark and copyrights. It states that OSHO® is a registered trademark of Osho International Foundation in many countries, in multiple trademark classes and for a wide range of goods and services. "The OSHO trademark mark is distinctive and identifies goods and or services originating from a particular source: Osho International Foundation as well as authorised licensees," the OIF states.

Fourteen types of meditations, many of Osho meditative therapies including Mystic Rose, No-Mind and Born Again, Rebalancing and Craniosacral Balancing stand protected by trademark as also Osho talks, audio video, and titles such as Osho International Meditation Resort, Osho Multiversity, Osho Mystery School, Music from the World of Osho, Osho Books and Osho Festival. The use of 'Osho', in combination with words like 'techniques' or 'Meditation Centers', is also protected.

The activities of various Osho Centres around the world are monitored by OIF's Osho Global Connections department which grants permission to start Osho meditation centres, institutes or information centres and "to use the mark 'OSHO' in this context". On copyrights, the OIF states on its website that OSHO International Foundation is the sole and registered owner of all the copyrights to all the published and unpublished words and works of Osho, as author, in all mediums.

OIF-Zürich, OIF-India and Neo Sannyas Foundation, also registered at OIF India's address at 608 Maker Chambers, Mumbai are the three trusts controlling the assets of the Osho Movement over the years. Each of these trusts has undergone changes over the decades (flow chart on p. 212).

Always ascribing its actions to "guidance from Osho" and sugar-coating its communication with the public and with Osho's followers, OIF says on its website Osho.info that when Osho "renounced all his former names in 1989, he requested that he should be known simply as 'Osho' and that no reference to former names should be made." Likewise, it said as early as 1989, Osho stated that "he did not want his Pune place to be called 'ashram'". Known as Osho Commune International till

2001, it was renamed OSHO International Meditation Resort thereafter. It is questionable whether Osho would pass such silly instructions when, in fact, "Shree Rajneesh Ashram" was the very first name of the Pune Commune.

In effect, Jayesh with his genius, charm, sleight and extraordinary business acumen has successfully transformed Osho into a multi-million-dollar business whose beneficiaries are not the devoted followers of Osho, or society at large, but a handful of foreign businessmen led by Jayesh and assisted by a handful of their Indian puppets who hold positions in OIF-India.

Journey of Osho's Intellectual Property Rights from India to Europe

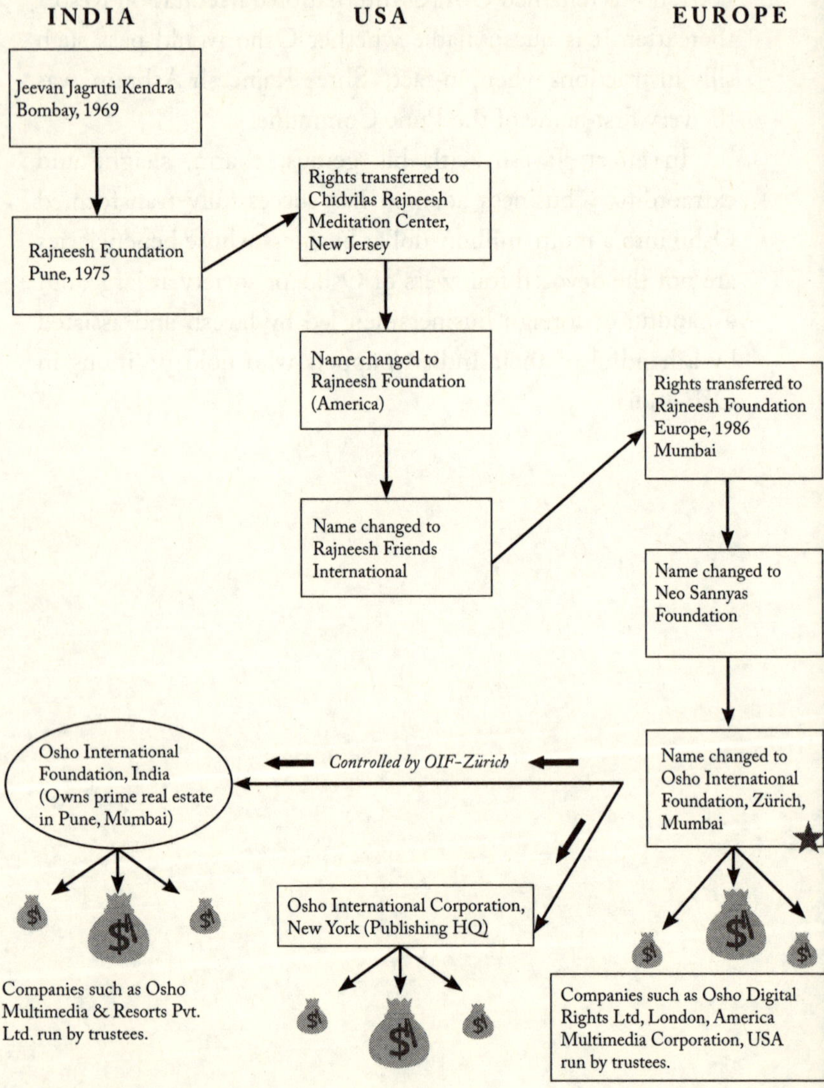

Flow chart by Abhay Vaidya

14

Will Osho's Bones Rattle if the Samadhi is Destroyed?

Since Osho was being celebrated and worshipped by his followers as an enlightened mystic, no less than a Buddha of our times, it was only fitting that a magnificent Samadhi of his was created for posterity. The Samadhi would serve as Osho's final resting place, creating a Buddhafield of the Master and a perfect place to meditate on his teachings. The Samadhi of an enlightened mystic with deep spiritual and esoteric significance has been a well-accepted part of Eastern traditions over the centuries and at the time of Osho's death, there was complete unanimity on this matter among his Eastern and Western followers. More so, as Amrito had announced that Osho himself wanted his Samadhi to be created on the premises.

On Sunday, January 20, 1990, a teary-eyed Amrito gave a detailed account in the Buddha Hall of Osho's last conversation with him. He spoke of Osho's desire for a beautiful Samadhi on the premises. The Pune Commune was the place where Osho had given form and substance to the Neo Sannyas Movement and the many meditation techniques and meditative therapies that he had created. This was the place where he had breathed his last after a tumultuous journey of 58 years. "Osho," said Amrito, "wanted his ashes to be preserved in an urn in his bedroom which was to be converted into a spectacular Samadhi."

As Amrito recounted before the assembled sannyasins in the Buddha Hall:

"He sat on the bed and I asked what we should do for His Samadhi. 'You just put my ashes in Chuang Tzu, under the bed. And then people can come in and meditate there,' He said."

The conversation on the proposed Samadhi continued, with Amrito and Osho discussing where exactly it should be located. When Osho asked him whether his existing bedroom would be good for the mausoleum, Amrito replied, "No. Chuang Tzu will be beautiful." Osho agreed and then said the Samadhi should be marbled and made beautiful.

Accordingly, every effort was made to create a dazzlingly beautiful hall where Osho's ashes were placed in an urn after they were brought to the Commune in a procession. The route from the crematorium to the Commune was lined by sannyasins who showered rose petals and celebrated with singing and dancing.

Shunyo, who had served Osho for many years on his personal staff, noted that preparations for the Samadhi were made towards the beginning of 1989 itself. It was Anando who had reported that Osho had given her instructions to transform the Chuang Tzu Auditorium into a new bedroom for him. "Osho had given instructions to Anando a couple of months before that He wanted Chuang Tzu Auditorium to be made into a new bedroom for him. She found people to do the work, the materials were ordered from all over the world and the work was progressing."[1]

This was originally a large open hall in Lao Tzu House where Osho had given discourses when he first arrived in Pune. As per the plans, a 20-foot diameter circular crystal chandelier became the main attraction of the Samadhi, reflected majestically on vertical sheets of dark blue glass panels that encircled the auditorium. Outside was a landscaped garden with rocks and a mini waterfall. The floor of the Samadhi was made of chemically-untreated marble brought from Madhya Pradesh where Osho, as a child, had been fascinated by the marble rocks of Bhedaghat near Jabalpur.

A marble platform was created at one end of the wall and the urn with Osho's ashes was placed inside this platform. A plaque on the platform carried the epitaph dictated by Osho himself: *Osho—Never Born, Never Died. Only Visited This Planet Earth Between December 11, 1931 and January 19, 1990.*

All was well till early 2000 when some drastic changes were initiated inside the Osho Commune. In 2002, when Osho's pictures were removed from the premises of the Commune, D'Arcy had told *The New York Times* it was done because "the dead guy's pictures" were putting off young people coming to the resort. Business interests had become paramount as the character, image and identity of the Commune were being overhauled and aligned with the "international meditation resort" tag. D'Arcy's remark reflected contempt and insensitivity for the sentiments of Osho's followers—especially Indians—who were appalled by the removal of Osho's pictures. There was still greater shock awaiting them when a few years later, word spread among the followers that even Osho's Samadhi was not being spared changes.

There were already strong undercurrents to suggest that the presence of the Samadhi was bothering the top managers.

One such indication, Tathagat recalled, was the difficult conversation that Chaitanya Keerti had with Amrito before he quit the Commune in 2000. Keerti had been insisting with Amrito that the sanctity of the Samadhi should be preserved and meditations with catharsis (the 'throwing out' of inner turmoil with screaming, shouting and abusing if necessary) should not be permitted. To this, Amrito had replied: "Keerti, do you think if we change the policy, Osho's bones will start rattling in that urn? Keerti, be practical; be a sannyasin. There's no rattling happening whether the bones are there or not there. It doesn't matter whether the Samadhi is there or not there. Why are you insisting on sanctity, that people should not do catharsis? That's all your Eastern concept."

While this was a "closed door" conversation that had happened some years ago, the Osho Commune responded to this particular criticism in its full-page advertisement in *The Indian Express* and *The Times of India* of June 28, 2000 in the following way:

"False allegation: Osho's Samadhi is being misused for No-Mind Meditation."

Facts: Osho No-Mind is a meditative therapy created by Osho himself during the last year he was in the body. It is a gibberish technique that has nothing to do with the alleged "violence or abuse." Osho specifically asked for this technique, and his Mystic Rose meditative therapy, to take place in the Samadhi. Ma Neelam's suggestion that it is more appropriate to have Buddha's Vipassana there rather than Osho's own meditations is incomprehensible."

By 2007, the Osho Meditation Resort managers had become emboldened enough to assert publicly that designating the Chuang Tzu Auditorium as "Samadhi" had been a "mistake". This assertion was made by Keerti's replacement and the Commune's new spokesperson Amrit Sadhana in an interview to the author as a reporter for *The Times of India*.[2] Sadhana, who insisted that she be referred to as "Member of the Management Team" and not the "spokesperson" had reluctantly agreed to allow me to visit Osho's Samadhi. She had insisted that I wear a maroon robe and white socks, take the blood test for HIV at the Commune's medical centre (HIV+ve people are debarred entry), and participate in the orientation programme before permission could be granted to enter the Samadhi. The orientation group which was led into some basic meditation routine in the morning, entered the Samadhi for a 'silent meditation' around 3 p.m. When asked about Osho's picture frame being replaced by a chocolate-coloured bust as reported by some sannyasins, Amrit Sadhana confirmed and explained that the wooden bust by a Chilean admirer had been much loved by Osho and had replaced the picture as "the edges had got frayed."

After the visit, Amrit Sadhana said: "We do not call it a 'Samadhi' but Chuang Tzu (hall) where Osho gave his first lectures after arriving in Pune in 1974. As per Osho's wishes, his ashes were put in an urn and buried there. Someone in the frenzy after his death called it a 'Samadhi'. We realised what a mistake it was."

Someone called it a Samadhi?

Why was a new story being created about the history of the Samadhi? What about Amrito's last conversation with Osho in which both had used the term 'Samadhi' and discussed it at length? What about the reference that Shunyo made to Anando about Osho's desire that the Chuang Tzu Auditorium be converted into his new bedroom to be beautified as a Samadhi?

Who was lying? Was it Amrit Sadhana? Or did Amrito concoct the Samadhi story and his last conversation with Osho?

On numerous occasions, Sadhana had said that the OIF was not in favour of providing public access to Osho's Samadhi as it could easily turn into a shrine like other Samadhis with prayers, fruit and flower offerings. This would be an insult to Osho and his philosophy, she said, as he was bitterly opposed to rituals, religions, customs and traditions. While that may be true, couldn't the trust insist on adherence to its rules while providing public access to the Samadhi?

By 2007, it was also noticed that the resort's website (osho.com) and promotional literature made no mention of Osho's Samadhi.

Keerti, who was based in Delhi, was among those who reacted sharply to this new development at the Commune and said Osho's disciples were suspicious of the Commune's motives in wanting to erase the memory of the Samadhi. "We feel that it is a long-term strategy to break the emotional link that sannyasins have with Osho's Samadhi and sell or lease the Pune property in future."

Tathagat said, "We are still not clear what is to be done, but everyone is deeply hurt."

Prem Anadi noted: "For 17 years, from 1990 to 2007, they were also calling it a Samadhi. But after 2007, suddenly they said it is not a Samadhi. Probably some real estate people had entered the picture and had advised that the Samadhi tag be removed."

Neelam, in her "Open Letter" on sannyasnews.com quoted Osho on the significance of the Samadhi:

"Slowly, slowly in all the countries where spirituality has flowered, people became aware that something happens...

So, people have preserved things that were used by these people, or just have made memorials of their bodies. In India bodies are burned, but you will be surprised to know that the remains left after burning a body are called 'flowers'. Ordinary people's ashes are thrown into holy rivers, but enlightened people's 'flowers' are preserved in Samadhis—in beautiful marble memorials. Just to go and sit there is in itself a meditation. But the trouble is that the world is ruled by those who know nothing of this."[3]

Neelam found it painful to see how Osho's Samadhi was being destroyed systematically by Jayesh and Amrito. According to her, cathartic group therapies were introduced in the serene atmosphere of the Samadhi in 1999, not paying any heed to protests from sannyasins. The Samadhi used to be cleaned with love by Osho's followers, but that was discontinued and hired labourers were brought in to do so. Neelam alleged that the marble plaque with golden inscriptions on it and Osho's photo had been removed and finally, the place was no longer called Samadhi. "They (Jayesh and Amrito) know if it is no more called Samadhi, then Lao Tzu House, his residence, where the Samadhi is, becomes merely a building. It can be sold or purchased. It can be demolished to erect a new building."

She asserted that Osho's followers won't let this happen as Osho's Samadhi does not belong to anybody: "It's not anybody's private property—it belongs to all the seekers in the world."

In the immediate years after Osho's death, Jayesh, as the custodian of Osho's dream cited his "guidance" to initiate several major changes such as moving the headquarters to Zürich, pursuing copyright and trademark protection and disbanding the Commune by discontinuing the free food pass and accommodation for a large number of sannyasins. In addition to Osho's "guidance", OIF trustees began justifying all their decisions by citing extracts from Osho's discourses. Thus, the 'Management Team' justified the removal of pictures from the premises, the rejection of the Samadhi, the dropping of the prefixes "Swami" for male sannyasins and "Ma" for the female sannyasins and the discontinuation of celebrations on special days such as Osho's birth and death anniversaries, his Day of Enlightenment and Guru Purnima—were done year after year with considerable energy. A handful of Indian functionaries such as Mukesh Sarda, Amrit Sadhana and Devendra Singh Dewal always supported these decisions and had been elevated to various positions as OIF trustees or directors in various private companies that had sprung up around activities relating to Osho.

The standard line maintained by the OIF was that Osho was opposed to customs and traditions.

However, New Year's Eve was celebrated with unfailing regularity with loud music, dancing and the free flow of alcohol. Most of the sannyasins who had fallen out with the Commune, or were seen as supporters and sympathisers of rival factions led by Neelam and Tathagat, were denied entry to the premises. They were simply told over the telephone at the front gate desk that they were "no longer welcome" and thus forced to turn back. The question of providing them with access to Osho's Samadhi or the old Buddha Hall for sentimental purposes just did not arise.

At a superficial level, this would appear as the "East-West Divide"—a clash between Osho's Western followers controlling the all-powerful OIF-Zürich and his Eastern, or specifically, Indian followers. In reality, the "clash" was more about turning Osho into a brand, taking the brand out of India and acquiring complete control over the 'Osho' business—along with the associated copyrights, trademarks and archives—with operations headquartered not in Pune but in Europe and America. In fact, the trademark battle in a European Court against OIF-Zürich was led by the German sannyasin Ramateertha from the Cologne Centre.

Likewise, the speculation among some senior Indian sannyasins—whispered in closed circles—that "Jayesh is an agent of U.S.-based Christian fundamentalists" who undertook to uproot and destroy Osho from his roots stood debunked by reality—far from Osho becoming irrelevant or forgotten, the interest in him over the last 27 years has grown manifolds across India and rest of the world.

Undoubtedly, there were undercurrents of an East-West divide in the Commune, the worst manifestations of which could be seen in some of the clashes among senior disciples. For example, Laxmi was bitterly opposed to the Westerners in Poona-I who were becoming increasingly influential with Osho. While Osho's cook was always an Indian, most of his caretakers, including his girlfriend Nirvano, physician Amrito, "laundry woman" Shunyo, dentist Devageet, and later, Jayesh, Hasya and Anando, were Westerners. The Western followers brought with them professional conduct and a range of professional systems which, senior sannyasins said, Osho loved. Osho was fastidious about punctuality with his food and discourse timings. If he wanted to be left alone and undisturbed, that is precisely what he meant. "But Indian caretakers would trouble him every now and then out of love and concern, which irritated him," said Neelam. Osho demanded a high degree of cleanliness and he expressed a clear preference for Westerners to serve as his caretakers. Most of them were English. Top

Western psychologists and psychotherapists worked with him on his meditation techniques and therapies; they brought in modern audio and video recording equipment, modernised the Commune and its operations, introduced excellent aesthetics, opened a window to the rest of the world and brought in resources through huge donations and contributions. All this took the Osho Movement to another level, paving the way for the ambitious move to the U.S.

After Laxmi's replacement by her assistant Sheela as Osho's secretary, there was no East-West friction but clashes born out of power politics. Sheela, who was deeply in love with the West and had settled in Europe after abandoning Rajneeshpuram, was more of a Westerner than an Indian. Thus, the entire range of actions initiated in Poona-II after Osho's death, starting with emptying the Commune of its Indian and non-Indian residents, and building up to the point of rejecting the Samadhi, was more to do with acquiring control over brand 'Osho'.

It was around mid-March, 2016 and the steel letterings on the façade above the front gate at 17 Koregaon Park proclaimed 'Osho International'. There were unmanned iron barriers to slow down vehicles on the narrow lane on both sides of the gate and a police picket with sand bags stationed near the Welcome Centre, on the right side of the entrance. The police presence was introduced after the German Bakery terror attack on the eve of Valentine's Day on February 13, 2010, which killed 17 people and injured more than 60. The restaurant was identified as a target by Pakistani-American Laskhar-e-Toiba operative David Coleman Headley because of its proximity to the Osho Commune and the Chhabad House.

The Commune of the past appeared dead and deserted, partly because the peak season from mid-November to mid-February had just ended. That, however, is not the only reason footfalls have reduced sharply on Koregaon Park Lane No. 1 which used to once buzz with the hustle and bustle of maroon and white-robed sannyasins, tourists, visitors and gawkers, amidst fusion music wafting in from the Buddha Hall. All that is missing today as there are just a handful of residents on the premises and the number of visitors has also dwindled. The daily minimum charge of Rs. 870 for Indians and Rs. 1,790 for foreigners which "includes the full-day meditation programme and the open-air classes in Buddha Grove" is one of the reasons why the 'meditation resort' has become unaffordable for many Indians. Premgeet felt that the charge is deliberately on the higher side for Indians to discourage them from frequenting the resort.

Amrit Sadhana failed to respond when asked about the number of sannyasins living inside the premises. The bookshop to the left of the entrance, is lifeless, but for an elderly lady at the counter. The large windows of the bookshop provide a glimpse inside the resort and reveal the presence of a solitary guard and a maintenance worker in a blue uniform. In the past, a guided tour that many tourists looked forward to would be organised for visitors to the Commune, but that was discontinued more than a decade ago. For the past many years, there has been a strong resistance to interacting with local journalists and hardly anything about the Osho Resort gets written in the local or national press.

Osho's followers were alarmed when they discovered that on September 19, 2011, OIF trustee Mukesh Sarda had made an application to the Charity Commissionerate, Maharashtra, seeking permission to gift a single-storeyed bungalow named Osho Sanai in Lane No. 1 to a New Delhi-based entity called Darshan Trust. The property with an estimated value of Rs. 8 crore was described by OIF as "excess space" not required by the OIF to fulfill its objectives and was "a burden" on the OIF.[4] The matter was challenged by Premgeet and Anadi who have been crusading against the OIF on many issues. There were plans for "gifting" of other properties belonging to the Osho Commune which came to light and were challenged in the Charity Commissionerate, Maharashtra and the Bombay High Court.

Where is all this headed to? Will hotels and service apartments come up on this property in place of the original purpose of promoting the Neo Sannyas Movement and innovative meditation techniques in the modern age? Only time will tell.

Lane No. 1 Koregaon Park: In previous years, this approach road to the Osho Commune used to be full of life, buzzing with the movement of sannyasins and tourists.

The lifeless façade on a Sunday afternoon in December, 2016.
The absence of the word 'Commune' on the 'gateless gate' is conspicuous.

With large, piercing eyes, a charming smile and jet black beard, Acharya Shree Rajneesh had a handsome personality and a magnetic appeal.

He was an itinerant monk and public speaker in the 1960s and early 1970s.

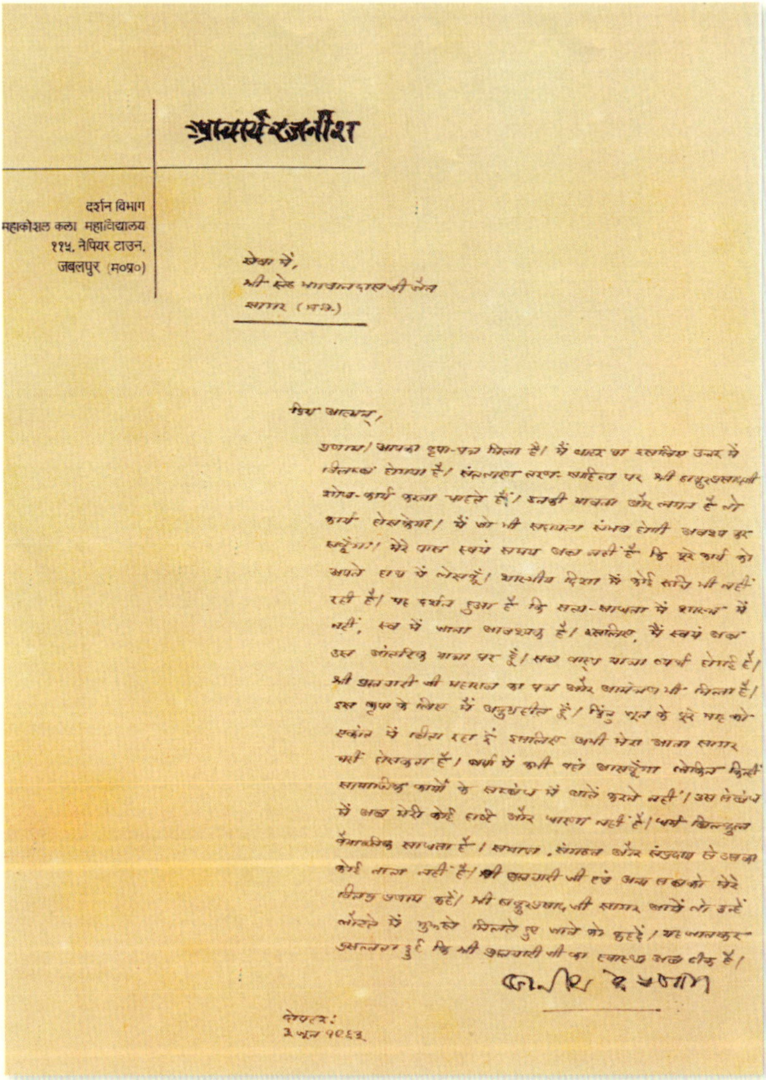

आचार्य रजनीश

दर्शन विभाग
महाकोशल कला महाविद्यालय
११५, नेपियर टाउन,
जबलपुर (म०प्र०)

Letters written by Osho in the 1960s and 1970s. His earliest signatures in Hindi read: 'Rajneesh ke pranam' (Salutations from Rajneesh).

acharya rajneesh

kamala nehru nagar : jabalapur (m. p.). phone : 2957

मेरे प्रिय,

प्रेम। तुम्हारा पत्र पाकर आनंदित हूं।

श्री० [illegible] और श्री० [illegible] के आमंत्रण भी मिले हैं।

मैं भी लोनावाला आना चाहता हूं। पर ही कठिनाई है कि उन्हीं तिथियों में मैं [illegible] से इंदौर, भोपाल, [illegible], अहमदाबाद आदि के [illegible] रूप से [illegible] हूं। फिर भी उनमें परिवर्तन की कोशिश करूंगा और यदि संभव होसका तो लोनावाला जरूर आजाऊंगा।

[illegible] आपको [illegible] हैं।

शेष शुभ।

सबको प्रणाम।

'[illegible] की ओर' का मराठी अनुवाद जैसे ही प्रकाशित होजाये मुझे भेज देना।

[illegible]

१२/१२/१९६८

acharya rajneesh

kamala nehru nagar : jabalapur (m.p.). phone : 2957

प्यारी कुसुम,

प्रेम। तेरा पत्र मिल गया है।
गर्मी के बाद जैसे धरती वर्षा के लिए प्यासी होती है, वैसे ही तू प्रभु के लिए प्यासी है।
यह प्यास ही तो उसकी बदलियों के लिए निमंत्रण बन जाती है।
और निमंत्रण पहुंच गया है।
तू तो बस ध्यान में डूबती जा।
उसकी करुणा की वर्षा तो होती ही।
जब इधर हम तैयार भर हों — वह तो उधर सदा ही तैयार है।
देख — क्या आकाश में उसकी बदलियां नहीं मंडराने लगी हैं?
कपिल को प्रेम।
अशोक को आशीष।

१५/२/१९७०

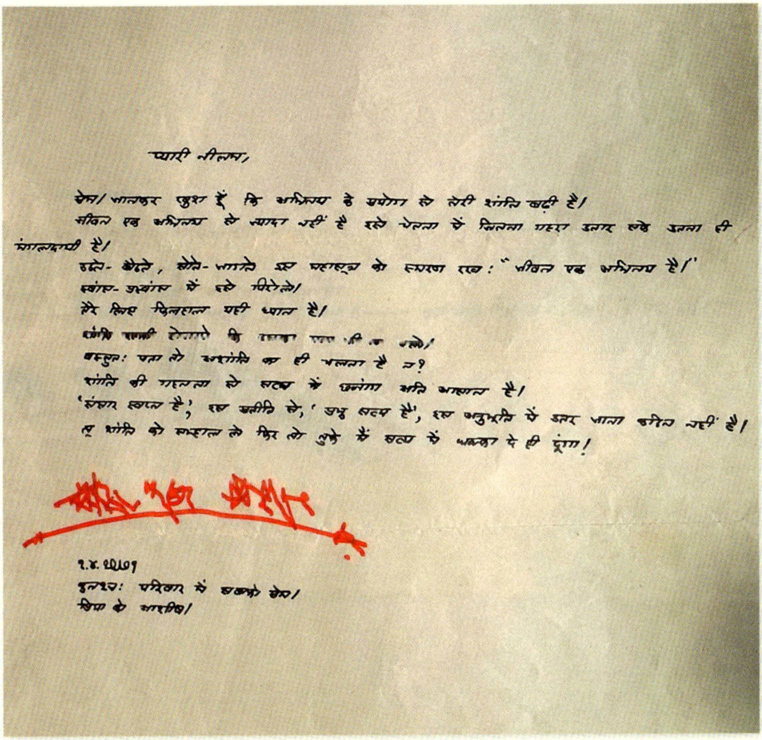

प्यारी नीलम,

प्रेम। जानकर खुश हूं कि अनित्य के प्रयोग से तेरी शांति बढ़ी है।

जीवन एक अनित्य से ज्यादा नहीं है इसे चेतना में जितना गहरा उतार सके उतना ही मंगलदायी है।

उठते- बैठते, सोते- जागते इस महासूत्र को स्मरण रख: "जीवन एक अनित्य है।"

श्वांस- प्रश्वांस में इसे पिरो ले।

तेरे लिए फिलहाल यही ध्यान है।

[illegible]

वस्तुत: पता तो अशांति का ही चलता है न?

शांति की महत्ता से सत्य में छलांग अति आसान है।

'संसार स्वप्न है', इस प्रतीति से, 'प्रभु सत्य है', इस अनुभूति में उतर जाना कठिन नहीं है।

तू शांति को सम्हाल ले फिर तो तुझे मैं सत्य में धक्का दे ही दूंगा!

१.४.१९७१

पुनश्च: परिवार में सबको प्रेम।

पिता के आशीष।

In later years, his signature became an indecipherable scrawl.

स्वामी शैलेन्द्र सरस्वती

swami shailendra saraswati

30.6.1971

Gadarwara . M.P. (India) .

Facing page: Letter written to his brother Swami Shailendra Saraswati in 1971.

The author interviewing Swami Shailendra Saraswati at his ashram Oshodhara Nanak Dham at Murthal, Sonepat in Haryana on July 28, 2016.

Rare archival photograph of the extremely elusive Jayesh (Michael O'Byrne) behind the left shoulder of prominent politician Sharad Pawar during a visit to Osho Teerth Park in the early 1990s. At extreme right is Atul Chordia, a prominent real estate developer from Pune whose corporate conglomerate Panchshil Group found a mention in the Panama Papers exposé of 2016.

Giving energy as Bhagwan Shree Rajneesh in Poona-I.

Rajneesh in Oregon in his specially designed winged robe.

The 97 Rolls Royces at Rancho Rajneesh in Oregon in the early 1980s grabbed the attention of the world media.

With his India secretary Neelam in Nepal, at the start of the 'World Tour' in 1985.

With his girlfriend Nirvano who died 41 days before he left his body.

Both Osho and Nirvano died in suspicious circumstances.

Osho's final journey on January 19, 1990.

The author interviewing ENT surgeon Dr. Gokul Gokani on December 14, 2015 in Baroda. Dr. Gokani had issued Osho's death certificate in questionable circumstances.

Left to right: Amrit Sadhana, Amrito and Jeffrey Archer in the Osho Commune Bookshop on May 23, 2008. This photograph was shared by the Osho Commune with the media.

The magnificent Osho Samadhi. An urn with Osho's ashes was placed under a marble platform. Osho International Foundation (OIF) later said it was a 'mistake' on their part to call this memorial a 'samadhi'.

OSHO
Never Born
Never Died
Only Visited this
Planet Earth between
Dec 11 1931 – Jan 19 1990

15

The Strange Case of Osho's Will

Such was the legal battle waged by Osho International Foundation, Zürich for the right to Osho's trademark, that, on June 4, 2013, it produced the most sensational document in its possession in a European Court—a true copy of Osho's Will dated 15th October, 1989, presented as 'Exhibit 4' in the 'Second Supplemental Witness Statement' by Philip Toelkes, also known as Prem Niren. Based in Santa Clara, Oakland, California, Toelkes was Osho's Personal Attorney from 1982 to 1990 and an attorney for OIF later. Prior to the European trademark case, he had deposed as witness in the Osho Friends International, New Delhi Vs Osho International Foundation (OIF), Zürich trademark case before the Appeal Board of the United States Patent and Trademark Office in which OIF had lost its appeal for registration of trademark in the U.S.

The appearance of Osho's Will, 23 years after his death, took the world of his sannyasins by storm. When Osho died in 1990, Amrito, who officially represented the Commune, was categorical that Osho did not leave behind any Will. He and the Commune's spokesperson, Chaitanya Keerti denied the existence of Osho's Will when specifically asked by the press. There was no mention of any Will by Osho in the 23 years that intervened, till it was produced in Spain. The case being heard in the Office for Harmonization in the Internal Market, Avenida de Europa, Alicante, Spain, otherwise known as the Trademark and Designs Registration Office of the European Union related to an application filed by Osho Lotus Commune e.V. (Cologne, Germany) for invalidity of 'OSHO' Community Trademark Registration No. 1224831 in Classes 41 and 42 in the name of OIF. In other words, one group of Osho's followers led by Ramateertha and opposed to the OIF, was pressing for cancellation of the Osho trademark held by the OIF in Europe.

Toelkes in his statement said that Osho's Will, executed shortly before his death, "clearly stated his intention to transfer any and all property rights or interests he had to OIF." The "breadth of the bequest," he said, "is clearly sufficient to transfer any and all rights to use of his name and likeness, as well as all of his work."

Toelkes said he drafted the Will and witnessed Osho's execution thereof, in the presence of the signing witnesses, Jayesh and Amrito, on October 15, 1989. "Osho asked questions about the legal effect of the document prior to his execution thereof, and was unquestionably mentally alert and in full possession of his faculties at the time of execution," Toelkes said in his statement. (See pp. 234–240.)

An extraordinarily terse document of 26 typewritten lines, the Will was presented on a ten-rupee stamp paper purchased in Bombay from the office of advocates and solicitors Champaklal D. Shah. Under the heading 'Last Will & Testament of Osho' the document is reproduced on pp. 232–233.

The second page of the Will carried three signatures—of Jayesh as the executor and Toelkes and Amrito as witnesses.

The Will carried the elaborate scrawl signature of Osho, seen in the letters that he signed in the 1960s and in the autographed books that he presented in subsequent years.

A number of questions arose in connection with this Will, the first and foremost being, why was it suppressed for so many years? Why was the second page of the Will bearing the signatures of Jayesh, Amrito and Toelkes not signed by Osho, validating the existence of the second page? How come Osho never mentioned or spoke about his Will to his India secretary Neelam, his International Secretary Hasya and to others close to him?

Suspicious that this Will could be a forged document, Osho's sannyasins in Europe and India sought to have it examined by forensic experts in India and abroad. In 2013, Osho's purported Will was submitted for forensic examination to Nicole Ciccolo, a graphologist registered in the List of Technical Consultants of the Civil and Penal Law Court of Bologna, Italy and member of the Association of Professional Graphologists.

Ciccolo was asked to compare whether Osho's signature on the Will matched with his signature that had been reproduced on the dust-jacket of the book entitled *Yoga: The Alpha and the Omega*, Volume 5, published in 1976.

Ciccolo said in her reports dated October 13, 2013 and October 28, 2014 that a forensic comparison of the two documents showed that "all the engrams are identical and perfectly overlap." She said: "A universally accepted graph logical axiom states that there cannot be two identical signatures, therefore, the signature bearing the name 'Osho' at the bottom of the Will is apocryphal and was executed by means of a photographic montage." She noted: "More specifically, the handwritten letter by Osho dated 1976 bearing a signature at the bottom was published in at least two Internet sites, therefore it has proved easy to find for making the false Will." (Report on pp. 241–246).

Legal experts pointed out that the document presented as Osho's Will was not attested by any legal agency approved by law in India and was also not notarised. As per law, each page of the Will had to be signed by the testator and the witnesses along with the executor, which was not the case in the document claimed to have been signed by Osho.

On November 18, 2013, Premgeet, Managing Trustee of Osho Friends Foundation, Pune filed a police complaint with the Koregaon Park Police Station followed by an FIR on December 8, 2013, accusing Jayesh, D'Arcy, Philip Toelkes, Amrito, Mukesh Sarda and Klaus Steeg of conspiring to forge Osho's Will. He cited Ciccolo's report along with reports from two other technical experts, namely, N.R. Parik, Examiner of Documents and Grapho Analyst, Aurangabad and J.K. Consultancy (Handwriting Expert and Document Examiner), New Delhi, both of whom were unanimous that Osho's signature on his Will was an act of forgery.

In 2013, a civil suit was filed in the Pune district court by Osho Friends Foundation, Premgeet and Anadi against OIF trustees, Philip Toelkes and Neo Sannyas Foundation seeking declaration of Osho's Will as null and void.

Finally, on January 2, 2014, OIF's attorneys submitted an application to the EUIPO stating that OIF was withdrawing its Exhibit No. 4 (Last Will & Testament of Osho) in order that the European Court was "not distracted from the key evidence and issues presented in the trademark registration cases relating to Osho."

This, however, did not end the controversy as there was trouble waiting to erupt in an Indian court. On June 20, 2016, Premgeet filed a criminal petition in the Bombay High Court complaining that no progress had been made by the Koregaon Park Police Station with respect to FIR No. 149/13 (dated 8.12.13). He pleaded that the High Court should direct the Pune Police Commissioner to give details of action taken on the FIR and also transfer the investigations to the CBI. This petition resulted in a flurry of orders from the High Court Division Bench of Justice Naresh Patil and Justice Prakash Naik in a series of hearings from August to October 2016. On August 3, the court reprimanded the Pune Police for tardy progress into the complaint and directed the Deputy Commissioner of Police (Crime) to supervise the investigations into the Osho Will case. The court expressed its dissatisfaction with the police reply that a copy of the Will had been sent to handwriting experts for verification in 2014 and their report was awaited. Reacting to this submission, Justice Patil asked: "It has been two years. You have not received the report and have not done anything about it?"

On August 12, the court asked the Pune Police to trace the original Will and bring it back to India. It also allowed petitioner Premgeet's plea to make the Reserve Bank of India (RBI) and the Enforcement Directorate (ED) respondents in the case in view of his allegations that Jayesh, Amrito, D'Arcy, Mukesh Sarda, Klaus Steeg and their conspirators were siphoning income rightly belonging to Osho's Indian trusts to Switzerland, U.S., Ireland and Europe. On October 7, the ED informed the court that it had begun investigations into this charge. The Pune Police also informed the court on that day that it had written to the central government for permission to issue Letters of Rogatory to a court in Spain to obtain the original Will of Osho. These were the developments till the time of finalising this manuscript.

On his part, Osho's younger brother Shailendra Saraswati had no doubts that the Will presented by the OIF was a forged document. In his interview to the author, he said: "It is clear that the Will is forged. When people become administrators of institutions, they have their own compulsions to do things to protect their power. They get caught in lies and falsehood. They can't think of any other way. It is very clear that the Will is forged." He cited forensic evidence which showed that "Osho's signature on the Will was digitally manipulated and reproduced from a book."

Community Trade Mark Registration
No 1224831 OSHO in Classes 41 & 42
in the name of Osho International
Foundation ("OIF")

- and-

Application for Invalidity No 6063
thereto by Osho Lotus Commune e.V.

Exhibit 4

10 Rs

16 JUN 1989

CHAMPAKLAL D. SHAH
ADVOCATES & SOLICITORS

LAST WILL & TESTAMENT
of OSHO

RECITAL. In 1975, 1978 and 1981, I executed assignments concerning my work. Also in 1981, I executed a broad power of attorney with the stated intention to divest myself of all worldly property, and also an amendment in 1982, with the result that all such property is now owned by Neo Sannyas International Foundation, a Swiss charitable entity. To be completely certain that all such property interests are so divested, I make this Last Will and Testament.

LAST WILL & TESTAMENT. Being of sound mind, and acting of my free will, I make this Last Will and Testament.

I, Osho, birth name Chandra Mohan Jain, formerly known as Bhagwan Shree Rajneesh, hereby devise and bequest any and all right, title or interest of any nature in any and all property of any nature and in any form, owned by me, now or in the future, including but not limited to, all ownership, publishing or related rights, to all my work, published to date or in the future, in any form, to Neo Sannyas International Foundation.

If for any reason that entity cannot or does not accept this bequest then the alternate beneficiary shall be a non-profit, charitable entity dedicated to the dissemination of my work, such entity to be designated by my executor.

EXECUTOR. I name as my executor Sw. Anand Jayesh, aka Michael O'Byrne.

Executed this 15th day of October, 1989, at Poona, India.

Osho

LAST WILL & TESTAMENT
of OSHO
(page 2.)

I agree to serve as Executor.

______________ Sw. Anand Jayesh

______________ aka Michael O'Byrne

Executed on October 15, 1989, at Poona, India.

ATTESTATION. We, the undersigned have witnessed the signatures of Osho and Sw. Anand Jayesh and each other, to this document on October 15, 1989.

______________ Sw. Amrito

______________ aka John Andrews

______________ Sw. Prem Niren

______________ aka Philip Toelkes

Community Trade Mark Registration
No 1224831 OSHO In Classes 41 & 42
in the name of Osho International
Foundation ("OIF") and
Application for invalidity No 5063
thereto by Osho Lotus Commune e.V.
("Applicant")

Second Supplemental Witness Statement

I, Philip Toelkes, also known as Prem Niren, hereby declare that:

1. All the statements made herein are true and from my personal knowledge and recollection. Where I have made statements from another source, I have identified that source and believe the facts to be true. I am competent to make this witness statement. My address is 90 Baywood Village Rd. #51, Sequim, Washington, USA 93882.

2. Scope of statement. This statement responds to questions raised by Lotus in its brief of January 4, 2013, and mischaracterizations of the documents of rights transfer and US copyright, contract and intellectual property. It will not restate the facts set forth in my earlier statements.

3. Qualifications. My first statement set forth generally my background and relevant experience. That material will not be repeated here. My qualifications to address the legal effect of the documents of rights transfers from Osho, as well as the subsequent transfer documents, under US contract and copyright law are set forth below in para. 5.

4. Introduction and Summary. Toelkes' statements factual. Lotus' intemperate characterizations of OIF's statements, including my own, wherein the use of such adjectives moved me to carefully review my earlier statements. I find nothing in the way of unsupported *ad hominem* attacks, as is unfortunately the case in the Lotus' brief. I find factual statements and some legal characterizations, to which Lotus has not offered controverting evidence, offering instead factually unsupported characterizations.

5. Toelkes' credentials re legal effect of documents of rights transfer. Lotus is correct in asserting that I have presented no bona fides as an expert in trademark registrations. I had no such experience or credentials in the early 1980s, at the time of the creation of the documents of rights transfers about which I opined, and I have little more now. But I had then a good deal of experience in drafting, working with, and litigating the kinds of documents in question: contracts, powers of attorney, assignments and licenses. In fact, it was the majority of my work in my legal practice.

6. Until mid 1981, I was a partner at Manatt Phelps in Los Angeles, then the fastest growing law firm in the United States, now one of the most respected firms in California and the United States. http://www.manatt.com/AboutUs.aspx I was a litigation partner with emphasis on financial institutions and entertainment companies, and prosecuted litigation in a wide range of areas, but primarily concerning contracts, real estate, and intellectual property, including copyright and trademark infringement and misappropriation of name and likeness, the first and last of which bear directly on my experience and competence in the areas in question as discussed below. I litigated several copyright infringement cases in federal district court, including the *Lear* case,

discussed below. As to trademark, I litigated one trademark infringement case in federal district court in Los Angeles. I was a research assistant for two years to Professor J. Thomas McCarthy on the first edition of his trademark treatise, *McCarthy on Trademarks and Unfair Competition* (published by Thomson-Reuters-West) researching a variety of issues relating to US trademark law. (A link describing Prof. McCarthy and his work is http://www.mofo.com/J-McCarthy/.) I litigated appropriation of name and likeness cases for several years on behalf of an actor named Shaun Cassidy and a singer named Linda Ronstadt against Universal Studios and the Mars candy company, respectively, as well as several other such cases. After leaving Manatt Phelps, I served as Osho's personal attorney and as the attorney for Rajneesh Foundation International for a number of years as is described in my initial statement in this proceeding.

7. Limited relevance of documents of rights transfer. Those qualifications are relevant here only in light of Lotus' legal characterizations and conclusions concerning the document of rights transfer: 1) the 1982 Assignment and Amendment to Power of Attorney ("Assignment/Amendment") (Exhibit PT2 to my initial statement. A copy is made Exhibit 1 hereto for ready reference.), and; 2) the 1983 Assignment from the agent under the Assignment/Amendment to Rajneesh Foundation International ("RFI") (Exhibit PT3 to my initial statement. A copy is made Exhibit 2 hereto for ready reference.) While the US law of trademark has no relevance to the decision before this body, the documents of rights transfer, addressed at length at pp. 12-18 of the current Lotus brief, are of some, albeit limited, relevance to the issues to be decided in this proceeding. They are relevant to Osho's intent, efforts at the time to give effect to that intent in the legal documents created at the time, and the rights transferred thereunder. While I would not presume *to brief the law on EU trademark, I am well qualified to address the controlling* US law of contracts and copyright as it relates the documents in question, in contrast to Lotus' apparent and understandable lack of experience with or understanding of the US law of contracts and copyright. In any event, in my experience, we do not expect courts or administrative bodies to take our word for the state of the law. Because of this courts unfamiliarity with the body of US copyright and contract law, I will briefly set out the relevant authority.

8. Legal effect and authentication of documents of rights transfer. Lotus questions both our earlier legal discussion of the 1982 Assignment/Amendment and the 1983 Assignment as well as the authentication thereof. (See pp. 12-18 of Lotus brief of 4 January 2013.) I analyze the issues concerning the intent and validity of the documents under controlling US authority in the paragraphs immediately following. Lotus' questions re authentication are puzzling in light of the lack of a formal authentication requirement in this proceeding, as that has been reported to me, and Lotus' total failure to offer evidence authenticating any document offered by it, precious few as actual supporting documents are. On review of my earlier statement, I note that I did provide authentication though not that required by a court of law in the U.S., because of the lack of formal evidentiary requirements in this proceeding. More complete authentication is provided in the paragraphs below where the documents are specifically discussed. I trust this will satisfy Lotus' legal devotion to OIF authentication, though Lotus' commitment to authentication does not extend to the documents upon which it relies.

9. Lotus brief on legal effect of rights transfer documents. The Applicant's core legal analysis/criticism of the documents of transfer may be found at pages 11 and 12 of their brief, as follows: "The 'legal documents establishing Osho's intent to exclusively grant the exclusive use of his name as a trademark to entities which give effect to Osho's

intention' ...do not exist." "The alleged assignment of 'all copyrights, trade names, trademarks and any other property' by Osho in 1982 ...is irrelevant as it does not contain any assignment of IP rights. The 'assignment' language in this document relates to the purported 'transfer' of powers of attorney and is merely part of the alleged amendment to an earlier power of attorney. Intellectual property rights are mentioned only in the grant of powers. In addition, this document could concern only rights which already existed in 1982.... It is amazing that a person who alleges to have practiced as an attorney for over 40 years does not know a Power of Attorney from an Assignment and does not know that one cannot assign a right that does not exist...."

10. In sum, Lotus states that there is no valid assignment, that there was no grant of IP *rights, that no rights to future work can be validly transferred, and that I am an* incompetent liar to say so. We will review the facts and law to assess the correctness of Lotus' statements.

11. Primary relevance here is intent, not legal effect. While I will show that the US law is conclusive in establishing the legal effectiveness of the documents in question, please recall that the primary purpose in offering the documents was to show Osho's intention and that of the assignees with respect to the right to disseminate Osho's words and meditations and to use Osho's *name* in commerce in that work. *I will present the law to* be applied to the analysis, and then consider the documents in light of the applicable law. But first I will address Osho's intent and that of the agent/assignee and subsequent *rights owners.*

12. Osho's intent was to grant exclusive control over the use of his name to OIF's predecessors in interest. The 1982 Assignment/Amendment states specifically that it grants a power of attorney and is also an assignment of all the property addressed therein: "I execute this document to more completely state **my intention** to maintain my separation from worldly activities and **divestiture of all worldly possessions. My grant** of power and authority to Ma Anand Sheela **includes not only the power** to act for me, but also the **transfer and assignment** of all such power and authority..." *The document* further states that the grant of authority and assignment specifically includes: **"11. ...my name, likeness, writings, copyrights, trademarks, trademarks, and any other *property...to which I am now legally entitled or shall become entitled in the future* as if such things were her own...."**

13. Osho was aware of the transfer of rights to OIF and the work OIF done by OIF related thereto and never acted to withdraw or modify his clear and total disposition of those rights. In my legal work for OIF from 1986 to Osho's death in 1990, I was personally present and participated in conversations with Osho wherein it was clearly communicated and understood that the work which had been performed in the United States was now being performed by OIF, initially under its earlier name. Osho understood that leaving the United States in November of 1985 resulted in such changes, and he approved same. While Osho was involved in detailed discussion of the *legal reasons for the structural changes, or the details of the corporate structures*, he did understand that the structures were created and used to implement and control the dissemination of his work and the related use of his name and likeness.

14. Intent of subsequent assignor similarly clear. The 1983 Assignment by the agent appointed under the Assignment/Amendment is clear. It refers to the 1981 power of attorney and the 1982 Assignment/Amendment as the source of authority. It also refers

to the assignment of rights to the agent. It then states: **"I hereby grant, transfer and assign to Rajneesh Foundation International (OIF's predecessor in interest) absolutely any and all right, title and interest of any description which is or may remain vested as of this date in Bhagwan Shree Rajneesh, or which may be or become vested in the future with respect to His name, likeness, utterances, writings, copyrights, trademarks and/or tradenames..."** The grant is broad and unqualified and applies to present and future works.

15. <u>In drafting the documents of transfer, the broadest possible transfer possible was requested by Osho and given effect in the documents so drafted.</u> In drafting the documents, we were following Osho's stated instructions, which were stated by Osho in my presence, to draft the broadest and most complete transfer of present and future rights that was possible. That is what we did, and the 1982 Assignment/Amendment reflects that effort to comply with the stated wishes of the client, Osho. In including "trademark" as well as "name and likeness" in the documents, we were drafting as broadly as possible, **even though Osho personally was not using his name as a trademark. He was, however, giving permission to use his name as a trademark, by giving permission to use his name and likeness to the foundation which does *all trading of his assigned IP Rights and work.*** *(See legal discussion below in* paragraphs 16 through 23.)

16. A US federal court accepted the 1983 Assignment as valid and admissible evidence, and, in reliance thereon, granted Rajneesh Foundation International, OIF's predecessor in interest, a partial summary judgment ruling that Rajneesh Foundation International was the owner of all the registered copyrights. The case, *Lear v. Rajneesh Foundation International*, was earlier discussed in my initial statement. The court stated as a basis for its decision: **"Rajneesh (Foundation International) is the assignee of a properly recorded instrument giving it all rights, title, and interest in and to the copyrighted works of the Bhagwan."** The court was referring to Exhibit 2 hereto, PT3 to initial statement, which was submitted as evidence by me in the case. (The partial summary judgment was entered prior to the partial summary judgment offered as Exhibit PT4 to my initial statement in this proceeding. A true copy of the partial summary judgment of October 1, 1984, is made Exhibit 3 hereto. It was obtained from the US federal court archive. I can also personally authenticate the document as having been received by me by mail as attorney for Rajneesh Foundation International in the case shortly after the date thereof and reviewed by me at that time.) **Thus it is established that the parties considered the documents to be valid and binding, as did a U.S. federal court.**

17. <u>US law to be applied to interpretation of rights transfer documents.</u> The 1982 Assignment/Amendment was executed by a resident of Oregon, U.S. granting power and transferring ownership to a resident of Oregon, U.S. as stated in the document. The 1983 Assignment was made by an Oregon resident to a US corporation then based in Oregon. Both documents were prepared by attorneys in Oregon to address and comply with Oregon and US law. Under choice of law principles, US law must be applied to determine the legal effectiveness of the documents.

18. *<u>Facts and law require application of US law.</u> The contacts and underlying interests* discussed support the application of US law in evaluating the documents discussed. In contrast, Applicant has no contacts with or interest in the documents, nor does this body have any policy interest in applying the law of the EU to documents created in the US by

US residents. C.f. *International Contracts, Aspect of Jurisdiction, Arbitration and Private International Law*, multiple contributors, London Sweet & Maxwell 1996.

19. Certainly an Oregon court would apply Oregon law. "The contract was made in Oregon, and must be construed and enforced according to our laws." *Washington Nat. Bldg., Loan & Inv. Ass'n v. Stanley*, 38 Or. 319, 341, 63 P. 489 (1901)

20. Under US copyright law and Oregon contract law, future works are assignable. The law of copyright in the US is clear that under both copyright and contract law, rights to future works may be assigned. *Saregama India Ltd. v. Mosley*, 635 F.3d 1284, 1290-93 (11th Cir. 2011) is an appellate copyright case addressing the assignability of future copyrights under both US law and the law of India, which is relevant here because the only other country with significant contact to Osho personally is India. In *Saregama*, the Court stated: "We assume without deciding that Indian law governs the assignment issue, since Indian copyright law of assignment is strikingly similar to U.S. copyright law. We would reach the same result under either Indian or American law. Under the ICA (Indian Copyright Act of 1957), the assignment of copyright ownership is described in these terms: **"The owner of the copyright in an existing work or the prospective owner of *the copyright in a future work may assign to any person the copyright* either wholly or partially and either generally or subject to limitations and either for the whole term of the copyright or any part thereof: Provided that in the case of the assignment of copyright in any future work, the assignment shall take effect only when the work comes into existence."**

21. US and Oregon case authority support the broad right to assign. As noted by the court in *Seragama*, US copyright law is to the same effect as India law. The relevant US statute requires an assignment of copyright to be in "writing and signed by the owner of the rights conveyed or such owner's duly authorized agent." *17 U.S.C.A. 204 (a)*. As to the language of assignment, no particular form of assignment is required, and an assignment of copyright will be given effect where the intention is clear, especially where the terms" assignment" and "copyright" are used. *Radio Television Espanola S. A. v. New World entertainment Ltd.* (9th Cir. 1990) 183 F.3d 922, 926-927. Oregon case authority is consistent with federal law. As stated in *Levins v. Stark*, 57 Or. 189, 191, 110 P. 980, 981 (1910): "Any declaration, either in writing or by word of mouth, that a transfer is intended, will be effectual, providing it amounts to an appropriation to the assignee. In equity the rule is that anything showing an intention to assign on the one side, and from which an assent to receive may be inferred on the other, will operate as an assignment if sustained by a sufficient consideration. The form of words used in making the agreement is not alone to receive attention, but all the circumstances of the transaction are to be considered."

22. The 1982 Assignment/Amendment is effective to support subsequent1983 Assignment. Under Oregon law, a power of attorney creates an agency and the acts of the agent will be enforced when within the scope of authority granted in the power. **A power of attorney creates a form of agency, and is interpreted according to the law of agency and of contract**. *Scott v. Hall* (1945) 163 P.2d 517. While powers of attorney are strictly construed, **"the intention of the donor of the power is the great principle that governs.**" *Capps v. Mine Serv. (1944) 175 Or Reports 248, 252-3; Ying Loi Ho v. Presbyterian Church* (1992) 116 Or App 115. The broad and clear language of the power of attorney and amendment fully support the subsequent assignment.

23. <u>The 1982 Assignment/Amendment is also effective as an assignment under the authority set forth.</u> The document uses the words "assignment" and "copyright" as well as "name and likeness" and "trademark" and uses broad language of transfer. It is therefore effective to transfer by assignment any and all rights described.

24. <u>Osho's Last Will & Testament negates Lotus' contentions re invalidity of documents of transfer.</u> Though Lotus' claims against the validity of the documents of transfer are shown to be against the applicable law and without foundation, the vulnerability of any of the documents of transfer would not defeat Osho's clearly stated intention to transfer any and all property interests to the persons and entities he entrusted with his work. Osho left a Last Will & Testament, which was created to address the possibility that any of the earlier transfers would not be effective to divest him of all property interests, as had been his stated intention.

25. A true copy of Osho's Last Will & Testament, ("Osho's Will") executed on October 15, 1989, shortly before his death, a copy of which is provided herewith as Exhibit 4, clearly stated again his intention to transfer any and all property rights or interests he had to OIF. His will devises "all right, title and interest on any nature in any and all property *including but not limited to all ownership, publishing or related rights, to all my work...in any form...*" The breadth of the bequest is clearly sufficient to transfer any and all rights to use of his name and likeness, as well as all of his work.

26. <u>Authentication of Will.</u> I drafted the Will, and witnessed Osho's execution thereof, in the presence of the signing witnesses, as can be seen on the face of the document. The copy provided is a true and correct copy of the Will, and the signatures thereon were made by the persons so identified and were made on the date indicated on the document. Osho asked questions about the legal effect of the document prior to his execution thereof, and was unquestionably mentally alert and in full possession of his faculties at the time of execution.

27. <u>Lotus' statement, quoted above, is thus shown to be incorrect legally and incomprehensible as argument.</u> **The 1982 Assignment/Amendment granted authority and assigned rights to present and future copyrights, name and likeness, trademarks and all other property rights. The 1983 assignment further assigned said rights as authorized. The language of the documents is clear and the law fully supports the actions taken.**

28. <u>While Osho did not use his name as a trademark, he was acting to protect and control that use by others in executing the 1982 Assignment/Amendment including the assignment and authority to use of his name and likeness.</u> And, as stated earlier, Osho was clear with OIF about how he wanted the name used and presented, which as trademark owner, they did. The attorneys included the right in amendment/assignment in light of US law on the subject. Lotus repeats again and again that Osho never used his name as a trademark. True, but not probative to show he did not transfer the right to use his name as a trademark in the Assignment/Amendment.

29. <u>Appropriation of name and likeness is a statutory and common law tort in the US, akin to *trademark*. Under that body of law, permission must be obtained to use the name of a person in connection with the sale of a product or service.</u> "Personality rights are generally considered to consist of two types of rights: **the right of publicity, or to keep one's image and likeness from being commercially exploited without permission**

or contractual compensation, which is similar to the use of a trademark; and the right to privacy, or the right to be left alone and not have one's personality represented publicly without permission. In common law jurisdictions, publicity rights fall into the realm of the tort of passing off. United States jurisprudence has substantially extended this right." Wikipedia article on publicity rights, https://en.wikipedia.org/wiki/Personality_rights. *Many states have passed statutes to* prevent such appropriation. **Cal.Civ.Code § 3344 provides that: "Any person who knowingly uses another's name, voice, signature, photograph, or likeness, in any manner, on or in products, merchandise, or goods, or for purposes of advertising or selling, or soliciting purchases of, products, merchandise, goods or services, without such person's prior consent, or, in the case of a minor, the prior consent of his parent or legal guardian, shall be liable for any damages sustained by the person or persons injured as a result thereof.**" "A common law cause of action for **appropriation of name or likeness may be pleaded by alleging (1) the defendant's use of the plaintiff's identity; (2) the appropriation of plaintiff's name or likeness to defendant's advantage, commercially or otherwise; (3) lack of consent; and (4) resulting injury**. (See Prosser, *Law of Torts* (4th ed. 1971) § 117, pp. 804–807; Witkin, *Cal. Procedure* (2d ed. 1971) Pleading, § 606, p. 2244.)" *Eastwood v. Superior Court*, 149 Cal. App. 3d 409, 417, 198 Cal. Rptr. 342, 347 (Ct. App. 1983)

30. Lotus categorically states: "...there was never a trademark "Rajneesh", and no trademark *"OSHO" before 1999." Lotus brief, p. 11. This statement is categorically* false – shown for example by existing TM registrations of 'Rajneesh' already in 1978 in Germany (Exhibit No. K56). I stated in my initial statement: "The names OSHO and RAJNEESH were always understood to be trademarks during the period of my representation, and were consistently so used in the ongoing publication and dissemination of Osho's works during the time of my representation." That was and is my understanding. And my understanding, then and now, is that in the US a trademark may be established by use even without registration. While the earlier US proceeding is irrelevant to the determination of this body, it is relevant that an unregistered trademark could exist in the US. The names were used to identify the source of Osho's work and were clearly a brand for products and services. It is an uncomfortable admission that my understanding of US law in this respect may have delayed the registrations in the EU and around the world.

The statements made herein are from my personal knowledge and I know all of the statements to be true.

Philip Toelkes Date: June 4, 2013

NICOLE CICCOLO
GRAPHOLOGICAL TECHNICAL EXPERT AND CONSULTANT OF THE CIVIL AND PENAL LAW COURT OF BOLOGNA
TEACHER OF EXPERT TECHNIQUES AT THE ADVANCED SCHOOL OF GRAPHOLOGY AGAS
MEMBER OF THE ASSOCIATION OF PROFESSIONAL GRAPHOLOGISTS
REGULATED BY LAW NO.4/2013
VIA RIVA DI RENO N.11 – 40121 BOLOGNA

INTEGRATION TO A TECHNICAL EXAMINATION REPORT

ON THE WILL DATED 15TH OCTOBER 1989 BEARING THE SIGNATURE "OSHO"

**** * ****

I, the undersigned Nicole Ciccolo, graphologist, registered in the List of Technical Consultants of the Civil and Penal Law Court of Bologna, and member of the Association of Professional Graphologists, regulated by Law No. 4/2013, have been entrusted by Mr. Alvaro Ruffo della Scaletta and Mrs. Vaidehe Vadgama to integrate my previous report, written in Bologna on 13.10.2013, with a technical examination aiming to ascertain:

- whether the signature bearing the name "Osho" printed on the dust-jacket of the book published in 1976 and entitled **"Yoga: the alpha and the omega" Volume 5,** is the same signature used in the will dated 15th October 1989 Poona – India **(produced as a photostat byKeltie LLP, London, UK, on 07/06/2013 at OHIM – Office for Harmonization in the Internal Market (TradeMarks and Designs), Avenida de Europa 4, E-03008 Alicante, Spain. References: Community Trade Mark Registration No. 1224831 OSHO in the name of Osho International Foundation – and -Application for invalidity No. 5064 thereto by Osho Lotus Comune e.V.)**

- moreover, whether it is possible to ascertain the date of the book **"Yoga: the alpha and the omega" Volume 5**verifying whether it was really printed in the

1970s, that is before 1989, the year reported in the will bearing the signature "Osho".

DOCUMENTS EXAMINED

*****

ENCLOSURE 1

WILL DATED 15TH OCTOBER 1989-POONA-INDIA

A copy of the will was submitted, which consists of 26 typewritten lines. At the end there is the signature to check, bearing the name "Osho".

ENCLOSURE 2

DUST-JACKET OF THE BOOK "*YOGA:THE ALPHA AND OMEGA*" VOLUME 5;

COPYRIGHT OF THE BOOK "*YOGA:THE ALPHA AND OMEGA*" VOLUME 5;

ENCLOSURE 3

TECHNICAL EXAMINATION REPORT BY FRANCESCO BORDONI, EXPERT OF THE TECHNICAL GRAPHIC SECTOR OF THE PENAL AND CIVIL COURT OF MILAN (No.8089).

As far as the first task is concerned, an analysis and a systematic comparison of the signature bearing the name "Osho" at the bottom of the will dated 15th October 1989 Poona-India and the signature at the end of the letter printed on the back side of the dust-jacket of the book **"Yoga: the alpha and the omega" Volume 5,** makes it possible to ascertain, without any reasonable doubt, that all the engrams are identical and perfectly overlap. A universally accepted graphological axiom states that there cannot be two identical signatures, therefore the signature bearing the name "Osho" at the bottom of the will is apocryphal and was executed by means of a photographic montage.

In addition to this, the same handwritten letter by Osho which bears the signature used in the false will at the bottom was already detected and examined in my previous technical examination report, having found it in the following website:

http://images.search.yahoo.com/search/images?_adv_prop=image&fr=yfp- t-303&va=osho+art+signatures.

MORE SPECIFICALLY, THE HANDWRITTEN LETTER BY OSHO DATED 1976 BEARING A SIGNATURE AT THE BOTTOM WAS PUBLISHED IN AT LEAST TWO INTERNET SITES, THEREFORE IT HAS PROVED EASY TO FIND FOR MAKING THE FALSE WILL.

The handwritten letter by Osho can also be found in the following Internet site:

http://famous-photos2.blogspot.it/2012/03/handwriting-of-acharya-rajneesh-osho.html

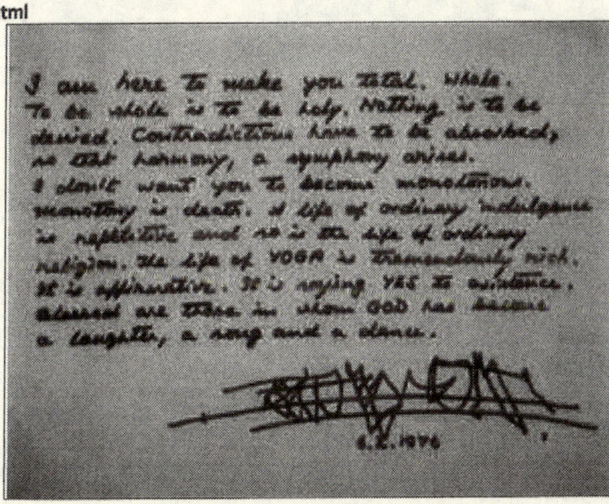

I am here to make you total, whole.
To be whole is to be holy. Nothing is to be denied. Contradictions have to be absorbed, so that harmony, a symphony arises.
I don't want you to become monotonous. monotony is death. A life of ordinary indulgence is repetitive and so is the life of ordinary religion. The life of YOGA is tremendously rich. It is affirmative. It is saying YES to existence. Blessed are those in whom GOD has become a laughter, a song and a dance.

6.2.1976

excerpt of the handwritten letter, written and signed by Osho in 1976 and published in the Internet site.

DUST-COVER OF THE BOOK "YOGA THE ALPHA & THE OMEGA" WITH OSHO'S LETTER PRINTED ON THE BACK SIDE.

Osho's signature printed on the back side of the dust-jacket of the book **"Yoga: the alpha and the omega" Volume 5. Published in 1976.**

signature to be examined, bearing the name "Osho", at the bottom of the will dated 15th October 1989 Poona-India.

MARCA DA BOLLO
Ministero dell'Economia
e delle Finanze
€16,00
SEDICI/00
Agenzia
Entrate
00022110 000052CA W0ZU8001
00021784 03/11/2014 14:46:29
4578-00088 3C4D6ADDA9ADE2F4
IDENTIFICATIVO : 01130428523091
0 1 11 042852 309 1

NALE CIVILE

It should be noted that in the signatures chosen for the comparison graphic groups characterised by a sequence of various shapes overlap perfectly and are perfectly identical to each other. This makes it possible to state, without any reasonable doubt, that the signature bearing the name "Osho" at the bottom of the will is false. **<u>This statement is technically certain, since it is a proven fake</u>.**

As far as the investigation of the date of the dust-cover of the book **"Yoga: the alpha& the omega" Volume 5** is concerned, I entrusted an expert, Francesco Bordoni, expert of the technical graphic sector, with this task. His whole technical examination report can be found in ENCLOSURE 3.

Francesco Bordoni's conclusions make it possible to state that **the dust-jacket of the book "Yoga the alpha and the omega – volume V" was produced in 1976, as reported in the colophon of the book in question.**

<u>FINAL EVALUATIONS</u>

*** * ***

IN THE LIGHT OF THE ABOVE OBSERVATIONS AND THE RESULTS OF THE EXPERT'S ANALYSIS, IT MAY BE CONCLUDED THAT:

- THE SIGNATURE BEARING THE NAME "OSHO" AT THE BOTTOM OF THE WILL IS THE SAME SIGNATURE WHICH IS PRINTED ON THE DUST-JACKET OF THE BOOK PUBLISHED IN 1976 AND BEARING THE TITLE "YOGA:THE ALPHA &THE OMEGA" VOLUME 5.
- THE ANALYSES CARRIED OUT BY FRANCESCO BORDONI MAKE IT POSSIBLE TO ASCERTAIN THAT THE DUST-JACKET OF THE BOOK "YOGA THE ALPHA AND THE OMEGA-VOLUME 5" WAS PRODUCED IN 1976, AS REPORTED IN THE COLOPHON OF THE BOOK ITSELF. (ENCLOSURE 3)

Bologna, 28.10.2014

In witness thereof

The Technical Consultant

Nicole Ciccolo

ENCLOSURE 1

WILL DATED 15TH OCTOBER 1989-POONA-INDIA

10 Rs

16 JUN 1989

CHAMPAKLAL D. SHAH
ADVOCATE & SOLICITOR
BOMBAY

LAST WILL & TESTAMENT
of OSHO

RECITAL. In 1975, 1978 and 1981, I executed assignments concerning my work. Also in 1981, I executed a broad power of attorney with the stated intention to divest myself of all worldly property, and also an amendment in 1982, with the result that all such property is now owned by Neo Sannyas International Foundation, a Swiss charitable entity. To be completely certain that all such property interests are so divested, I make this Last Will and Testament.

LAST WILL & TESTAMENT. Being of sound mind, and acting of my free will, I make this Last Will and Testament.

I, Osho, birth name Chandra Mohan Jain, formerly known as Bhagwan Shree Rajneesh, hereby devise and bequest any and all right, title or interest of any nature in any and all property of any nature and in any form, owned by me, now or in the future, including but not limited to, all ownership, publishing or related rights, to all my work, published to date or in the future, in any form, to Neo Sannyas International Foundation.

If for any reason that entity cannot or does not accept this bequest then the alternate beneficiary shall be a non-profit, charitable entity dedicated to the dissemination of my work, such entity to be designated by my executor.

EXECUTOR. I name as my executor Sw. Anand Jayesh, aka Michael O'Byrne.

Executed this 15th day of October, 1989, at Poona, India.

Osho

LAST WILL & TESTAMENT
of OSHO
(page 2.)

I agree to serve as Executor.

_______________ Sw. Anand Jayesh

_______________ aka Michael O'Byrne

Executed on October 15, 1989, at Poona, India.

ATTESTATION. We, the undersigned have witnessed the signatures of Osho and Sw. Anand Jayesh and each other, to this document on October 15, 1989.

_______________ Sw. Amrito

_______________ aka John Andrews

_______________ Sw. Prem Niren

_______________ aka Philip Toelkes

Ministero dell'Economia e delle Finanze
MARCA DA BOLLO
€16,00
SEDICI/00
Agenzia Entrate
00022110 000052CA WDZUB001
00021782 03/11/2014 14:46:20
4578-00088 45B8684ED3AE7950
IDENTIFICATIVO : 01130428523115
0 1 13 042852 311 5

TRIBUNALE CIVILE E PENALE

TRIBUNALE CIVILE E PENALE

ENCLOSURE 2

DUST-JACKET OF THE BOOK "*YOGA:THE ALPHA AND OMEGA*" VOLUME 5
COPYRIGHT OF THE BOOK "*YOGA:THE ALPHA AND OMEGA*" VOLUME 5

I am here to make you total, whole.
To be whole is to be holy. Nothing is to be denied. Contradictions have to be absorbed, so that harmony, a symphony arises.
I don't want you to become monotonous. Monotony is death. A life of ordinary indulgence is repetitive and so is the life of ordinary religion. The life of YOGA is tremendously rich. It is affirmative. It is saying YES to existence. Blessed are those in whom GOD has become a laughter, a song and a dance.
YOGA alpha & the omega
5
BHAGWAN SHREE RAJNEESH
BHAGWAN SHREE RAJNEESH
talks on the YOGA SUTRAS of PA
YOGA the alpha & the omeg
VOLUME V

Copyright
United States Copyright Office

Help | Search | History | Titles | Start Over

Public Catalog

Copyright Catalog (1978 to present)
Search Request: Left Anchored Title = Yoga:the alpha and the omega
Search Results: Displaying 10 of 89 entries

previous | next

Labeled View

Yoga : the alpha and the omega : v. 5 : discourses on the Yoga sutras of...

Type of Work: Text
Registration Number / Date: TX0001092120 / 1982-10-19
Title: Yoga : the alpha and the omega : v. 5 : discourses on the Yoga sutras of Patanjali / Bhagwan Shree Rajneesh ; [compiled and edited by Swami Prem Chinmaya].
Edition: 1st ed.
Imprint: Poona, India : Rajneesh Foundation, 1976.
Description: 252 p.
Copyright Claimant: Rajneesh Foundation
Date of Creation: 1975
Date of Publication: 1976-07-17
Copyright Note: C.O. correspondence.
Variant title: Yoga : the alpha and the omega : v. 5
Names: Prem Chinmaya, Swami
Rajneesh, Bhagwan Shree, 1931-
Rajneesh Foundation

previous | next

Save, Print and Email (Help Page)
Select Download Format: Full Record ▾ Format for Print/Save
Enter your email address: Email

Help Search History Titles Start Over

Contact Us | Request Copies | Get a Search Estimate | Frequently Asked Questions (FAQs) about Copyright | Copyright Office Home Page | Library of Congress Home Page

ENCLOSURE 3

TECHNICAL EXAMINATION REPORT BY FRANCESCO BORDONI, EXPERT OF THE TECHNICAL GRAPHIC SECTOR OF THE PENAL AND CIVIL COURT OF MILAN (No.8089)

Ministero dell'Economia
e delle Finanze
MARCA DA BOLLO
€16,00
SEDICI/00
Agenzia Entrate
00022110 000052CA W0ZUB001
00021781 03/11/2014 14:46:15
4578-00088 37086F3F11DZE066
IDENTIFICATIVO : 01130428523126
0 1 13 042852 312 6

francesco bordoni
ex teacher of chromatology, industrial systems, graphic technology
Registered in the Roll or Experts of the PENAL
AND CIVIL COURT OF MILAN under No. 8089
with a specialisation in the TECHNICAL GRAPHIC SECTOR

Registered office: p.le Lagosta 2 – Milan, Italy
Operating address: c/o Ci. Ti. O. s.a.s.
36060 Romano d'Ezzelino (VI)
via Don Giovanni Minzoni 19
tel. +39 0424 501884 - fax +39 0424 501624
mobile: +39 335 6536604
e-mail: bordoni.perizie@citio.eu

VAT Number 07388533015 1 – Fiscal code: BRDFNC51R11F205T – Chamber of Commerce, Industry, Crafts and Agriculture (MI) 30-0001317

I, the undersigned Francesco Bordoni, registered in the Roll of Experts of the Technical Graphic Sector of the Penal and Civil Court of Milan under number 8089, upon request by Nicole Ciccolo, Graphological Expert at the Civil and Penal Court of Bologna, living and registered in via Riva Reno n 11, 40122 Bologna, as an assistant of the Court Graphologist who entrusted me with this task, have drafted this

TECHNICAL EXAMINATION REPORT

bearing the following title:

dating of the print on the jacket of the book "Yoga the alpha and the omega – volume V"

The book has the following characteristics:

- size closed: 150mm x 225mm (size of the cover)
- 264 pages plus endpapers, plus cover, plus jacket
- print inside the book: 1 colour on the recto (black) and 1 colour on the verso (black) with an offset lithographic printing process
- photograph printed by means of an offset lithographic process, with a four-colour process, enamelled print, the photograph was printed separately (not at the same time as the signatures in the book) and glued on the left page of the book title page
- hardbound cover, covered with silk-like cloth, printed with 1 colour (black)
- jacket print with 5 colours (four-colour process + orange) only on the recto, with an offset lithographic process
- plastic-coated jacket
- book thread stitching with red headbands

The book in question is shown in a photograph below:

francesco bordoni
ex teacher of chromatology, industrial systems, graphic technology
Registered in the Roll or Experts of the PENAL AND CIVIL COURT OF MILAN under No. 8089 with a specialisation in the TECHNICAL GRAPHIC SECTOR

Registered office: p.le Lagosta 2 – Milan, Italy
Operating address: c/o Ci. Ti. O. s.a.s.
36060 Romano d'Ezzelino (VI)
via Don Giovanni Minzoni 19
tel. +39 0424 501884 - fax +39 0424 501624
mobile: +39 335 6536604
e-mail: bordoni.perizie@citio.eu

VAT Number 07388533O151 – Fiscal code: BRDFNC51R11F205T – Chamber of Commerce, Industry, Crafts and Agriculture (MI) 30-0001317

Method of analysis

In order to carry out the task I was entrusted with by the Court Graphological Expert, that is the purpose of this technical examination report, namely to ascertain the period when the book jacket was produced, I applied the following method:

1.- the printing date reported in the book in question was checked;

2.- the technology used for producing the body of the book (inner part of the book) was checked;

3.- the technology used for producing the jacket was checked;

4.- a comparison was made with printed matters produced after the printing of the book in question.

I believe this methodology to be objective, since it makes it possible to identify the period when the book in question was produced objectively, due to the evolution of technologies and the subsequent disappearance of previous technologies. Moreover, the geographic location of the printers ensures the use of certain precise technologies through the years.

1.- Printing date reported in the book in question;

The book in question reports "1976" as its printing date, as shown in the photograph below, which reproduces page "iv" (not numbered):

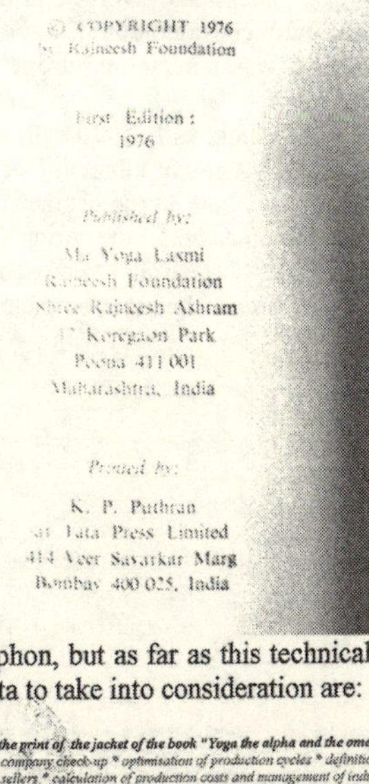

© COPYRIGHT 1976
by Rajneesh Foundation

First Edition :
1976

Published by:

Ma Yoga Laxmi
Rajneesh Foundation
Shree Rajneesh Ashram
17 Koregaon Park
Poona 411 001
Maharashtra, India

Printed by:

K. P. Puthran
at Tata Press Limited
414 Veer Savarkar Marg
Bombay 400 025, India

The page reports the full colophon, but as far as this technical examination report is concerned, the fundamental data to take into consideration are:

francesco bordoni
ex teacher of chromatology, industrial systems, graphic technology
Registered in the Roll or Experts of the PENAL
AND CIVIL COURT OF MILAN under No. 8089
with a specialisation in the TECHNICAL GRAPHIC SECTOR

Registered office: p.le Lagosta 2 – Milan, Italy
Operating address: c/o Ci. Ti. O. s.a.s.
36060 Romano d'Ezzelino (VI)
via Don Giovanni Minzoni 19
tel. +39 0424 501884 - fax +39 0424 501624
mobile: +39 335 6536604
e-mail: bordoni.perizie@citio.eu

VAT Number 07388533015 1 – Fiscal code: BRDFNC51R11F205T – Chamber of Commerce, Industry, Crafts and Agriculture (MI) 30-0001317

a.- the book was printed in India (Printed by K.P. Puthran at Tata Press Limited, ... *omissis* ..., Bombay 400 025, India);
b.- the book copyright dates back to 1976 (copyright 1976 by Rajneesh Foundation);
c.- the first edition of the book was in "1976" (First Edition: 1976).

This information says that the book was printed in 1976, or at least this is what is specified in the colophon.

2.- Technology used for producing the body of the book (inner part of the book)

For producing the book, prepress, printing and packaging technologies were used. From a visual point of view, packaging technologies have not changed in the last 50 years, therefore it is extremely difficult to identify the date of a fold, stitching, cover. Conversely, prepress and printing technologies have changed remarkably, therefore the examination focused on these processes.

In the early 1970s, the prepress process was exclusively photomechanical and manual. Reproducing a photograph in the press was a complex process, whose results were rather far from the contemporary ones.

In order to perform a printing operation, it is necessary to make printing plates which will have to be inserted into the printing press. Through the years, technologies for producing printing plates have evolved enormously. In addition to this, technologies for making printing plates have evolved in different ways in different geographic areas. If we take into consideration Europe, the United States, Asia (excluding Japan), the evolution was similar in Europe and the United States, whereas Asia (again, excluding Japan) lagged decades behind the other two above-mentioned Continents. In the 1960s and early 1970s, the method for making printing plates was based on the chemical incision of bimetallic or trimetallic plates. Therefore, chemical incisions were imprecise, both in the characters of their texts and in the halftones of the images. In order to check the printed matter in question, I made some photographs using a 320X electronic microscope (320 magnification). A microscope photograph of part of a text character on page 163 of the book in question is shown below.

16

The Need for a SIT

Osho died in extremely tragic circumstances and the possibility that he was murdered cannot be ruled out. There are far too many inconsistencies in the official version of Osho's death, too many contradictions and damning eye-witness accounts which cannot be ignored or wished away.

"How does it matter now?" asked Satya Vedant, one of the highly accomplished disciples of Osho who had spent the best years of his life in the Master's shadow. There was helplessness and a sense of resignation in his voice. Life for him, and thousands others like him, had moved on. They felt there was little they could do now and they had reconciled themselves with the past. There was, nevertheless, a lingering sorrow and unrest in the soul because the story of Osho's death was still awaiting closure.

"This is why it matters," the author told him, because what has been told to the world, what has been presented officially as the story of Osho's death, could be a big lie. Would it be right to want to perpetuate and leave behind a lie for posterity?

There are too many loopholes in the official narrative of Osho's death for people to believe that Osho died naturally and peacefully on January 19, 1990. There are so many questions that need to be answered: Why was the doctor who issued his Death Certificate not allowed to see him? Why was Osho cremated in a tearing hurry? What about Osho's Will that surfaced after 23 years of his death, mentioning Jayesh as the executor of the Will and Amrito as one of the witnesses? This Will which has been examined forensically and found to be a forged document was presented by the OIF-Zürich while fighting a trademark case in a European Court. It was withdrawn after a public uproar that it was a forged document. How can the people who presented this allegedly forged document continue to run the public charitable trust that ought to have been headquartered in Pune?

In addition to Osho's death, there was the unnatural demise of his former girlfriend and caretaker Nirvano which was suppressed by the Commune in an extremely crass manner. Why? Why was she cremated in a hurry? What explains the gross discrepancies in her name in the records of the Pune Police and the Pune Municipal Corporation?

It has been 27 years since Osho's death. Most of his followers who stood by him courageously, as young men and women in the 1960s and '70s, have either passed on or are in their late 60s, 70s and 80s. For the sake of thousands of Osho's followers the world over, for the sake of history and for the sake of truth and justice, the truth behind Osho's death, that has eluded people all these years, needs to be firmly established.

This truth can emerge only if fresh investigations are undertaken by a court-appointed Special Investigations Team.

Endnotes

Chapter 1: Osho's Death: A Fairy Tale Account?

1. Khushwant Singh, 'Foreword,' in *Life's Mysteries: An Introduction to the Teachings of Osho*, 1995), pp. 15–16.
2. Human Growth Potential Movement: This movement became popular in the U.S. in the 1960s and grew out of the "Humanistic Psychology" school which was distinct from other schools of psychology such as Behaviourism and Psychoanalysis. The Human Potential Movement sought to free the mind of its conditioning to reach the highest capabilities of creativity, happiness and fulfillment in individuals. The leaders and practitioners of this school did not hesitate to experiment with drugs to explore the other dimensions of the human mind. The Esalen Institute in California was the hub of this movement. In the late 1960–early 1970s, Osho's Dynamic Meditation and other meditation techniques which had a strong component of catharsis, and his assertion that sex could be a path towards super-consciousness caught the attention of the leading practitioners of the Human Growth Potential Movement

in the West. Many of them came to Pune, took sannyas and experimented with several individual and group therapies during Poona-I.

3. Ma Chetan Unmani and Swami Chaitanya Keerti, "Vision 2000: Interview with Ma Garimo, coordinator of Osho 2000 Festival," in *Allah to Zen—An insight into the world of Osho: The Real Man of the Millennium*, ed. Ma Chetan Unmani and Swami Chaitanya Keerti, New Delhi: Diamond Pocket Books, 2000, p.21.
4. Neo Sannyas or 'Nav Sannyas' as Osho called it: An important concept in Hinduism, *'sannyas'* which originates in Sanskrit, means renouncing worldly life in the pursuit of the ultimate truth. He turned the concept of sannyas upside down by saying that his sannyasins would not abandon the world but lead a worldly existence while seeking to pursue the truth. As a part of their initiation into the Neo Sannayas Movement, they were given a new sannyas name, mostly Sanskrit in its origins. They were committed to wearing ochre robes and a beaded *mala* with a locket bearing Osho's picture.
5. George Ivanovitch Gurdjieff (1877?-Oct. 29, 1949) was a Greco-Armenian mystic and philosopher. He held that man lives and dies in sleep which he called "waking sleep" and that each individual has to work upon himself to awaken his consciousness. Gurdjieff composed sacred dance forms with music, called "Movements". Swami Anand Lokesh, one of Osho's earliest followers since 1975 wrote: "Osho was greatly inspired by Gurdjieff and many times he spoke highly of him. Osho was not the kind of speaker who often revealed the sources of the material he used to help compose his discourses or add to

his often radical ideas. Had he done so he would certainly have mentioned *The Chronicles*," sannyasnews.org, http://sannyasnews.org/now/archives/3669.

6. Ma Prem Shunyo, *My Diamond Days With Osho*, New Delhi, Full Circle, 1999, p.7.
7. Pierre Evald, "Part One: Raja Rajneesh,"*OSHO Source Book: A bio-bibliography 1931-1974*, www.oshosourcebook.com, p.25.
8. Evald, *OSHO Source Book: A bio-bibliography 1931-1974*, p.47.
9. *Ibid.*, p.47
10. *Ibid.*, p.27
11. Vasant Joshi, *Osho, The Luminous Rebel: Life Story of a Maverick Mystic*, New Delhi, 2010, p.30.
12. Pierre Evald, *op. cit.*, p.38.
13. *Ibid.*,p.140.
14. *Ibid.*, p.143.
15. Vasant Joshi, *op. cit.*,p.96.
16. Ma Yoga Laxmi, *The Journey of the Hear*t http://www.sannyas.wiki/index.php?title=Ma_Yoga_Laxmi, p. 22.
17. *Ibid.*, p. 26.
18. *Ibid.*, p. 35.

Chapter 2: Poona-I: A Commune Is Established

1. Located 190 km southeast of Mumbai, the name of the city Poona changed to Pune in 1978.
2. 'Dynamic Meditation' was among the earliest and the most popular forms of meditations devised by Osho. The Osho Commune International Press Office described 'Osho's

Approach to Meditation' in a detailed press note issued in October, 1989:

Osho describes meditation as "the first and last freedom", the key to self transformation. He emphasises the use of active meditations in which the stillness and silence traditionally associated with meditation are preceded by dynamic physical activity. This may sound like a contradiction. Activity and meditation? What have they to do with each other? But this unusual combination reflects Osho's insight that meditation is essentially an energy phenomenon, and that the basic law of energy is that it moves from one polarity to the opposite.

DYNAMIC MEDITATION: Nowhere is this understanding better demonstrated than in Dynamic Meditation, a unique method developed by Osho and used by his disciples for many years. "Dynamic Meditation is a contradiction," he explains. "Dynamic means effort, much effort. And meditation means silence, no effort, no activity." Like most meditations developed by Osho, Dynamic lasts one hour. It begins with three active stages, each lasting ten minutes:

Stage one: Breathing deeply and rapidly in and out through the nose, concentrating on the exhalation. This builds up a tremendous pressure of energy inside the body.

Stage two: Releasing the energy in catharsis, using the voice and the body to let go of everything that needs to be thrown out.

Stage three: Jumping up and down, with one's arms raised above the head, shouting the mantra "Hoo! Hoo! Hoo!"

This completes the three active stages. At the word "Stop!" the meditators freeze in whatever position they find themselves. For 15 minutes they watch everything that is happening to them: thoughts racing through the mind, emotions pounding in the heart, heat flooding the body after so much effort. This state of watching is known as "witnessing"—the art of being a silent observer to everything that is going on inside yourself, and outside, without opinion or judgement. This process creates a distance between the witnessing consciousness and the mind, emotions and body, bringing the meditator to the centre of being.

The final stage of Dynamic lasts 15 minutes and is devoted to dance as an expression of gratitude for whatever has happened during the meditation.

KUNDALINI MEDITATION: Another popular form of active meditation devised by Osho is Kundalini Meditation. This is usually done in the evening, at sunset, while Dynamic is usually done in the early morning. Kundalini lasts one hour and has four stages:

Stage one: Shaking your body in a relaxed yet total way, so that you are taken over by the shaking.

Stage two: Dancing, letting the body move as it wishes.

Stage three: Sitting or standing still, eyes closed, witnessing.

Stage four: Lying down with eyes closed, being still.

THE MYSTIC ROSE MEDITATION: In April 1988, Osho developed the Mystic Rose Meditation. He called it "the greatest breakthrough in meditation in 2,500 years, since Gautama the Buddha's Vipassana Meditation." Thousands of people have now participated in the Mystic Rose Meditation, not only at the commune in Poona, but also at Osho Meditation Centres around the world. "I have invented many meditations, but this will be perhaps the most essential and fundamental one. It can take over the whole world."

The meditation lasts for 21 days, as follows: one week of laughing for three hours a day, one week of crying for three hours a day, and one week of watching or witnessing for three hours a day.

During the first two stages, the participants simply laugh and cry for no reason at all, breaking through the layers of inhibitions, repression, and pain. This clears a space where silent witnessing can happen. After the cleansing of laughter and tears, it is easier not to become identified with or lost in whatever comes by: thoughts, emotions, body sensations.

As Osho explains it: "The whole of humanity has gone a little cuckoo for the simple reason that nobody laughs fully. And you have suppressed so much sadness, so much despair and anxiety, so many tears, they are all there, covering you and destroying your beauty, your grace, your joy. What has to be done is to break through these two layers. Then the witnessing simply opens a pure sky."

Medical science has recognised that laughing and crying are immensely healthful, not only physically but also psychologically. Scientific studies done during and after the Mystic Rose Meditation groups reveal that participants experience profound and lasting changes in many dimensions of their lives. These include a deep inner relaxation, improvement in a wide variety of psychosomatic conditions, and a greater ability to feel and express their emotions in daily life and at the same time to be detached from these emotions—to become a witness to their experiences.

NO MIND MEDITATION: No Mind is a two-hour meditation with two stages. In the first stage, which lasts one hour, participants talk continuous nonsense, emptying the mind of accumulated garbage. There is no contact between participants. In the second stage, they sit silently, eyes closed, witnessing everything that happens.

BORN AGAIN MEDITATION: Born Again is also a two-hour meditation with two stages. During the first stage, which lasts one hour, participants re-enact their early childhood, playing, giggling, kicking, rolling around. There is no contact between participants. In the second stage, participants sit silently, with closed eyes, silently witnessing.

Osho Commune International Press Office, "Factsheet, 'Osho's Approach to Meditation'," (Pune, October, 1989)

3. Satya Niranjan (P.C. Bagmar), *I Leave You My Dream... Osho Memoirs*, Pune: Sakshi Publications, 2012, p. 77.

4. Iain McNay, "Clare Soloway 1—'Life Changes'—Interviewed by Iain McNay," conscious.tv, https://www.youtube.com/watch?v=TCBP1wlsMMo
5. George Meredith, *Bhagwan: The Most Godless Yet The Most Godly*, Poona: The Rebel Publishing House, 1987, p.62.
6. *Ibid.*, p.65.
7. *Ibid.*, pp. 41–42.
8. *Ibid.*, p.44.
9. Hugh Milne, *Bhagwan: The God That Failed*, London: Caliban Books, 1986, p. 160.
10. Ma Anand Sheela, *Don't Kill Him: The Story of My Life With Bhagwan Rajneesh*, New Delhi, Fingerprint, 2012, pp. 171–172.
11. Vasant Joshi, *op. cit.*, p.143.

Chapter 3: The Lure of the United States

1. Biographical note on Osho "Factsheet—Biography of Osho" released by Osho Commune International Press Office, October, 1989.
2. Testimony by Ma Prem Hasya before the Wasco County Grand Jury on October 15, 1985
3. Criminal trial testimony of Swami Krishna Deva, Mayor of Rajneeshpuram, also known as David Knapp and 'K.D.' before the U.S. District Court in Portland. https://commons.wikimedia.org/wiki/File:Criminal_trial_testimony_of_Rajneesh_member_David_Knapp.pdf
4. Ma Dharm Jyoti's interview with the author at Osho Dham, New Delhi on 17 February 2016.
5. Ric Dolphin, "Jayesh Michael O'Byrne,"*Saturday Night* magazine, February 1997, http://www.n0by.de/2/rst/jayesh.htm

6. "Rajneesh and company pull up stakes from Oregon as guru's vision in desert becomes a mirage", *The Oregonian/ OregonLive*, 30 December, 1985.

Chapter 4: Poona-II: A Reluctant Retreat

1. Ma Prem Shunyo, *op. cit.*, pp.134.
2. *Ibid.*, p.138. Vasant Joshi writes on page 189 of his book *Osho The Luminous Rebel: Life Story of a Maverick Mystic* that "Kulu-Manali was not the place to receive expert medical advice" and unease about Osho's health grew among Osho's doctor and caretaker.
3. Vasant Joshi, *op.cit.*, p.211.
4. Ma Prem Shunyo, *op. cit.*, p. 198 and p.163.

Chapter 5: The 1989 Coterie: Jayesh, Amrito & Anando

1. Ma Anand Sheela, *op. cit.*, pp. 35–38.
2. Antar Navjot, "20 May, 1989 Migraines", Blog: *A Year in Lao Tzu—1989*, https://orangegirloklaotzu.wordpress.com/2016/01/21/20-may-1989-migraines/
3. Ma Prem Shunyo, *op. cit.*, p.10.
4. Witness Statement, Klaus Steeg before EUIPO on July 6, 2011.
5. Witness Statement by Jayesh before EUIPO on July 19, 2011.
6. Ma Anand Bhagwati, *Creating a Vision for the Himalaya of Kumaon*, Osho World Online Magazine, January 2012, http://www.oshoworld.com/onlinemag/jan12/htm/Media_Watch.asp

7. Swami Prem Amrito, Osho's Medical History 1987–1990, February 8, 1990, Osho Commune International Press Office, 17 Koregaon Park, Poona.
8. James S. Gordon, "A Letter from Poona, November, 1989," in *The Rajneesh Papers: Studies in a New Religious Movement*, ed. Susan J. Palmer and Arvind Sharma, New Delhi: Motilal Banarasidass Publishers, 1993, p. 148.
9. James S. Gordon, *op., cit.*, p. 149.
10. Vasant Joshi, *op. cit.*, p. 216.
11. Ma Prem Shunyo, *op. cit.*, p. 280.
12. *Ibid.*, p. 282

Chapter 6: The Suspicious Death of Osho's Girlfriend

1. Ma Yoga Sudha, Interview by Sudha with Vivek, December 17, 1978, http://www.sannyas.wiki/index.php?title=Interview_by_Sudha_with_Vivek
2. "Nirvano's body was taken to the burning ghats by the river and, at Osho's request, only a few of her friends attended," writes Ma Prem Shunyo in *op. cit.*, p. 299.
3. Ma Anand Sheela, *op. cit.*, pp. 251–252.
4. Testimony by Nirvano before the Wasco County Grand Jury on October 18, 1985.
5. Ma Anand Sheela, *op. cit.*, p. 37.
6. Ma Prem Shunyo, *op. cit.*, p. 297.
7. Antar Navjot, *10 May 1989 Lao Tzu authors and putting Nirvano to bed,* Blog: "A Year in Lao Tzu—1989," https://orangegirloklaotzu.wordpress.com/2015/12/24/10-may-1989-lao-tzu-authors-and-putting-nirvano-to-bed/
8. Shantam Prem, Blogpost under the thread, *Vivek's death at 40, and how was it untimely?* December 7, 2015 at 10.02 p.m., http://sannyasnews.org/now/archives/5566

Chapter 9: Osho's Death: A Fabricated Account?

1. Ma Chetan Unmani and Swami Chaitanya Keerti, "Keeping Osho—24 Karat Gold: Excerpts from an interview with Swami Satya Vedant, in *Allah to Zen—An insight into the world of Osho: The Real Man of the Millennium*," p. 28.

Chapter 10: Did Drug Overdose Kill Osho?

1. Ma Shivam Suvarna, "Keeping Osho—Going For The Diamonds," in *Allah to Zen—An insight into the world of Osho: The Real Man of the Millennium*," p.71.
2. Press Release: "The people who destroyed Osho's body are now using the media to destroy his international vision, says Ma Yoga Neelam," Osho Commune International Press Office, 17 Koregaon Park, Poona, February 9, 1990.
3. Ma Prem Shunyo, *op. cit.*, pp. 266–267.
4. *Ibid.*, pp.306–308.

Chapter 12: Disbanding Osho's Commune

1. Antar Navjot, *18 May 1989 Self-sufficiency in the Garden of the Beloved*, Blog: "A Year in Lao Tzu—1989," https://orangegirloklaotzu.wordpress.com/2016/01/17/18-may-1989-self-sufficiency-in-the-garden-of-the-beloved/

Chapter 13: It's All About Money, Honey

1. Witness Statement, Klaus Steeg before EUIPO on July 6, 2011.

2. *Ibid.*, p.25.
3. Witness Statement, Ursula Hoess, also known as Vatayana before EUIPO on May 21, 2011.
4. Witness Statement, Klaus Steeg before EUIPO on July 6, 2011.
5. Waldman, Amy, "Pune Journal; Old Rajneesh Commune Lightens Up in Afterlife." *The New York Times*, December 10, 2002.
6. Ramateertha, "*Open Letter to the Inner Circle*", September 1, 2010, http://satyaprem.com/blog/open-letter-to-the-inner-circle-from-ramateertha/
7. Witness Statement, Jayesh before EUIPO, on July 19, 2011.
8. U.S. National Arbitration Forum, Decision, Osho International Foundation v. Osho Dhyan Mandir and Atul Anand, Claim No. FA0006000094990, July 28, 2000. http://www.adrforum.com/domaindecisions/94990.htm

Chapter 14: Will Osho's Bones Rattle if the Samadhi is Destroyed?

1. Ma Prem Shunyo, *op. cit.*, pp. 268–269.
2. Vaidya, Abhay, "Cultures Clash Over Osho's Samadhi." *The Times of India*, August 9, 2007.
3. Ma Yoga Neelam, "Open Letter to Jayesh, Amrito and Anando," July 11, 2000.
4. Application filed by Mukesh Sarda, Trustee, Osho International Foundation, before Charity Commissioner, Maharashtra, September 19, 2011.